W9-BBY-398

Love
and
Houses

a   n   o   v   e   l

Marti Leimbach

Simon & Schuster

SIMON & SCHUSTER

Rockefeller Center

1230 Avenue of the Americas

New York, NY 10020

SIMON & SCHUSTER and colophon are registered trademarks of Simon & Schuster Inc.

DESIGNED BY BARBARA M. BACHMAN

Manufactured in the United States of America

10   9   8   7   6   5   4   3   2   1

Library of Congress Cataloging-in-Publication Data

Leimbach, Marti.

   Love and houses : a novel / Marti Leimbach.

      p.   cm.

   I. Title.

   PS3562.E4614L6   1997

   813'.54—dc21   96-49273

                                                                            CIP

   ISBN 0-684-83670-X

For Alastair

Love and Houses

CHAPTER ONE

ONE OF MY FRIENDS PIERCED HER BELLY button, took a lover, and then moved from an adobe-style four-bedroom in Playa del Rey to a Georgian cottage in Greenwich, not Greenwich as in New York, but Greenwich as in London, leaving the lover with a very long commute. Another, bound by custody laws to remain in her home, gutted all three stories of her vast, architecturally perfect glass and timber house and rebuilt the entire inside so that not one brick or fragment of mortar from her marriage remained within her new living space. A third, this one rather pathetic, took up with a guy she met from work and bought the house next door to him. So when my own husband, Andy, left me my thoughts went immediately to what I was going to do in terms of real estate. My best friend, Carla, asked me what I was going to do—she said, "Now, Meg, what are you going to do?" drawing the words out slowly in that psychoanalytic way of hers. She's a shrink—she's not *my* shrink, but being great friends with a shrink means you are kind of de facto going to one. Anyway, when she asked me what I was going to do I assumed she meant with the house, or rather with the houses which Andy and I owned, or at least owned in theory. In fact, Citibank owned most of both of them; in the manner of all young couples with heavy real estate investments we were deeply in debt. Our apartment was on the market and we'd secured a bridging loan for our new house, an eighteenth-century former schoolhouse, an enormous beautiful structure that needed a great deal of work, and we'd even finagled a loan for that.

I told Carla, "Well, I'm going to cancel the contractors for the patio on the new house—I think the patio idea was thoroughly tasteless and was only going through with it for Andy's sake—he's always wanted a pergola. I'm going to have to think practically, perhaps a butcher's block island and a disposal in the kitchen? I can't believe how long I've lived without a disposal. Of course, central heating would probably be a good idea. Can you imagine how the previous owners lived on open fires and freestanding electric heaters?"

"Not about the *house*," Carla said. "And don't get

an island. I've got one and all I do is bump into it. What are you going to do about *you?*"

"Oh, me—ha ha," I said, "I have no idea."

Most of my friends are recently divorced or separated or recently unseparated or remarried, one is even remarried to the man she divorced, so I had any number of models to work from. One thing I definitely would not do, I decided, was pierce my belly button as I was about seven months pregnant when Andy left me and I felt if anyone pierced anything I would simply deflate across the room like a balloon. Also, I would not buy real estate adjoining that of any man whom I'd only known three months, which is what my other best friend, Beth, did. When I told Carla about Beth she said, "Oh, so needy," in her dismissive way. I often wonder what it is like for Carla's patients, do they confess that they can't leave the house without checking that the lights are all off, the oven off, the iron put away, all of these confessions given over in forlorn hope that she might help them, only to have Carla mumble, "Oh, so obsessive," and look bored with the whole thing?

I told Beth when she bought the little ranch house—a perfectly ordinary three-bedroom with a green door and a cellar that floods—that this was perhaps the most pathetic move ever made by a newly single woman.

"You've been talking to Carla," she said. She finds Carla difficult, and Carla finds Beth somewhat embarrassing. The three of us were roommates in college, along with another woman whom none of us speak to now, and they didn't really get along then, but neither would they be separated. Nothing much has changed over the years.

"Well, Carla's right this time. It sounds like you are afraid to live alone."

"I'm already moved in," she said, knowing as she does that practical always beats psychoanalytical. Carla and I could think what we wanted, Beth saw it as a skilfully executed plan to win her man. Which man didn't actually seem to matter to her.

"Either it works with Mark and we eventually build some sort of bridge between our identical ranch-style homes or David becomes unaccountably jealous and insists I go back to him," she said.

David, I reminded her, was now heavily involved with Diana—or Short Fat Diana, as we'd taken to calling her—and was unlikely to be jealous over her budding affair with Mark, who though not especially fat had splayed feet and a lot of hair on his back—monkeyish, not *my* type, but Beth liked him all the same.

She took a long breath and then rolled her eyes. Beth has a tiny heart-shaped face and enormous Liza Minnelli eyes which she decorates with a number of dazzling shades of red and gold all mixed together like autumn leaves on her eyelids. "Here's the deal," she said. "The current party line is that Men, and I say that with a capital M, don't want a *commitment*. Once there is a commitment, love—which you might like to know is now considered a *leisure sport*—anyway, *love* becomes work and they are fed up with work." She paused and waved her hand in front of her face, a gesture that comes quite naturally to Beth who has lovely hands and a collection of outstanding rings, mostly gifts from assorted exes including her now ex-husband. In the months before the divorce, when David tried to get me on his side—or at least to explain that it really wasn't his fault that he fell in love with another woman (of course, it was *Beth's* fault)—he said he fell in love with Beth because of her hands. And even though he could see that half a dozen men before him had dropped a small fortune decorating those hands, he had felt compelled to do the same. "What does all this mean?" Beth continued, as though lecturing to a class, "It means that when eventually Mark and I need to take that next step into the commitment stage and he says he just cannot do it I will point out to him that he already has done it. We own houses fifteen feet from one another, I'll say, we share a *property line.* This is a commitment and we still have great sex, don't we? So what's the problem?"

"You have great sex with him?" I asked. I couldn't help myself. Monkeyish, I'm telling you. I had the sudden blinding image of beautiful petite Beth in a sequined Fay Wray shift being ravished by Mark, the miniature King Kong.

"Fair," she said, and did a little *comme ci, comme ça* gesture. "But did I ever tell you that Mark has a bit of plumbing knowledge? I've never been with a man who knows plumbing. Plumbing is tricky, it takes a special kind of man who is willing to delve into the hidden complexity of waste pipes and water tanks. With Mark you could have a blocked toilet and it would not be a crisis," she said. Her dramatic eyes grew wide and she whispered, "With Mark you could possibly *renovate*."

"Oh please, you barely know him, you're not ready to talk about renovating. Renovating is for senior couples."

"It's a *thought*."

"It's a far-fetched thought. What happens after you give the commitment speech to Mark and it doesn't work?"

"It will work."

I envisioned a situation in which both little houses were on the market within six months. "Personally," I said, "I don't see it working."

"*Personally* I know it works. It always works. I point out the property line, how we already share a street, a neighborhood, a lifestyle, and then . . ."

"Yes?"

"Then I get the serious jewelry."

Perhaps of all the stories of what to do when you find yourself suddenly on the brink of divorce, my favorite was one told to me by my mother. My mother comes from a very fancy part of Chicago and was brought up on loads of money that she has spent most of her life discarding as quickly as possible through donations to various charities and animal rights groups. She has pretty much reached her goal now of total poverty and lives on a goat farm at the border of Massachusetts and New York State. The goat farm she created herself from two ewes and a billy goat; she attempts to farm organically and live on

yogurt and goat's milk, foul stuff she neither pasteur-
izes nor sweetens, insisting that food is best left near-
est to its natural state. The fact that goat's milk is not
meant to be consumed by humans and that a carrot's
natural state is in the ground does not occur to my
mother, who set up a farm stall at the end of her long,
dirt driveway and sells her wares on an "honesty" system, which means any passing motorist can take what
he wishes from the stacks of beets and cabbages and
the stocks of goat's milk and plain yogurt kept in a refrigerator she runs off a generator right there by the
road, and leave whatever he feels like in a ceramic
bowl next to a Thank You sign.

Well, my mother's divorce story is the best, because it is my story, too, or my story before I started
my own unique tale of tragedy in love. I was three
years old at the time, my brother was four, and my little sister was about six weeks gestated inside my
mother's stomach. We were living in New York, in
the city, of all places, where my parents owned a
brownstone in Chelsea and my father worked as a
public defender. It is precisely because he would do
something as nonlucrative and ultimately unreward-
ing as being a public defender in New York that my
mother married the guy and despite her own degrees
in psychology and sociology from Barnard, stayed at
home to raise the children. I've often said, and
Mother agrees, that had Dad stayed home and *she*
gone to work, setting up a clinical practice—which is
what she'd assumed she'd do before meeting Dad and
embarking on a mission to emulate June Cleaver—

she'd have been raking in considerable cash and by now she'd be so rich she could invent charities of her own. Also, had my father and mother hung on to that brownstone, which they paid something like twenty thousand dollars for, they'd have been able to buy some serious property in today's market. But neither of these things was to be. We lived off the tiny salary my father brought in and the dwindling supply of my mother's inherited money, which she continued to dispatch to beggars and hostels and now to my father's clients— people they both knew were criminals—without thought to the tide of attention that psychology would attract or what property markets were likely to be twenty years hence, let alone the value of money.

In addition to monetary donations my mother also gave a great deal of her time to good causes. She cooked for the homeless and brought her creations to them in the back of our station wagon. The homeless were always happy to see her; the homeless were often not homeless at all but runaways from fancy addresses who chose to live on the street. It was these opting-for-homeless people who most loved and appreciated Mother's culinary creations—brick hard homemade bread, grainy whole-meal pasta, casseroles of lima beans and tofu, whole-nut peanut butter, the kind that hides under a sea of oil, which she personally ground in a Mr. Peanut machine—all of these concoctions very much entrenched in my childhood memories as we were brought up on the same. The real homeless, the hungry, wanted meat pies and chicken legs, food which would fill them up, food that was not ethically farmed. They would have rather been handed canned beef stew than my mother's lovingly stir-fried sprouts and lentils, but they didn't have much choice. Whenever they asked for meat my mother, in that careful and patient voice she has, a voice that never hurries through a sentence, but takes time over each syllable and pauses between each sentence—you would think whoever she was talking to had to write down what she was saying—anyway, she would explain how for every pound of meat consumed it takes six times that much out of the land, how all the world could be fed if we used the land differently and how meat was the problem . . . it never ended. It was the same speech I heard half my life and which, no matter how carefully outlined, how intricately described were the evils of carnivorous appetites, never stopped me from consuming great quantities of hamburgers whenever I could steal away to a McDonald's.

We took in a lodger—we took in several lodgers, all teenage types who needed someplace to rest on their way elsewhere, to communes and friends' farms, to Europe—but in particular we took in a girl of about twenty who called herself Rocky (Why? Why would anyone, even in the sixties, call themselves Rocky?). Rocky was skinny and long-legged, with a porcelain complexion and straight, jet-black hair. She was the type of girl who could look quite stunning or could look like a member of the Addams Family, depending on the light, and though she lived with us only for about six months, this was as long as I could remember. To me Rocky was a permanent fixture in our house and I could hardly recall a time when she didn't live in the tiny room on the third floor (a room we later converted into a bathroom when Father was gone and Mother redecorated in an Arts and Crafts style, which perfectly suited the house's nineteenth-century details), from where sheaves of scented smoke rose up, clouding the hallway so that it always looked as though the place was on fire. She used my mother's lipstick to draw flowers on my forehead and cheeks, she showed me how to weave Indian beads into a bracelet, and how to use stencils to create geometric shapes. She gave me things—a leather pouch, a box with a hidden drawer, a silver dollar—things I kept like treasures in the top drawer of my bureau. Other stuff I just took.

"Can I have your leather ankle bracelet?" I'd ask Rocky.

She smoked clove cigarettes she rolled herself and sat cross-legged on a cotton rug, her hair in two shining braids over her shoulders. The top of a mayonnaise jar served as an ashtray. Her toenails were painted and decorated with decals in the shape of butterflies.

"It's not *mine*. It just *is*," she said of the anklet, which meant I could pocket it.

Of course, you've guessed already, she was having an affair with my father. Mother found out and suddenly Rocky was thrown out of the house and my father disappeared for long stretches on the feeble excuse of business trips. Business trips? I sometimes wonder what kind of mind a cheating husband has that he thinks he can lie with such a lack of verisimilitude. I seem to remember my mother asking what kind of business trips did a public defender in Manhattan make? Then he disappeared altogether and my mother got on with the task of divorcing him outright and otherwise raising us just as before, except now entirely on the diminishing coffers of her inheritance.

That is all I remember, the rest is what was told to me. Apparently it had never occurred to my mother previous to the onset of separation from my father that marrying a lawyer has several disadvantages, especially when you get to the divorcing stage. Not only did he want to pay no alimony or child support, but he also wanted a third of her money and joint custody of my brother and me (he did not yet know my mother was pregnant). As funky and alternative as my mother was, she was enough Episcopalian, enough private school, enough of her own country-club-going parents' daughter to realize that she did not want to part with a nickel of her cash so that my father could live in style with Rocky—who now that she'd taken up with my father properly was living on the Upper West Side and calling herself Esther—and, even more to the point, there was no way Mother would share her children half the time with him or anyone else. She did not care tremendously about material things; he had taken the silver and the Spode and most of the decent furniture (no doubt to furnish the new place he shared with Rocky/Esther), he'd drained their joint accounts and cashed in on their joint life insurance. He had done all this without any particular protest from my mother, but when it came to the children—to her *babies*—she was not going to give.

However, my father knew the law. He knew perhaps that he would look very bad in the eyes of the court, having run off with a beatnik (albeit a beatnik who was now wearing designer clothing and taking cabs all over the city and doing lunch) but he also knew he could paint a very different picture from the one that really existed. He quit his job as a public defender and joined a corporate firm. He bought new suits and worked at a mahogany desk. Planted in his big chair overlooking midtown he harassed my mother daily with phone calls. He told her that court was a magical place where great transformations took place. In court she would not look like a regular housewife with a strong moral sense and a dedication to aiding the impoverished, but like a demented hippie mother so alternative and impractical as to appear incompetent. The house, with its beaded doorways and moonlamps and tapestries, its kitchen full of lentils and brown bread, its occasional lodgers, offbeat and in transit, could be described, he claimed, as unsuitable for children. The way Mother packed us all into the station wagon and took us to deliver food to the homeless could be construed, he said, as negligent. And the way she gave away money, the way she threw it at any cause whatsoever without discretion could easily be seen as foolish, if not actually mentally unsound. He would take her to court, where all of this would be seen exactly as described, he claimed, unless he got the children at least three days and three nights per week, which for a time was how my brother and I lived—between two homes—half the time at our house in Chelsea and half the time in Esther and Father's apartment on the Upper West Side. Esther no longer made me beaded bracelets, but shut herself away in her private bedroom, a room separate from the one she shared with my father, whenever we came to stay. Father, for his part, suddenly appeared to have no normal means of communicating with us. Overnight he'd become skittish and private, not like our father at all. We spent evenings in the apartment quietly playing together or watching television until it came time to return home, which we did with great relief, rushing into Mother's arms or sulking upstairs, with no idea why we'd had to take to this peculiar living arrangement.

What I did not know at the time was that my mother had a plan. What she planned was to have him killed. My mother is like that, you see. She is a strong woman, and one of extremes. She might campaign for peace at all costs on a *global* scale, but when it comes to her personally, she doesn't take a lot of guff. She is a radical Democrat, really a socialist, but I believe that deep inside my mother there lives a rather reactionary Republican, a part of her person she might not be proud of but which can be reliably called upon when push comes to shove. Right now she lives on a goat farm—one can see that as living in an alternative, creative way in sync with nature, or as living in much the same way as a survivalist, who hoards canned food in a nuclear shelter and puts a gun in every room. The two at their most extreme become almost indistinguishable. Father, in his arrogant manner, had failed to remember what his wife was made of, this woman who did not fear Alphabet City in New York, who regularly dropped off food in Harlem. She was not afraid and she would not be bullied. He'd smashed to pieces the family she'd worked hard to create, taken her money, forced her to part with her children three days and nights out of each week, and left her pregnant. Did he think that she would do *nothing?* Mother is an extremely moral person and though she does not necessarily believe in divine retribution, she certainly believes in retribution. She had no choice, she explained to me, but to buy for him a cheap single-engine airplane—a gift thinly disguised as a peacemaking gesture—in which she hoped he would be killed. An airplane was what he'd always wanted, always dreamed of the way most control freaks, particularly lawyers, do, and she bought it for him in the autumn as winter was fast approaching and encouraged him to use it as much as possible, especially when there was a heavy frost.

"I bought a radio with a twenty-four-hour channel to weather reports on the East Coast; it sat in my apron pocket eight hours a day, squawking about gale forces and barometric pressure. Whenever it mentioned ice storms or poor visibility I got excited. I kept seeing his little plane crashing to the ground, preferably before our divorce was finalized so that we would inherit back all the money, less the airplane, of course, which I assumed would be a write-off. I did my research and made sure to get a model with a particularly bad crash record."

"That was wicked of you," I said tearfully. I'd traveled four hours to my mother's farm to tell her about Andy, finding myself exhausted and crying in the kitchen as the baby kicked inside me. I was definitely not crying over my father, whom I only vaguely remember having loved at all. "I do admire you," I sniffed.

"He was damaging you and your brother. I had to do *something*. I didn't want him to die, but really I couldn't think of an alternative."

"Very brave of you," I said.

She paused and looked at me with a *you got to do what you got to do* expression and for a moment I actually believed my father was killed in that gift airplane. Then I remembered that after he died we had to sell the plane—how could we have sold a wrecked plane? Suddenly my tears stopped. I looked at my mother suspiciously.

"But Mother. Dad died in an *automobile* accident, not a plane crash."

"Yes, I know, but he was on his way to the airport."

"But then you didn't kill him."

She looked at me, almost in surprise, and said with authority, "Well, I tried awfully hard."

The funny thing about my mother's confession of how she tried to kill my father, or if you believe her version, effectively did kill him, was how it totally changed the way that I now remember the entire childhood legend involving my father. You see, Mother always maintained that we were a perfect family until, tragically, Father was killed in an automobile accident near the airport. She always said "near the airport" and until now I never understood why that particularly bit of geography mattered. She also insisted they were a perfectly matched, perfectly happy couple—this I partly still believe—and that was why she could never remarry. To do so would be a step down from the fabulous coupling she'd had with Father.

All of this washed very well with my little sister, Delilah, who never even met her father. Whether Delilah was named with a rather morbid reference to Samson or whether it was just a name Mother liked, I do not know. I know that my father, had he had any say in the matter, would never have allowed it. Father had this idea that he was from Scottish ancestry and that this was important despite hundreds of years of mixed blood since his "family" emigrated to America. He insisted we all have Scottish names. I am Margaret, though I am called Meg; my brother is Alastair, though he would rather live with the name Al than go through all the confusion and spelling, not to mention the embarrassing explanation of why he was named Alastair. Delilah thought, and still thinks, our father was a hero and a family man, a good sort who was tragically killed. My brother and I have our memories and they run rather counter to Mother's insistent recollection of total family bliss. Throughout our childhood and adolescence we repeatedly quizzed her on this fantasy she maintained was our family, although to her credit she never once faltered.

"Why did Dad have his own apartment then?" Al asked.

"He didn't have any apartment—don't be silly!" was my mother reply.

"What about Rocky!" I cried. "He was in love with her!"

"We *all* loved Rocky. Sadly she failed in her bold effort to become a New York society woman and is now a drunk."

"But they lived together!" said Al.

"Lived where? She lived with us for a time."

"In that apartment!"

"That was his *workplace,* honey. She helped keep it clean for him. She was a cleaner."

We gave up and, in the end, actually believed her. Believed, for whatever it mattered, that we came from a strong nuclear family, from good stock and circumstances. It wasn't until Andy left me and I went to Mother's farm to tell her that I'd been left—been rejected, along with our unborn child—that she told me the truth about Father and I began to realize just what a woman on the edges of divorce was capable of doing.

This whole notion, that of being powerful, being effective, being strong and decisive and getting what you want—I mean Mother wanted the man dead and *presto* he was dead—took a while to really sink in with me. I could not be like that, for one thing I did not want Andy dead. I did not want him to die and me to have his baby and be reminded of his horrible death. But what I could do, I realized, was change super-markets. This was important, because although Andy had left me, left me hugely, left me pregnant and with a new house I couldn't pay for and an apartment I could not sell, and a really bad track record in love, he had not left the local Star Market where we did all our grocery shopping. Never mind that our apartment is in Newton and Andy was living in a studio flat in Brighton, he still drove four miles each direction—he even paid the turnpike toll—to shop in Newton. Why did he do this? To torture me? To humiliate me? To further crumble my already broken heart? No. He claimed it was too much trouble to relearn the order of aisles in a new grocery store.

"Too much trouble!" I said, my voice booming through the fresh produce section on that first day I caught him, cowering behind an island of winter vegetables. "It wasn't too much trouble to move out, to pack your things and find an apartment, but it is *too much trouble* to get used to eggs being on aisle nine in-stead of aisle two!"

He looked at the floor and then glanced to either side of him like a true criminal. In the harsh fluores-cence of supermarket lighting the dark circles under his eyes looked even more pronounced than usual and I felt secret glee at this solid evidence of his advancing insomnia, an affliction he suffers from even at the best of times, but that really gets to him under stress. One look at his face and I knew he was under serious stress.

"It's just that the store in Brighton is, you know,

so downmarket," he whispered. "For one thing it's not a Star, it's something else, some sort of supersaver economy store. You can't buy *one* of anything. Family-sized economy packs in huge cartons, that is all you can get. Toilet paper comes in rolls of twelve. Orange juice is sold in a container so large you have to set it in the refrigerator like a vat and run it off a removable plastic tap."

"Oh, so they cater to *families*—is that what is making you a little uncomfortable?"

"No, no, it isn't just that," he said, patting the air with the flats of his palms, keeping his voice in a low, controlled whisper. People around us were beginning to stare. Did he think I cared? Did he think he could calm me with hand gestures? "Also, they don't mist the vegetables. I mean, look around you, the lettuce here is misted every ten seconds, the cucumbers have such a dewy sheen. And there are no mirrors either."

"What mirrors?" I was about to explode. I was at that stage right before explosion when your face goes red and you find yourself spitting with every word. "What are you *talking about!*"

"You see, *here* at the Newton Star Market there are mirrors running along the top of the food stores so that you get the reflection of the greens from above. They don't have those at the Eco-Save in Brighton. You don't realize how much you need mirrors in a vegetable aisle until you don't have them. And in the Eco-Save there is hardly any selection. It's mostly cabbage and dry-looking corn on the cob. No mist, no Easter-basket plastic green hay around the squash and turnips. The shopping carts have graffiti on them. Armed guards stand by the doors. It's just not a nice place."

Our baby was likely to be born within the next six weeks and what did he care about? He cared about vegetable presentation. He cared about fake hay. He cared about *mist*. I was fuming. If he said another word about the merits of the Newton Star Market, if he mentioned the fresh baked goods or the newly built glass and chrome cheese counter with over two hundred types of cheese from all over the world, if he so much as hinted at the luxury of the ready-cooked meals, the freshly baked Mexican fajitas, the bouillabaisse, the eggplant Parmesan, and how he sat in his dark little room in Brighton missing all those things, those Star Market things, and not me and our life together, I felt, truly, that I would burst into flames.

"You are crazy!" I screamed at him.

"I think you should stay calm," he said.

"Calm! Why should I stay calm? You've wrecked our marriage and ruined my life and now you are invading my local chain, *why should I stay calm!*"

"It's just that there's a guard coming our direction. This being Newton, he is unarmed, but really, Meg—"

And there was, too. A guard. He asked me to leave the store. Doesn't that beat everything? He asked *me* to leave the store and he let Andy remain, let Andy the traitor, who does not even live in Newton anymore, stay and shop while I, the bereft pregnant tax-paying resident, had to return to my car.

I sat in my car wishing I knew how to make a quick bomb out of car parts and bobby pins. For some reason I hated Andy even more for having gotten me thrown out of the Star Market than I did for leaving me altogether. And I hated the guard even more than I hated Andy because it was as though he'd suddenly become the arbiter in the whole affair. The guard throwing me out was like saying that I was the guilty party, I was the shrew, I was the one in the wrong, not just in yelling at my husband in fresh vegetables, but in my marriage generally. The thought that Andy was still in the Star Market pushing his shopping cart gingerly past the baguettes and bagels and ciabatta bread, past the bakery windows of almond croissants and chocolate chip cookies and gingerbread men, around to my favorite aisle—the one with the cereal—an aisle I love because cereal boxes always make me feel so safe and secure—was like saying he was the innocent one, the good one, the one in the right. There he was among all those bright colors and crowing roosters and promises of wholesome goodness and natural ingredients, pretending that he, too, was good. And he doesn't even like cereal! It's me, *I* like cereal, I like it because my mother, the crazy woman, used to make her own out of oats and organic raisins and sunflower seeds. But I wasn't even allowed in the store.

Then I saw him. I saw him and I thought, *he must be punished.* I clambered out of my car as fast as my enormous stomach would allow, searching my purse for a striking instrument—a nail file? a lipstick tube?—

and settled on hairspray. Hairspray which I have never dreamed of actually using on my hair but that I keep in my purse as a weapon. I found the hairspray and went charging across the parking lot to get him with it when I suddenly realized that Andy didn't have any bags with him. Normally one would expect at least one and possibly two shopping bags, but Andy held nothing. And when he saw me, running (such that I could) at him, he didn't back away. In fact, he looked relieved.

"I'm sorry about that," he said as I reached him. If he thought it odd that my open purse was hanging off my elbow and the can of VO5 hairspray in my right hand was just about at the level of his eyes, he did not say. Instead he looked apologetic and outraged and concerned and fatherly. He looked like the man I love and with whom I planned this child—*we* planned this child—and I felt a terrible sadness and a terrible amount of love. He said, "I told that guy it was outrageous for him to throw you out and demanded to see his supervisor. He gave me some song and dance about how his supervisor wasn't there right now and I'd have to come back. What a jerk! Can you believe it! To think, you've been shopping there for five years!"

"You yelled at him? You yelled at the security guard?"

"Of course I did. I told him you were heavily pregnant and very emotional and you didn't need a bully like him throwing you out of the only decent place to purchase groceries for miles."

"You did that?" It was almost too much for me. Was it possible that somehow this confrontation in front of the zucchini had brought magic back into our lives? That my being thrown out of a supermarket would result in the realignment of our marriage? I held out the VO5 for him to inspect. "I thought you were in there shopping. I was going to spray you in the eyes."

"What? Like a mugger? You were going to spray me?"

I was laughing. He was laughing. "Yeah! But you were in there standing up for me."

"Well, I had to. Hey, does this work? Hairspray? Would I have been blinded?"

"Not, you know, *permanently,*" I said.

We walked back to the parking lot. He took me to my car and it suddenly felt like a date, or like we were back inside our marriage again and he would put me in the passenger side and go over to the driver's side. We would drive home together in happiness, albeit without groceries, and make love in front of the fireplace, which is something we used to do but we stopped doing, and everything would carry on like before, just as though he'd never moved out. I felt so sure this would happen that I was surprised—offended, even—when he stopped ten feet from the car and said, "Well, goodbye then."

"Goodbye? That's it? Now you're just going to scoot away."

"Well," he said, pointing over his shoulder. "My car is over there."

"So?"

"So I better go to it."

"Why?"

"So I can go home," he said. The word "home" had stuck in his throat a bit and he realized he'd made a major gaffe.

"Home to Brighton."

He said nothing. I said nothing.

"You told the security guard I was heavily pregnant and very emotional. He should have treated me differently. He should have treated me well. So why not you? Why don't you treat me well? I am your wife, Andy. I am wedded to you!"

His face was dark; he could not look at me. He turned, his head bent toward his chest, and began to walk away.

"Here wait!" I said and scrambled toward him. He turned, registering a bit of fear—as well he should have, given that I had come within an inch of dousing him in hairspray not ten minutes before. But I didn't have the hairspray now. I reached him and started tugging at my wedding ring. "I want you to have this!" I said, still pulling. "Because obviously I'm not going to need it anymore!"

He stood. I pulled. I pulled and pulled. I could not get that ring off. My fingers had swollen with the pregnancy and I could not have gotten that ring off without chopping my finger at the knuckle. So after a good amount of grunting and bruising myself I had to admit defeat.

"Oh, fuck it," I said, and went back to my car.

O F ALL THE PEOPLE I KNOW, MEN AND WOMEN
alike, I am the only one whose spouse left them *not*
for another lover. To have driven away a man single-
handedly, without rival, is a very damning reflection
on one's character, I suppose, and it puts me in a special class of bad wife. However, for some reason I also
feel rather proud. I can look at my marriage, my
dead marriage, the slaughtered ruined corpse of my
marriage, and say *I did this*. At least I have done *something*. In most of my girlfriends' cases there was not
only another woman but an advanced love affair, almost to the marrying stage, into which their husbands

fled. In other words it was not their fault, it was not their doing. They were the victims of conniving Other Women, the notorious libidinal excesses of men, and a bit of bad luck. The men I know who have been left were *all to a one* left for other men, although the women in question pretended this was not the case. I don't know why women should be so squeamish about admitting their affairs while men are given to lengthy confessions. Men tell all. Months if not years of total silence, of stealthy calculated utterances, of practiced distance and excuses of fatigue and overwork and then, once you get them talking, they admit not only to the affair but inform you of every incident of the affair, filling in dates and times and degrees of love until you want to ram a two-by-four down their throat to shut them up. I know this because my first serious boyfriend, a man with whom I shared a studio apartment in Kenmore Square, ran off with my former college roommate—the one that neither Beth nor Carla speak to either—and he was pretty clever at keeping up appearances with me, of covering for his whereabouts, of being kind, if a little closed, of maintaining both relationships without breaking into a sweat, until I found her underwear in my laundry basket (he was so stupid he thought it was my underwear, even though she is two sizes smaller than I am, and put it there himself) and he started talking like he was in a verbal race.

I find the complicated psychological world of an adulterer (a wonderful word, so damning and classic and somehow at once both enticing and bad) endlessly fascinating and have made a small, personal study of the subject. It would seem that women adulterers (adulteresses?) pretend they haven't actually done it. Yes, they might be interested in someone else, but they haven't in fact slept with him, or so they claim. Perhaps they *don't* sleep with him—I don't know—but I have a feeling that these protests of chastity are akin to those made similiarly in high school and that in every case they are full of shit. Of course they've slept with him, a man whose name comes up frequently in conversation, a "friend," usually a work colleague, who just happens coincidentally to have something vaguely to do with any subject that you care to mention from ski resorts to wall grouting, and there's that little bit of electricity surrounding the name when it is spoken, as though the very utterance of his name comes with a pinprick, a painful but sweet reminder. Even to her best friend a woman might swear that he is only a friend, this man with the electrical name, until the divorce is well on its way and then, *kismet,* this friend is now a lover, and the two are practically living together.

With Andy there was no other woman. This makes me happy, *happy* being a relative term in my case, *happy* meaning, at this precise moment in time, not fitfully depressed, not grievously pained, not ready to kill or be killed. One reason I am "happy" is that when I am lying in bed alone feeling the baby doing head butts against my bladder at 5 A.M. it gives me some small satisfaction to know that Andy is also alone, and probably awake as he has early morning insomnia, and perhaps, if I am very lucky, he is suffering, too. I like the idea of his suffering—this may mean that I don't love him (I do) and that I never did (I did), but at the moment every small dissatisfaction on his part, and especially actual physical pain, creates in me a fleeting joy. Despite earplugs, an eye mask, a machine that creates "white noise," a humidifier, and a prescription, he rarely is able to sleep past four-thirty.

Downstairs, in a room which should be the dining room, there is a library of over a thousand books, all of them quite ancient and in various states of disrepair. Back in the days of our marriage, in the morning while the rest of the world slumbered toward seven o'clock, Andy could usually be found in his boxer shorts, perched on a chair in front of what should be our dining room table, though of course it has never been used as a dining room table, has never had a single morsel of food served upon it because it is already occupied as a work desk for Andy's collection of ailing rare books. There, for hours, he performed his particular alchemy, rebinding and regluing, treating the leather covers with special hydrating oils, applying special highly toxic solutions—some of which he makes up himself—to remove mildew and dirt and long-ago spilt food from the pages, which he finds precious, if unreadable. Andy does not read his collection, but ministers to it. The books he *reads* are stacked in our bedroom and in the second bedroom and in the linen closet, which houses no towels, just books.

In the early months of my pregnancy when I was highly sensitive to smells I used to wake up with the feeling that alcohol was being poured down my nostrils and I knew then, as I scrambled for the toilet, that Andy was downstairs, awake, treating one or the other antiquarian book. Half asleep, deeply ill, I hobbled from toilet to stairs, taking each shaky step as quickly as I could, given that I was exhausted, with a peptic taste in my mouth and the definite feeling I would throw up again at short notice. I appeared like an apparition at the threshold of the dining room, where the smells of liniment and horse glue and oils swam in the air so thickly that I might have fainted had I not been fueled with a serious amount of adrenaline and a determination to kick Andy's ass for making me sick for the fourteenth time with his stinking, nauseating, thoughtless, diabolical morning ritual.

"What are you doing!" I yelled.

"Oh, hi, honey. You look a little green."

"I am about to throw up and you know whose fault that is?"

He looked at me innocently. "The baby's?"

"No, you moron. I've told you a hundred times that I cannot, I *cannot,* wake up to this kind of stink stewing in my head. I've already been sick this morning because you felt you had to fix these goddamned books!"

I picked up one of his books, threw it down hard on the table, immediately regretting it. He'd treated the leather with some sort of buttery concoction which was now all over my hand. "Aach!" I screamed, staring at my contaminated fingers.

"Now what's wrong? And why are you manhandling *Barthelme's Fair*?"

"Why do you have to do this at five in the morning?" I demanded, though of course I already knew that he had to do this at five in the morning because he was a neurotic and why he was a neurotic was that he had a neurotic father and a cloying mother and a background full of complicated people who were always having breakdowns and needing shock therapy and disappearing for long stretches in their cars. But I asked him anyway because I was angry and because, at thirty-nine years old, he really should have been able to put all that to one side and become a normal, or *normalish* person.

He looked around the room at his book collection, housed in brick and timber frames he created himself, which stood precariously in front of all available wall space. "I don't know," he said philosophically. "Should I make you some tea and dry toast?"

This last part was spoken hopefully, like a suddenly remembered remedy, chicken soup for a bad head cold, whisky for a sudden shock, and dry toast for morning sickness. It is because Andy is capable of being screamed at and called a moron without violent reaction and self-defense, and because he suddenly recalls a single castaway detail from an article I asked him to read on the subject of pregnancy, its ills and their cures, and offers like a gift and a gesture of peacemaking something as sweet, and at this point useless, as dry toast and tea that I love him and am perpetually frustrated by him.

But I present this as though all Andy and I ever did was fight. Already not one but two accounts of my screaming at him. Actually, prior to the onset of my pregnancy (which Andy could not handle) and his actual leaving (which I could not handle) we were a pretty happy couple. We did couplish things. I recall a specific week in December during the few days between Christmas and New Year about six months before everything exploded and we became miserable with each other. This particular Christmas we decided that rather than buy each other a gift, we'd buy each other an experience.

"Let's get each other a midlife crisis," I said. Andy looked at me like I had lost my mind. "But not the crisis part, just all the stuff."

"Oh, you mean a Porsche?" he said. "We can't afford a Porsche."

"We can't afford to *buy* a Porsche but we can afford to *rent* one."

"And we could get Rollerblades!"

"And haircuts that are too young for us!"

"And you'll buy dresses that are too tight and show a lot of cleavage!"

"And we'll wear sunglasses all the time, even in bed."

"Yeah, and you'll buy dresses that are too tight and show a lot of cleavage!"

"Yeah!"

And that's what we did, too. We flew to Fort

Lauderdale and rented a white Porsche convertible which we drove at speed through the Florida Keys. We donned wetsuits and went snorkeling, holding hands as we worried great schools of fish. We ate at expensive restaurants and talked about which couples at nearby tables were married and which were having affairs. We did daredevil things. I dared Andy to go skinny-dipping in the hotel pool at dawn. He dared me to go to a casino and gamble every penny I'd brought with me to Florida. My new haircut was short, androgynous, and very sleek, not so good at first but sexy as my skin turned brown. His was long at the sides and back, perhaps a little too much like a Bee Gee, but the long parts went blond in the Florida sun and I kind of liked that. I wore a toe ring, he got an old army chain with dog tags. He wore it in bed and I called him my soldier. He turned me over and over in bed, his hands in my cropped hair, and called me his whore, but he said it nicely, sweetly. For the first time in our marriage, we were really bad in bed. Not bad as in bad, but bad as in good—which is a miracle considering various troubles we'd had early in our married life and on which I will elaborate a little later. Anyway, we fell in love freshly, we kissed each other and bit each other's lips and I spent two weeks with whisker marks on my chin. We went Rollerblading on the beach, me in a bikini top and leggings, him in Bermuda shorts and his dog tags. In Florida we did not look weird, we fit in. We were normal. But on the plane home we realized we did look weird. We looked so weird people thought we were foreign. We went with that. We spoke in a vague foreign accent of our own invention. Then we went home and decided things were so good between us, so fun and lush and potent, that we ought to have a baby.

One day, about three months into my pregnancy, at a time when I knew that there was something very wrong with Andy but didn't know exactly how serious it was, I called my friend Sarah who has several children and is almost always somewhat depressed. It pays to have at least one morbid and depressing friend because if all your friends are upbeat and confident, if they all have high self-esteem and a fundamental love of life, then you have nowhere to go if all you want to do is complain without acting. Certainly I could not speak to Carla who would want to know what I was *going to do*. Nor to Beth who would have some really stupid instant solution that would solve nothing but might get me a diamond. At that point, when all I had to go on was Andy's peculiar way of looking at my body, as though it had suddenly become a suspicious and unnatural thing, his disregard of all subjects related to the baby (which admittedly was at this point, even in my mind, a hypothetical baby), and a distance I felt had opened between us, a distance which increased each day such that I felt pretty soon I was going to start carrying around a photograph of him and dialing 1 before attempting to speak with him, all I really wanted was to complain without action, to *kvetch,* to unload.

"I'm feeling depressed," I said to Sarah. "Don't tell Carla. She'll prescribe something."

"Would she prescribe something for me?" Sarah asked. "I could use it."

"Andy doesn't appear the least bit interested in the baby. Nor does he take seriously how ill I feel."

"You're depressed about *that?*"

"Yes."

Sarah sighed. Sarah is a really practiced sigher and does many different sighs, a the-world-is-doomed sigh, a never-mind-me sigh, an isn't-that-beautiful sigh, a frustrated sigh, and a sigh of great anger, exactly the kind of sigh you imagine God made before he damned the world with forty days and nights of rain. But the sigh she reserved for me that day was her nothing-is-wrong-here sigh, which made me relax immediately because I believe in Sarah's sighs. I believe in their power and wisdom, and I believe they have gotten her, and many people close to her, through a lot of tough times. She sighed and then she said, "When Phil comes home he goes into his study and plugs his headphones into his portable CD player and refuses to come out for hours. If I knock on the door he says *Leave me alone! Can't I have any peace and quiet?* I tell him no, he cannot, because he is father to three children. After a few hours he can be persuaded to come out. Now, does that give you some perspective on your supposed problems with Andy? Do you feel better now?"

"A little better, but still a little depressed, too. Keep talking."

"Okay, look, there's nothing yet to be depressed about. The baby is hardly a baby yet. It's a thing the size of a prawn. Wait until you show, wait until you waddle around like a giant penguin and he realizes that a single one of his sperm produced so great a change in you. It's a real testosterone charge for them and that's when they get interested and start talking about *our* baby rather than *your* pregnancy. If he's anything like other men I know he'll start getting really possessive about it. You'll eat a Snickers bar and he'll say, 'Do you think the baby *needs* a Snickers bar? Wouldn't he rather have a tempeh salad?' He'll talk about your fitness, urging you to exercise and pay no attention whatsoever to your claim that getting in and out of a chair *is* exercise. He may even buy you a fitness-in-pregnancy video, which of course you must break in two over his head. He *may* even take to sitting beside you talking *to the baby*. Or worse, he'll be one of those types who studies childbirth practices in different countries and expects you to discuss seriously the merits of acupuncture as a form of pain relief. And just about the time he becomes such a pain in the ass that you are ready to divorce him, you'll go into labor."

"You're sure about this?"

"Oh yes. It's what sends you into labor usually. In two out of three cases I went into labor while yelling at Phil."

"What about the other one?"

"I was out looking for him to yell at him. He was walking the dog and I didn't catch up to him before the pain started, I mean labor pain, not the general pain which is my life."

At that moment I heard a toilet flush and Sarah scream and one of the children yell "Bye-bye" and I knew that her youngest son, Oliver, was flushing another of Phil's incredibly expensive saltwater fish down the toilet. Once, months previously, one of the smaller fish had died and Phil, not realizing the implications of his actions, flushed the dead fish down the toilet. Oliver had watched this, transfixed by the idea that fish can swim (or float, in this case) in the toilet and then be whisked away to the Great Beyond.

"Where is the fish going?" he'd asked his mother.

"To heaven," said Sarah.

"You get to heaven through the toilet?"

"Fish can. Fish have a special relationship to God."

Since then Oliver had sent half a dozen fish to heaven. I don't like to think what Freud would say about the fish, the toilet, potty training, and the outlook for young Oliver's sexual future. But I know that I am fortunate to have learned from Sarah and Phil's mistake and that, if I ever have the impulse to flush anything that was previously live down the toilet, or to keep fish, I will wait until my children are in college.

But back to Andy and the baby and me.

Let me assure you that this was a planned baby. Andy and I always said we'd have a baby someday and then I turned thirty-seven and Andy turned thirty-nine and we did the Florida midlife crisis thing. We were standing in line for bungee jumping (and for those of you new initiates into that "sport" I do recommend a support bra) next to the only couple over thirty-five, other than us. The woman, who was just a hair on the wrong side of forty gave me an enormous smile and said, "Isn't it great when the kids are gone and you can do all these things?"

"Gone?" I said.

"Ours are in college now. We can do anything we want!" she exclaimed.

Her husband, a bit older than she, stamped his foot and snorted just like a horse. "As long as it don't cost nothing," he said.

I couldn't quite admit that we were still waiting to have children, that we hadn't really noticed that our fecund, fertile years were dwindling in supply, so I nodded and smiled and pretended that I understood exactly what she meant and had children who were "gone," too.

That night we looked at each other. We were happy and healthy and tanned and it seemed that the "someday" when we should have children had really been a Wednesday in September back in 1989. So, we tried. And tried. And then we really tried. Six months later I missed my period and the little window on my home pregnancy test turned pink.

Andy was at work and I spent all day wondering how I would tell him. Would I fix him a drink, sit him on the couch and say, in that fifties wife sort of way, "Darling I have some wonderful news for you . . ."? Or would I don my shortest black number, make reservations at the restaurant on top of the Hyatt Hotel, the one that revolves slowly, allowing for views all over Boston, and tell him that beneath my lace stockings and suspender belt there was a very tiny life beginning? Or would I tell him in bed while we were making love, or just afterward, or just before? Or would I save it and grow from a size ten to twelve to fourteen to sixteen until he guessed himself?

Hundreds of scenarios crossed my mind but what happened was this. Andy came home earlier than I expected and started going through the garbage looking for an article in the Sunday papers which I'd thrown out, an article on antiquarian bookstores in Dublin. I came upon him in the kitchen surrounded by mashed milk cartons and take-out bags, chicken bones, and disused cans. He was sitting on the floor with a section of stained newspaper over one knee and coffee grounds in his lap. The pregnancy test, which I'd thrown out that very morning, was on the floor, its pink dot inches from his big toe.

"What's this?" he said, holding it up.

"A pregnancy test."

"Oh," he said, looking newly at the white plastic tube which housed evidence of our future daughter. "I thought that kind of thing required a test tube or a rabbit or something."

"I'm pregnant," I blurted out. I hadn't meant to say it like this. I'd wanted to say something like "We're going to have a baby." Or, "You're going to be a father." I hadn't thought I'd tell him like that, as he sat on the floor amid all of the week's garbage. And I hadn't expected his response, which was "Oh, no."

Ｎone of my friends took me seriously when I told them that Andy's response to my pregnancy was not normal. In fact, it was truly negative and hostile, but hostile in that sneaky passive way that men do so well. I spoke to Carla and she asked what I was going to do. I said, Have the baby, and she said, That's right, and I hung up feeling confused and thinking that this didn't sound like the solution that Carla clearly thought it was, though looking back on it that was the only and obvious solution. But most of my friends simply took the opportunity to tell me how much worse their own husbands were and how lucky I was to have Andy who was cute and eccentric and really very loving, even if he wasn't interested in the pregnancy. They said different things but basically they all agreed that men respond badly to the female body at the best of times, especially when it is a body inhabited by a tiny life form for which they know they will be responsible, in one way or another, for the rest of their lives. One friend, Suzanne, had a reverse response. Her husband was happy enough about the prospect of being a father, but what he was *really* happy about was the new breasts his previously flat-chested wife suddenly sprouted out of the sea of hormones which is your body when you are pregnant.

Suzanne had never had any breasts to speak of before she was pregnant; she is one of those pencil-thin women with bony shoulders and a magnificent face, with high cheekbones and almond eyes, and lots of auburn hair she piles on her head. She wears tunics and tank tops and a swimsuit you could fit in the palm of one hand. Classic, I've always thought. A real beauty. She'd once had her clothes stolen out of the dryer at a laundromat and we all thought this was phenomenal because what thief could possibly have fit into them? Anyway, we always assumed that Suzanne's long, elegant frame was one of the major reasons why men all gawked at her when she entered a room and why she'd managed to snare a really gorgeous, sexy, wildlife photographer, Dan (her husband), while the rest of us went out on hopeless dates with insurance salesmen.

But when she was eight weeks gone with her first child, she didn't just have breasts, she had BREASTS. She'd gone from an A cup to a D cup and was still growing (she got to a DD underwire job with extra support through the shoulders before the whole thing was over) and Dan was delighted. Dan was ecstatic. He was so happy he kept feeling her up whenever he got the chance. Exactly like a high school boy, she said, except much worse because it wasn't just Saturday night but every night of the week and she had to live with him, knowing as she now did, that he must have found her previously petite breasts rather pathetic and unattractive if this was how he responded to her new large breasts.

She told us this while we were sitting in the courtyard garden at the Museum of Fine Art during

the Thursday night outdoor concert series, waiting
for a jazz band to come on. This was years ago; I was
engaged to Andy but not yet married to him. I'd left
him asleep in my apartment—we were having that
clumsy frantic all-day sex new couples often do—and
he was near collapse when I'd hauled myself from bed
and rushed to the subway platform. I had to do it because I was the one holding the tickets and, though I
realized it was perhaps not good behavior to leave
Andy at such an intimate postcoital time, I felt that his
sudden marriage proposal and subsequent procrasti-
nation at actually setting a wedding date bode omi-
nously for the future. I reasoned that he was way too
interesting and nice and generally fun for me to snare
and keep. Okay, he was also paranoid and unbalanced
and this might knock him down a few pegs with
other women who are more choosy about the mental
state of their partners, but I felt certain that some
other slimmer, more cultured woman with better
skin and a snazzy dress sense—a woman not unlike
Suzanne herself—would scoop him out from under
me even as I did my best in every way, cooking
gourmet meals for him and ravishing his perfect body
with incredible gusto any night of the week he cared
to call. Except that night, as it was concert night.

Beth was there—she was still married to David at
the time. I mean, she's still married to David now, but
they were happily married then. Sarah was not there
(she was just about to have her first baby and found
sitting on the ground a physical impossibility). Carla
was there, looking broody and dark in a black sum-

mer dress and a cotton shawl and bare feet. She always looks bored at these events, bored and preoccupied with thoughts much more interesting than any which our company might provide, though she swears this is not the case and she is deeply interested in all of her friends. She was especially interested that night in George Lambrick—he is married to Lori Marshall, who is a surgeon and therefore almost never there— because he'd brought along another woman, named Gloria, whom we all speculated about in silence, wondering if he was having an affair with her and, if so, why he'd been so brazen, so stupid, as to bring her to an event at which half of Lori's friends would be. The answer, of course, was that he was not having an affair with Gloria—Carla told me this during the intermission—she could tell by his body language. Naturally, Carla was right, she is the smart one who is always right, and the reason why Gloria had come with George to the concert (we found out later) was because he wouldn't dare bring Claire, with whom he *was* having an affair. Even then, before our suspicions were confirmed, the thought did cross our minds that there might be another woman, but not Gloria. There was lengthy telephone coverage following the event during which we called each other on flimsy excuses and had conversations that started *we must have lunch together soon and who was that Gloria person anyway* and then went into long debates as to whether Gloria was the woman he was having an affair with or was she the *cover* for the actual woman, the decoy he positioned to confuse us with, which is what she turned out to be.

Suzanne, whose large breasts pressed in a painful-looking way against her summer dress, sat down next to George and Gloria on the picnic rug and said, "Bastard can't get his hands off them. I feel like a scratch post for a cat."

"Oh, let him have his fun," Beth said. "Soon he'll get bored and go back to reading *Newsweek* in bed."

"Actually, there was an article about sex in last week's *Newsweek,*" I said. "Apparently American sex is visually oriented whereas sex in other nations is driven more by the tactile and olfactory senses."

"It's the media. It's destroying our fundamental animal drives," said Carla.

"I don't know about that," George said. "I think men are very tactile. Isn't that what you are complaining about, Suzanne?"

"The point is that it is not *me* he's touching," Suzanne said. She looked down at her front. "He's touching *them, these,* and they are not really mine. They belong to the pregnancy."

"That is an interesting statement," Carla said, perking up a little.

"I wouldn't mind having them even if they weren't mine," I said.

"But they are yours," George said, looking right at Suzanne's chest. "They are part of you."

"Get him a rubber doll," Beth said. "I got one for David as a joke but I think he really liked it."

"One of my patients uses a doll," Carla said, yawning.

"It's not David, is it? He's not seeing you?"

"No."

"Excuse me," said Gloria, "but I don't really think I know any of you well enough to be talking about this."

We thought she was having an affair with George so we all looked at each other like *Oh please* and continued.

George pointed at Suzanne's left breast. "If they aren't part of you then can I touch them?" he asked.

"You are sick," Suzanne said. "And no, you may not."

"See, *I may not*. That's exactly what I thought you'd say. Which means that you *do* think they are part of you, no matter what else you might claim."

We paused, considering this.

"It might seem unkind," I said, "but in the scheme of things I find it a little ungrateful of you to go around having a perfect body—tall and thin with enormous breasts—and complaining about it, even if the breasts are only temporary."

"Per*haps*," Suzanne said.

"A lot of couples use, you know, equipment. This is just natural equipment," Beth said. "I don't see a problem."

Carla gave Beth a disapproving look. "I can assure you that your not seeing a problem means very little to Suzanne at this time."

Beth clucked her tongue. "Says you, Dr. Spock."

"Dr. Spock is a *child* psychologist," Carla said. "He had very little advice about sexual aids."

"I really wouldn't mind if we changed the subject," said Gloria.

Because we thought she was having an affair with George we gave her a really hateful look and then continued.

"Dan is a sexy guy. He likes breasts. You probably just have to go with it," I said.

"Nothing wrong there!" George said.

"Plenty wrong," said Carla.

"Oh Carla, you are such a stick in the mud. Think of Dan, you are going to ruin all his fun," George said.

Carla shrugged. "I have a great sex life with James. And we use nothing artificial, not that I wouldn't be open to it if he wished to introduce such an item to the relationship."

"Bullshit," George snorted. "You'd send him into therapy."

"Therapy is not a punishment."

"Oh, stop."

"I will stop, because I don't think we are helping Suzanne."

No, we could not help Suzanne. And tension mounted in her household with each passing month. Dan continued to lavish attention on her DD cups, while Suzanne, like most pregnant women, became less and less interested in any display of sexual interest, especially those centered around breasts which she really felt she'd only borrowed from the world and would have to return. Eventually the whole thing was resolved—their daughter was born—and the breasts that Dan had so loved became her domain until they eventually diminished back to their original size, if not slightly smaller. Suzanne returned to wearing tunics and strapless dresses and a swimsuit so tiny you could use it as a bookmark and Dan, for reasons that I think are obvious, insisted they have another baby.

Suzanne now has four children and is no longer a nubile young thing in thongs and sashes. She isn't fat either, just normal in shape except that her once pert, tiny breasts are now somewhat elongated and when unclothed she has come to resemble an African woodcarving. Of all my friends she was the only one who agreed with me that Andy's response to my pregnancy was not normal. On the phone I explained to her his initial response and then his brooding silence, and then how when I'd asked him if anything was wrong he got this maniacal smile on his face and said, in a totally fake and unbelievable way, "Oh no, darling, why should anything be wrong?"

"Does he talk about the baby?" she asked.

"No."

"Does he touch your stomach?"

"No."

"Does he touch you *at all?*"

"No."

She paused and took a breath, kind of like a doctor who while examining you finds something a little wrong and takes that moment to breathe before asking you pointed questions about your diet and lifestyle.

"Has he told his parents you are pregnant?"

"I told them. They got so excited they had a car accident."

"You didn't tell them while they were driving?"

"Of course not. But as soon as they knew they insisted on driving eight hours from Illinois to come and see for themselves, though I did explain that at thirteen weeks there was nothing to see."

"Has he told anyone? Work colleagues, friends?"

"No."

"And of course he won't talk about it."

"No," I said. "Do I have a problem?"

"I think you do, but I just want to emphasize at this point that many fathers have no interest in their children until they are school age and that the mothers do survive, although I have to admit I have no idea how."

She recommended childbirth classes. She told me that if Andy got involved with a group of other expectant fathers it might have a cheerleading effect on him. I agreed and made some calls. The last thing I really wanted to know about was labor—I was in heavy denial about that particular part of pregnancy and had already decided that the form of pain control I wanted was general anesthesia. My mother had all her children under general and, though we may have lost some IQ points on the way, we were basically fine and she thinks, even to this day, that childbirth is a lovely experience. That is, what she can remember of it, which is waking up to a room full of flowers.

That was how I wanted it to be, too, but modern-day medicine frowns upon those who simply won't participate in the birth of their children, and I realized I needed to make some concessions in the direction of consciousness during the proceeding. A childbirth class was probably a good idea. I might learn techniques to persuade the doctors to put me out and Andy might learn that other people look forward to the birth of their children and this might point him in the right direction. So when I was seven months pregnant we drove up to a little house in Brookline where four other couples, four other women of approximately my own size with their relatively skinny partners, sat propped up on various couches and pillows listening as the teacher, a very tiny woman named Gail who spoke with a low, meaningful voice and nodded a lot as she introduced us to the world of third trimester pregnancy and asked us each our names and due dates.

"I'm Donna, this is Paul. December second," said the first couple.

"My name is Elaine. Stewart and I are not actually married. In fact, he is not the biological father of this child, but we met in July and are now life partners, so I want you all to think of him as the father of this child."

I couldn't help myself. Without even so much as raising my hand I said, "That would have been a lot easier if you hadn't told us he definitely wasn't the father."

"I know," said Elaine, nonplussed, "but I've been through a lot of group therapy and whenever I get in a circle of relative strangers like this I can't stop myself from being painfully honest."

"That's real brave of you," the teacher, Gail, said.

"Thank you."

"No, thank *you.*" Gail nodded.

"I'm John Frank. This is my wife, Valerie Frank. We're due—when, honey?—December sixteenth."

We're due? Where did this guy get this idea that *we're due?* It turned out that John Frank had all sorts of ideas about what *we,* meaning his mousy little wife Valerie, was going to do by way of childbirth and that the reason Valerie insisted they went to childbirth classes was the exact opposite of why Andy and I were there. She was trying to get him less interested in the pregnancy. She was trying to convince him, at least, that he himself was not pregnant.

"I'm Marcia Brady. This is Greg—and before you laugh and make comments about *The Brady Bunch,* let me assure you we can't help having this name. It's our parents' fault. Our baby, which we already know is a boy, is being named Connor. Oh, and he's due on the third."

Then it was our turn. Andy looked at me in a slightly panicked way. I said, "I'm Meg, this is Andy. The baby is due December thirteenth."

"Lucky thirteen!" Elaine piped up.

"Oh shut up," I said.

We went every week. Wednesday nights. Gail had an extremely messy house and either never attempted to decorate or had a very bad, a really pathological, sense of what goes with what. In fact, the only decoration as such came from her three children's finger-paints and collages and pictures made out of seeds. Added to those works of "art," as October arrived, were Halloween black cats with chalked eyes and whiskers, witch hats made from construction paper, ghosts with dangling legs (why do ghosts need legs?). The furniture was a mishmash of different styles and fabric designs, plaid against florals against paisley, and we sat there in our clothes, some of which had designs of their own, with ghost legs dangling in our faces and the light fixture—a brass and frosted glass contraption embellished with balloons from one of the children's parties—shedding harsh yellow light onto our tired faces. After the second session Andy said he got a headache from the visual chaos and couldn't stand going back.

I didn't know if it was the decor or the subject matter that had this effect on Andy but I had to admit that I, too, was practically incapable of sitting for two hours in that room, a tiny, hot room with flocked-on foil wallpaper and all those clashing prints and colors, and people with *Brady Bunch* names and that Elaine person, who really did think she was in group therapy and talked about her relationship with her mother, her relationship with her sister, her relationship with her previous shrink—who it turned out was the biological father of her child—and, worse than *anything,* she talked about sex during late pregnancy, which she apparently had with this Stewart character, her "life partner"—what a sick bunch of grapes he was—no matter how much we—okay, *I*—reminded her she was not in group therapy and we (I) had no interest in any of the above. The decor problem *was* bad—I'd taken to wearing black from head to toe on Wednesday nights so that at least I'd done my bit not to add to the esthetic disaster that was Gail's living room, but the day Marsha Brady turned up in an enormous tent dress in blue and green tartan *with a fringe* and then sat on a red and mustard leopard-spot couch *also with a fringe* and Elaine talked about doggy-position sex in late pregnancy, I went rushing to the toilet.

I returned, flustered and supremely embarrassed, hoping that I didn't smell.

"Is vomiting normal in late pregnancy?" Donna asked. Donna was a computer analyst; she and Paul were the only somewhat normal couple in the group, and I don't really know why they were there at all. She already knew everything about pregnancy and spent most of her time sitting in front of a terminal coaxing information from the Medical Forum on the Internet. She knew better than Gail that vomiting was not normal in late pregnancy, although it probably was normal given Elaine and Stewart, who, you could tell just by looking at them, were counting the minutes before the class was over and they could go back to her apartment and have a lot of sex on all fours.

"It can be a sign of labor," Gail said. She was holding a set of life-size pictures of the newborn descending from the uterus. The one we'd gotten to before I'd been sick was of the first part of second-stage labor. The baby's head was being squeezed into the size and shape of a small pear and the vaginal opening, so clear and exposed, so humiliatingly delineated in pen and ink, had the circumference of a Bic pen. Andy was staring with horror at the drawing, just as he'd stared in horror at the one previous to that, which really only showed a baby in a large oval uterus, and I thought I was probably in trouble.

"Are you feeling any pain?"

"No," I said. "But I think I better go home anyway."

This was not a good time for me. It was winter and I wore sweaters and a heavy coat everywhere I went, even in our kitchen, which is very cold. They say pregnancy makes you hot, but I did not find this to be the case. I was always cold, cold even as I wore my size 22 thermal long underwear, even as I wore my mountaineering socks. Each day I went out into the world resembling in both size and shape a refrigerator, or one of those grannies with an enormous bust and girth, or a bag lady. That was me from a distance. Up close my skin had become a road map of veins and my stomach actually appeared bruised it was so dark in places. I developed a sudden allergy to all metals and couldn't wear my engagement ring. My wedding ring was also slightly aggravating but I felt I had to wear it or else I would look unwed, as well as all the rest.

I was tired, a condition that I now understand lasts for eighteen years after the initial conception. Freckles appeared out of nowhere; my face was hidden in a rust color that would not wash off. My hairdresser threw up his hands in despair. At night, festooned by my enormous stomach, which like the moon had taken on a dark and light side, I waited for the thigh which suffered from a pinched nerve to go crampy and ache. My craving was for oranges; I ate fruit like a monkey. I was miserable and everyone at my childbirth class could see I was miserable and that Andy was like a zombie—he never talked in class, he never once offered his opinion on anything—and in this condition, him a zombie and me looking like a bloated meatloaf, we packed ourselves into the car outside Gail's House of Fabric only to discover that someone, probably kids anticipating Halloween (a "holiday" which really ought to be abolished in inner cities where, let's face it, every night is Halloween) had taken all the air out of our tires.

This was very bad because this meant that our fight—which we were bound and determined to have regardless of circumstances—had to take place in the back of a cab.

"Did you see all those people in there, every one of them actually is looking forward to the birth of their child?" I said for openers.

He said nothing.

"The men involved, they listen to the explanations about birth and they ask questions."

He said nothing.

"If you didn't want to have a baby then you might have said something before I got to the *third trimester*," I said.

There was a long pause and then Andy spoke. "I thought having a baby sounded like a good idea."

"When did it *stop* sounding like a good idea? It's not like we even have the baby yet. It's not like we can look at it and then say to ourselves, 'Oh, this one really isn't so good.'"

"We would never say that."

"Exactly, so why can't you participate in this pregnancy?"

Andy opened his mouth to speak—thank God, I thought—and just as he was about to confess either that he didn't want the baby after all or that he thought he was participating enough in the pregnancy just by agreeing to attend classes in which his head throbbed from two hours of having to align Indian mosaic prints with ancient, fraying floral chintz, while a strange woman named Gail droned on about the magical qualities of the uterus, the cabdriver interrupted us. "I got three," he said.

"What? Who is talking?" I knew it was the driver but I wanted to make a point. The point is this: we pay cabdrivers to drive and they do not pay us to include them in our conversations. The reason I hate cabs—the reason I only take them if the car has been vandalized and I am too pregnant to walk to a subway station—is because for some reason they always talk to me. If I am with another woman they say, "So, where're you girls off to?" and then have some comment about anywhere we might name. If I am by my-self they start giving me advice. *Don't buy furniture at junk shops—it's always shot through with woodworm. Don't use Drano, it kills your pipes, don't buy fuel additives, they're a scam.* But until that night they'd always kept quiet when I was with a man.

"I got one boy and two girls. Girls are better. The boy had earaches for the whole first year, screamed all day and all night. We took him to the doctor, doctor couldn't tell us anything. We took him to a specialist, but this specialist was for stomach upsets and so that didn't do us any good. We took him to the emer-gency room one night, just so we could be with other people who were up at three A.M. We didn't have a single night of peace. It was hell. It was *living hell.* My wife and me couldn't have a meal together, couldn't even have a conversation! I started driving a cab just to get out of the place. I used to have a day job, I was a mechanic, but I'd rather drive all night in this stink-ing city than listen to that kid scream . . ."

We made it home despite the cabdriver's speech on parenthood. I made it up the stairs despite swollen ankles and tired knees. We undressed in the dark, in silence. I remembered what I'd read that morning in the obstetrician's office, in one of the women's mag-azines from three years ago that for some reason col-lect in the waiting room of doctors' offices. The latest survey on adultery reveals that 60 percent of men have affairs and that these affairs most often begin during their wife's pregnancy or soon after the deliv-ery of a first child. That's what it said, in black and white in the obstetrician's waiting room. I looked at Andy suspiciously. I looked at myself, my huge self, and for a moment I felt as though my shape was the correct shape, while other women, women with normal figures, seemed oddly like aliens from some sex planet, here on a mission to steal my man. Could Andy be having an affair? His stomach was flat, his muscles were unhampered by layers of water retention, placenta, baby, developing tissue, and just plain lard. Perhaps he, too, belonged to the sex planet, and I was in an orbit all my own.

We went to bed, him hugging one end of the mattress while I, and five pillows, took up the rest. In the morning I woke to find that he had gone.

CHAPTER THREE

YOU MIGHT WONDER WHAT I DO FOR A LIVING. I've saved this part for as long as I can because when you announce outright that you write fiction for a living people have one of several responses. First, they stop taking you seriously that very second because, after all, you don't do anything serious with your life, you simply make up stories about other people's lives. This is what they think, even if they don't say it, and what they also think, and an uncanny number actually say, is that you *steal* other people's stories and weave them into novels that you then sell for a mint. Some people consider this to be good—they want their lives stolen and immortalized on the page—and some think it is bad—they wish writers would mind their own damned business. How anyone could believe that what happens in their lives is so interesting that I would steal it and sell it is well beyond me, considering that nothing worth mentioning ever happens to most people, while my imagination can summon up any number of bizarre happenings without too much trouble.

"You would never believe who Darla Phillips is having an affair with! You could use this in your next book, she's having an affair with the window man!" This is from Glynnis, the local alumni coordinator in my area. Despite my having never given a dime to my alma mater, she still invites me to all her teas.

"The window man?" I asked, mildly interested. "Who is the window man? Is he like the Calgonite man? Does he live in my windows?"

"The guy who cleans the windows in her office building! Isn't that amazing? Isn't that just like something out of a novel?"

Not any novel I would read, but Glynnis isn't the only one who thinks she has a literary tidbit to add to my life.

"I went to this wonderful party two weeks ago. I'll tell you about it—maybe you can use it in your next novel!"

Can you imagine more hopeless material? A party that I didn't attend? A friend of mine, to whom things *do* happen, in fact she is the one with the pierced belly button whom I spoke of in the first line of this book, the one who got the boyfriend and then moved away from him to live in the Georgian cottage instead of the adobe house, which I always felt was a charming house because I'm the sort who likes terra-cotta floors and plain walls and really hates wallpaper (Carla says this is because after my father died in the car accident on the way to the airport, my mother went seriously into the Arts and Crafts movement and for many years we lived with three different William Morris prints in every room of the house, so I associate death with intermittent patterns of fruit and birds, but it's a debatable point)—anyway, *she* does tell me some awfully good stories that I'd like to swipe. Trouble is I can never seem to fit them into anything I am writing. For example, she had a boyfriend, an ex-boyfriend, who befriended a gay man without knowing he was gay (or so he says) and this other fellow, Claude, fell in love with her ex, the way gay men often do fall in love with straight men, which is the way women fall in love with disinterested, emotionally closed men with good jobs, and spent months trying to get Arthur, my friend's ex, interested in sex. It is pointless to recount all the antics that poor, enamored Claude got up to trying to reveal to Arthur all the secrets and spoils of gay love, because nothing about it has any relevance whatsoever to the rest of this book, but let it suffice to say that the climax, if you don't mind my calling it that, was when Arthur was convinced that he ought to inspect Claude's butt for a possibly melanomatic mole which Claude claimed was just to the inside of his left cheek. Not only inspect, but take pictures of, because the doctors in the area (who knew Claude, and knew he had no such mole) had long ago refused to treat him.

The other thing about being a fiction writer is that nobody quite believes what you are saying, which is what happened the morning I woke up to discover that Andy had left me. My editor called to ask when my manuscript was going to be finished and when the baby was due, these things being easily interchangeable, if not exactly the same thing, in my editor's mind. (During my pregnancy I often wondered if Bill understood that I was actually going to give birth to a human baby *as well as* a three-hundred-page document, but never mind that.) He caught me at a particularly bad time, precisely one and one half hours after I'd woken to discover Andy had abandoned me, and I'd been weeping around the house dying for the phone to ring and it to be Andy and for him to explain. Any explanation would do. He could say he simply forgot where he lived, and woke up thinking he'd fallen asleep in the wrong house. He could say he had thought I told him to meet me in Oklahoma for dinner when really what I'd said was what time are you going to be home for dinner. The particulars didn't matter.

But no such call came from Andy, who it turned out was driving around aimlessly in his car, much like his father before him, who apparently spent most of Andy's childhood driving aimlessly around in his car. If you've ever driven into the parking lot of a 7-Eleven and seen a man with disheveled gray hair and three days' beard growth and eyes like a German Shepherd talking into the backseat of a gold Ford sedan as though there were someone back there, which there is not, there is only a great mass of empty Chinese take-out bags and Dunkin' Donuts bags, Styrofoam tubs and plastic-domed trays from Wendy's and Arby's and a few McDonald's Happy Meals, and that same guy is still in the parking lot when you return *the next day,* it is probably Andy's father, Sam Howe, who set the example for Andy, who was indeed doing a latter-day imitation of his father, driving hopelessly around the Boston metropolitan area, wondering where he would go now that home was not an option.

When Bill called about the book I could not even summon up the tiniest bit of regular conversation and dove straight into my problems with Andy, how he had closed up like a fan the minute the pregnancy started, how he went into a kind of catatonia when we attended childbirth classes, and how I'd woken up that very morning to an empty bed and a note of apology. Andy was gone, I explained. He must have opened one sleepy eye, caught the silhouette of his enormous wife—a previous size 8—and decided to bail before she blew.

"You are making this up," Bill said.

"Just because I *can* make things up doesn't mean I made this up," I said.

"But nobody would act like that, certainly not Andy. Andy is a workhorse. Andy is a solid man."

"Ha ha, that's what he's like at *work*. At work he is

confident and thrusting and totally in control," I said. "A man at work is a different animal altogether from the pitiful bag of anxieties that appears at the doorstep around dinnertime each evening."

Bill and Andy know each other separately from me—they worked together when Andy was sales rep at the same publishing company in New York where Bill was an editor. In fact, that is when I met Andy. I moved in with him in New York and then, when he decided to switch repping for bookselling, we moved here to Boston where he owns his own store. I didn't realize at the time exactly what it would mean to live with the owner of a retail outlet that sells one's very own product. I'd thought perhaps it might mean my books got a better position on the shelf. But basically what Andy does is figure out which books deserve what floor space based on figures he extracts from an enormous computer that tracks sales, tax, employee payroll, you name it. This computer has proved to be my enemy. This computer can tell Andy just how long it takes to sell a single copy of my book (too long) and what the value of it is in terms of quarterly reports. I hate this computer, and in a way I hate Andy's job. These days sales reps from publishing companies come to him to shop their wares and when they arrive, all brimming with love for a new book, a book with honesty and balance and poetry and wisdom, a book like the type I try to write, he's the guy who gets out the calculator.

A great job—owner of a Boston bookstore. He's invited to dinners and publishing parties and asked quite often for his opinion of up-and-coming new authors. But for me it's not so great. He brings home a lot of proof copies, sent to him by over a dozen different publishing houses. They all look very impressive to me and are accompanied by letters from editors and advance praise from major reviewers, saying how great the book is, how brilliant the author is, how much it will sell, all that. These proofs fill me with envy. For one thing, they are finished, bound books just waiting for their final jackets, while my own book is still stacks of marked paper in a drawer. For another, if you believe all the letters and smarm, everybody desperately wants to see these books published and read; they are willing to pay great sums and print enormous quantities of them, while my books take a lot of effort to sell and fetch only a small pittance by comparison.

The whole thing can get pretty demoralizing. While I spend all day filling my computer screen with all my beautiful words, he spends his day filling his computer screen with ISBN numbers and formulas which delineate the bottom line and conclude, one way or another, that no, I'm never going to make a penny. He can prove beyond a reasonable doubt that the books that make editors drool, the literary books that brought them into publishing in the first place, the books that we all should be reading except we are too busy watching *I Love Lucy* reruns, all those books are just not economically viable. What is viable are the plot-thick novels about beautiful lithe virgins who meet tall dark strangers and fall prey to sweeping passion—A-format paperbacks with gold-embossed writing and a picture of a woman bending backward in the brutal embrace of some semi-tyrant in leather—*those* are the only books worth hawking to the public these days if you have any interest in turning a profit. Andy, who claims to love books, who spends half the night resurrecting dead books by dead authors, is the guy who gives over only a table in New Fiction to major, established novelists, sets up great dump bins and posters for Jackie Collins and Judith Krantz, John Grisham and Danielle Steel, and then hides new writers in the stacks by alphabetical order where they will never be seen or bought. Then, he reports his sales to the publishing houses, who use these criteria to make sure that they next time they publish new writers they pay them so little money that the next book they write has to be written between shifts at Superdrug. Andy claims it isn't his fault—he is simply reflecting the public's taste—but it seems to me he does an awful lot to ensure that brand-name authors sell in big numbers while the real talents are left behind. I should have been *glad* he left me; I should have thrown a party. When I think about what he has done to the careers of authors like me, I should have *left him,* not only left him but maimed him badly if not outright killed him.

But I didn't feel that way at the time. What I felt was desperately alone. Alone and heavily pregnant and scared.

"Maybe he went out to get a paper. Maybe he had an early meeting," Bill said.

"No, he's left. And it's serious, too, because he took his electric blanket and his de-ionizing machine and his wave sound simulation machine and a bottle of sleeping pills."

"Do you think he's going to try to off himself?"

"No, he always takes sleeping pills. But if he'd left spontaneously, impulsively, if he left not really *wanting* to leave he'd never have remembered the pills. The fact that he remembered the pills means he planned this out."

There was a pause and then Bill said, "Hmm," and I could tell he had drifted away from this conversation and was now thumbing through the mail on his desk.

"What are you writing again?" he asked. "I keep forgetting the storyline of your new book."

I sighed. There is no point in telling a man about your marital problems. They may make sympathetic noises but what it comes down to is they think, Gee that's tough, without thinking this might actually happen to them or have any relevance in their lives. A woman, on the other hand, wants to know everything and wants the conversation to go on as long as it takes to get everything, because she is comparing her situation to your situation. Even as she sobs with you on the phone and tells you that you are beautiful and he's a fool and he'll come back and who needs him anyway, she is *multitasking;* she is doing complicated mental analysis to determine whether her husband is about to walk out on her, too. If Bill had been a woman he'd have wanted to know every gritty detail from when I first noticed a change in Andy's behavior to what we had for supper the night he left. But not Bill. Bill was an editor and a man and he was a man at work, so all he wanted to know was about the novel.

"It's about a woman historian who relates her marital problems to the history of marital problems in a kind of funny, anecdotal fashion."

"People don't want to read about bygone ages."

"It isn't bygone. It's happening now," I said.

"Oh well, *somewhere.*"

What Bill meant was that it wasn't happening in New York City right this minute. More than that, it wasn't happening right now to the people Bill has lunch with. He and his lunch pals were not at the moment thinking about marriages in Victorian times, in Chaucer's times, in Napoleon's times, and remembering that some very famous marriages were actually a shambles and thinking about what this says about the contemporary situation we all find ourselves in. In other words, it wasn't happening to *him.* Nor had anyone faxed him to say it was happening to them. In fact, *he* wasn't even married at the moment, so why should he be interested in books about the subject? The person he wants me to write like is Theo Clarkson, his whiz kid, my contemporary and onetime lover, who writes anything that sells and has recently hit on westerns, which he writes in a trendy way. I admit that it is a real feat to write westerns in a trendy way if only because there is nothing trendy *per se* or even remotely interesting about westerns, which I might have reminded Bill are indeed from *bygone ages,* but Theo conjures up the semi-tough, die-in-the-saddle heroes that men like to read about, and all his heroines are under twenty, and nobody is married, and everybody is extremely sexually charged. The men wear boots and spurs, the women are barefoot. A heroine is likely to step delicately outside with the bare earth as her floor, holding a bucket of lemon-scented water with which to wash herself as the sky bleeds orange and red, innocently exposing her perfect naked form to the boot-and-spur man. In these books women have slim thighs and need no sexual arousal prior to penetration, people make love on sand, which we all know is uncomfortable, but discomfort is not mentioned. *GQ* did a spread of Theo in his underwear and a pair of leather chaps—I recognized him from his appendicitis scar, which once upon a time I knew intimately—and at the moment he's like a writer/pop star. He lives in New York but pretends to live in Montana, which he visits on occasion and hunts big game and pals around with Richard Ford, who also pretends to be a cowboy. Bill wants me to be like him, but then he wants all his authors to be like him. I keep trying to tell Bill that this is impossible, if only because I am slightly afraid of farm animals, like the goats my mother keeps, and can't ride a horse—not that Theo, the "cowboy," has ever actually sat on a horse in his life.

"Bill," I said. "It's pointless talking to you. I'm hanging up now." I said this, knowing that I was acting a little mean, but someone once told me that if you bottle up your emotions you get cancer early in life and so I use that as an excuse to vent anger at my whim. Besides, Bill was a man and, although he'd never done anything to hurt me personally, he had undoubtedly hurt innumerable other women who'd never had the opportunity to hurt him back quite hard enough for whatever he'd done to them, so it was fitting and right that I was a little mean to him.

I got off the phone with Bill and I looked around at our apartment, which is part of a larger house, a nineteenth-century Victorian that stands stark and tall on the middle of a chestnut tree–filled road in West Newton, where we'd moved because we'd heard the schools were good back in the days when our marriage was young and alive and we planned great masses of children. Days very much *before* I learned that Andy has a pathological fear of pregnancy, of childbirth, and if one cares to take it a step further (and I think it is safe to do so) of children themselves. Days like now.

Because I was feeling desperate and unhappy I went straight for the kitchen to eat my own weight in chocolate. A pregnant woman always has an ample stock of chocolate and other related junk food and I lit into a box of Hostess cupcakes without further ado. I like our kitchen. Our apartment has a beautifully handmade kitchen that the previous owners, the Andersons, went to a lot of trouble and expense to create. We bought the apartment for that kitchen, which is constructed out of antique pine cabinets that the Andersons gutted from the house of a relative who died and left a perfectly untouched nineteenth-century farmhouse behind for them to pick the cabinets off, and the paneling, and the balustrade, and the fireplace surrounds, and the leaded glass, and the front door. These items, and many others, were then hauled to a U-Store-It, and our apartment got the cabinets before the Andersons decided they really needed a bigger house to store all their antiques. They ended up buying a newly built Federal-style house—new for the sake of the plumbing and wiring and plasterwork—which they doctored up with authentic old things—old so it could look charming and tasteful and homey, which it would have if you could ignore the fact that the Andersons live in it and the Andersons are grabby and gauche and think going to EuroDisney is "visiting the Continent" and actually use phrases like "visiting the Continent." They even tried to take *back* the kitchen cabinets after the contract was signed and it took *three* lawyers and *five* real estate agents to convince them that they could not do this.

So we have the handmade kitchen and an adjoining breakfast room, which is a lovely sunny room with a picture window looking out over the backyard, which even in November is quite beautiful. We have a cherry tree which has never seen a cherry in its life, but offers up by way of apology the most awesome golden red leaves in autumn. There is an oak which the neighbors keep threatening to cut down (they say it ruins their view) and a small vegetable garden that the woman who owns the rest of the house,

Mrs. Russell, a lovely older woman with long steel-colored hair she coils on top of her head, tends to with great love and care. The oak tree was planted by her from one acorn over seventy years ago.

We love the kitchen with its perfect New England backyard so much that we never really bothered to do anything much with the living room, which mostly just functions as a kind of theater for the television. It has a working fireplace, however, and because I was feeling extremely depressed and weepy I took my package of Hostess cupcakes with me into the living room and sat in front of the fireplace remembering, remembering exactly, how the first winter after we'd moved into the apartment five years ago was spent collecting logs and twigs for the fireplace, which we lit and made love beside the way all new couples do. Every night we did this, and some afternoons as well, until one day I woke up and realized that kicking around the backyard looking for kindling had become foreplay and we never made love anywhere else.

"It's all become too contrived," I told Andy. "I go to kiss you and you're already feeling in your pocket for matches. I'm thinking 'Are the logs dry? Where are my rubber boots?' It's got to stop."

That was true. It was also true that on one occasion we'd positioned ourselves too close to the fire and halfway through what would have been our finest lovemaking session on record, we were forced to turn our attention to a peculiar smell, which we discovered was my hair, which was on fire. Also that both our backs had developed bruises the size of silver dollars and that we had a brand-new king-sized bed upstairs that we'd hardly ever been in since getting married.

"Okay, I'll tell you the truth," Andy had confessed then, "I don't like our bed. I don't like it because your mother gave it to us and so whenever I look at it I think about her and how you are her daughter and I am sleeping with you."

"But you are *married* to me. When you're married you aren't sleeping with the person, you're married to the person."

"But still," he said, "your mother."

"She *bought* the bed. She sanctions the whole thing! She gives it her blessing."

"I think she's, like, *in* the bed. Don't start talking about Freud now. I'm not going to talk to you if you mention Freud."

"No," I said. "This is a fake-out. I'm not saying you don't have some fleeting thought of my mother but she is not the problem here. I know this because if she were you'd never have been able to get it up all those times we stayed over at her farm. There's something else going on. Something you aren't telling me."

"Okay," he said and gave a huge sigh. He took out the pen he always, but *always,* keeps in the breast pocket of his shirt. It's one of those pens that you can flick in and out of its casing by pressing a toggle at one end. When Andy is nervous about something, when he's on the phone to somebody at work or can't quite crunch his numbers correctly, he flicks the pen, and he was flicking furiously now. "Okay, I'll tell you. Eloise and I had the exact same brand, with nearly an identical headboard. When I look at the bed, I think it is cursed. Also, that Eloise is in it. Eloise and your mother, and me and you."

Eloise is Andy's ex-wife. She is a tall bosomy blond—that is Andy's word, *bosomy*—I can't imagine describing anyone as bosomy in this day and age—with glued-on plastic fingernails and a collection of glass figurines of unicorns and kittens. She had a (real) toy poodle she kept under her arm because it made her feel "society" and she thought that being glamorous meant wearing rhinestones and a tight black dress. She used to leave little messages of the most stupid and trite variety all over the house for Andy to find. *Love conquers all—why don't you conquer me tonight?* when she wanted him to seduce her. Or, *The world is our oyster, let's take off somewhere* when she wanted to go to Ocean City, Maryland, which is where she is from. She cooked using recipes she found on the backs of Fritos bags and could not tell fake jewelry from real ("Look at this beautiful pearl necklace," she once said to Andy, "it was only sixteen dollars! Can you believe it! And all those women spending hundreds!"). They went to the same crummy beach hotel every year and she would insist they go to the beach and just lie there, every morning, every afternoon, while she soaked up the rays and drank diet Dr Pepper. She wore white zinc on her lips and eye patches so that no sunglasses lines would appear on her temples. At night when they got back to the hotel room she would slather her body in aftertan lotion, and stand naked in front of a mirror evaluating the deepening color of her skin.

The hotel was a wreck of a place, with a lock on the television so nobody could steal it. You could get doughnuts in the front office in the morning but otherwise the only food was from vending machines in the hall, and those were often dysfunctional because the kids tried to rob them. Andy hated the beach, though he is exactly the sort of person who bronzes beautifully within the space of a day, and he couldn't sleep in the hotel because he can't sleep anywhere and, besides, Eloise kept putting quarters in the Magic Fingers box and he woke up thinking there was an earthquake. One week and then home again. Eloise told all their friends about the romantic time they had, but really it was just a tanning project.

"Do I look like one of those models in *Sports Illustrated*?" she would ask him on the plane ride back.

Her skin had gone from creamy peach to practically black, with rich glossy lipstick and new eyelashes that fluttered all the way up to her eyebrows, Andy told me. New freckles, new burgundy-colored neck skin, new blonder, frizzier hair. She wore skirts the size of a postage stamp and white sandals with three-inch heels. She didn't look like *Sports Illustrated*, he told me, she looked like a transvestite.

"Wow, and you were married to her," was my frequent refrain, when he spoke of Eloise. I was never jealous of her—how could I be jealous of a woman who painted not only her own toenails, but those of her toy poodle, Bebe?

He'd married her when he was nineteen, a simple mistake of youth, a simple mistake that five other men have made since. It was easy enough to see the reason behind divorcing Eloise—she bought Hall-mark cards with photographs of actual couples, em-bracing in hazy soft focus, with crude, embarrassing limericks inside. She gave them to Andy signed in her loopy scrawl with the "i" in her name punctuated with a tiny heart. When she wrote her little messages, "Love conquers all," et cetera, she had to look up "conquer" in the dictionary. It was easy to understand why he left her, but why marry her in the first place?

I might have thought to ask that *before* I married Andy. Instead, dumbshit that I am, I waited until half a year into the thing when it suddenly occurred to me that we never made love in our bed—and it was then revealed that Andy *could not* make love in our bed—and he could not because of Eloise. It turned out the reason Andy married her was because Eloise was great in bed, great as in *totally* great. Not adequate, not good, not willing to do her part, not orgasmic and easy to stimulate, but *out of control* fantastic. She did all those things that I could never do. She wore stockings with black suspender belts and leather boots and lace bras. She wanted to be tied up, she wanted to be spanked. She bought a videocassette player and watched dirty movies—not because Andy asked her to—she watched them *on her own*. When she was twenty-nine she met Andy and told him she was twenty-four. She tried out all her practiced sex on him, one act after another, until he went so weak in the knees he agreed to marry her. And then, after they were married, she continued to be totally dedicated to him—hundreds of candy hearts and Hallmark cards and new undergarments to turn him on. She wanted to fuck so much that she considered his insomnia to be a good thing. She had a high school education and thought Puerto Rico was the capital of Portugal—but he stayed married to her because she gratefully gave him forty minutes of oral sex on a regular basis and she did it in the exact model and size bed, with approximately the same headboard that my mother had bought us for a wedding gift.

All this I learned after we were married. Isn't that sad? Isn't that the nightmare scenario? I have mentioned that Andy is good-looking, but when I say good-looking I really mean he is drop-dead handsome. He is six foot two and has glossy blond hair and green eyes and perfect teeth. He has a deep, resonating voice and dresses in a casual, slightly scruffy, totally sexy way. He's funny—he's got an acerbic wit that had, until that day, been used to entertain me endlessly about tales of Eloise, how she put doilies on every table in the house and bought plastic flowers and changed her name every few years—she'd been Candy and Scarlet and Kimberley—she'd picked Eloise because she had thought *it sounded French* and I think this last comment really sums up Eloise. She thought she could go to Paris and fit right in with that name. She even tried to inflect a little French accent into the name Eloise and nobody ever disillusioned her about the name. However, her biggest crisis occurred when the truth was brought forward about the gender of her dog, Bebe, her toy poodle, who turned out to be a castrated *he*. Apparently Eloise never looked at the key area which would have clued her in earlier, relying on the poodle's peeing habits to determine for her if he was male or female. Bebe was a squatter, not a cocker, and assumed to be female until one day in the park when a female in heat aroused poor castrated Bebe with painted toenails—Bebe who was indeed a transvestite through no fault of his own—and Eloise was cast into a state of shock and confusion such that she woke up each day unable to make a decision. I still laugh when I think of Eloise, a grown-up Barbie doll, parked in front of her vanity table with its jars of makeup and curlers and hair remover cream, all perfectly arranged under a semicircle of round starlet lightbulbs, unable to decide whether she should buff or file? Mousse or gel? And it was Andy who made me laugh about it in the first place. He's funny because he understands that a good joke is almost always at someone else's expense.

Okay, mentally, he's a little messed up and, in my ignorance and deluded self-glory, I thought this was enough reason for why it was fitting that he should marry someone average looking like me instead of the beauty queen you would expect him to marry. But no, it turns out that the beauty queens were all more clever than me. They found out early on that his previous wife was a nymphomaniac. They found out, made their excuses, and they left the party. Only I was too dumb not to inquire, with the result being that six months into the marriage I learned just how really doomed I was.

"But I really regretted marrying her," he said, after he'd finished telling me all the finer points of their extraordinary love life.

"Because you have found every woman since a great disappointment?" I queried. "Including and especially me." I'd adopted the rather sarcastic and despondent tone that I reliably call upon when my life has taken a tumble for the very much worse, and spoke as though I really didn't care at all about Eloise and Andy, what she did with him, how he loved it, and how he and I could never ever make love again, because even if he weren't thinking about her, I would be.

"No, no, no. Because I should never have married her. I didn't love her."

"Oh, what a surprise, and why would that be? Too much Shalimar?"

"I didn't love her and one day I met this other woman on the train and we had a conversation—"

"A conversation, how unusual. I'm sure you and Eloise didn't have time for such a thing—"

"We talked all the way from Boston to New York—"

"—between all the sex and her having to look up the words."

"—and I realized how much I'd been missing out

on, how much I needed to talk to a woman. It was fantastic just to talk and laugh and be friends. Four hours on the train and I realized I could not go back to Eloise."

And then it struck me.

"Name?" I said. Andy looked confused. "The name of the woman on the train?"

"Adrian."

"Adrian as in the-girlfriend-you-had-before-me-Adrian?"

"Yes. So?"

"*So* you know exactly what *so*. I am married to someone whose previous wife was a nymphomaniac with a perfect, albeit sunburnt body, which in the first place means that I can never have any strange or unusual sex in my life if I wanted to—which now, of course, I emphatically *do not*—because anything I'd care to do you and Eloise would already have done and it would all be a big yawn to you. And in the second place, you left Eloise for another woman, you left the nymphomaniac who has ruined our sex life from now until eternity, to run off with Adrian, who happens to have a one hundred sixty IQ and be the curator at a major New York gallery. So I'm fucked either way. I can't be the sexy one or the smart one. I can only be the dull one. I want a divorce."

One evening around that time we had Beth and David over for dinner. It was a cold night following a snowstorm, so of course we wanted to have an open fire going when they arrived. I came downstairs and found Andy hunched up in front of the fireplace rolling a paper log out of the *New York Times*. I wasn't having sex with him, I hadn't since the Eloise argument five days previously and I thought, what? *Now?* Before we've resolved the Eloise disaster and fifteen minutes before Beth and David arrive? But then I realized that the fireplace had ceased to be a talisman for love and simply become another period feature. We never made love in front of it again, though we did trade in the bed for a different model and resume normal relations.

But before that, before the fireplace became just a fireplace, I remember Beth and David coming over and Beth saying, "Tell me what it's like to be in love. To wake up not believing your luck, to hold your breath as your love enters the room. I miss it so."

She and David had been married five years. They'd come over the day of their anniversary to help us move some furniture and in the course of the afternoon had mentioned in passing that it was their fifth anniversary. The fact that they were helping us move furniture on such an important day, and that we'd asked them at the last moment, not knowing that it was their anniversary and that they'd agreed because they didn't have any other plans, should have made me stop and think that maybe they weren't so happy together. But when you are at that drooling in love stage you think everyone else is, too. Beth had been married five years and I assumed it was just like it was between Andy and me, just five years more of it. I remember I'd felt jealous—to be married five years seemed to me a real marriage while Andy's and my few months was just a kind of warming-up period—and I wanted to feel totally married. Like Beth and David, who were hardly speaking to one another, not that I noticed that because I was too busy being starry-eyed about my new husband, going around using the word "husband" whenever possible, and buying him little presents—a new shirt, a pocket flashlight, a silver frame to house our favorite picture of ourselves together—oh, yes, I was that sickening.

"Oh, *Beth,*" I said, like she was telling some sort of joke.

"Are you in each other's pants all the time? Just tell me. David and I hardly ever do it anymore."

"You are so funny," I said, still not getting it.

"I'm thinking maybe I should have an affair. This is not a voluntary thought. It's just that when I sit on the subway and I see a nice-looking man I wonder if he kisses well and if his underwear is clean or whether he's the type who makes all those horrible grunting noises, all the same thoughts I used to have when I was single except that back then I used to also wonder if he had a career in anything interesting or was he living with his mother. Now, I don't care about the career or the mother, what I want to know is can I get it with him, get *that feeling,* you know the one."

I didn't know what she meant. Of course I *did* know, I was living it, but I'd grown so used to romance, so used to love, that it had ceased to seem a thing separate from myself. I always compare love and houses—there's something essentially the same about them—a new marriage is almost always followed by a new house and that same house is sold like old junk when the marriage collapses. There's that old expression *If walls could talk. . . .* Want to know what walls would say if they could talk? Well, they'd say don't paper me in brocade, but they'd *also* say, *Marry in a bad market, divorce in a good one.* That would be any house's advice to a prospective couple. A corollary to my theory on love and houses is that you can tell love is waning in a couple's life when real estate has been elevated beyond the practical interest stage and into the dream house state. When couples fantasize about houses and areas and gardens and double garages, they are drifting past the romantic part of their lives and into a new, more dull, and much more permanent one. This is because being freshly in love is a little like living in the most beautiful house in the world and waking up each morning feeling enchanted by the house and also comfortably at home, wandering dreamily over the parquet floor and thinking how every inch of it is yours. Walking from bedroom to bedroom, admiring the dormer windows and the walk-in closets (not that I've ever lived in such a house—this is only a metaphor) and going downstairs to breakfast in your beautiful conservatory with views over the garden, thinking how lucky you are. If you've ever experienced this you know that it is exactly like feeling in love, becoming aware of all the normal everyday things in life as though they are unique and magical. Here I am opening my sash window with the original leaded glass. Here I am stepping into my twenty-one-foot bedroom. It's a bit like when you used to look at your husband and think, Wow, there he is in his boxer shorts reading the paper. Or, there he is washing his hair in the shower. The thought that he uses shampoo, that he takes the bottle and tips it upside down and lathers the shampoo in his hair, makes you feel almost weak. It seems so endearing, so intimate, almost heartbreaking.

Well, that doesn't last too long. But you think at the time that everyone is feeling the same way about their man, that they find everything about him wonderful, his face rough with whiskers, the hair on his toes. And you assume that people with particularly lovely houses feel the same way you do when you are in love with your own house. You don't realize that someday you'll take beamed ceilings for granted, that the Victorian claw-foot tub will just seem like a regular bathtub, that a slate roof is not going to permanently awe you, in fact you are not even going to notice it except when it leaks. You cease to feel lucky except by comparison to others who might be living in tract houses, and one day you find yourself wandering through the real estate section of the papers circling ads with a pen.

That's where Beth was, not with her house particularly (though that would come) but with David. She was browsing the real estate section and I didn't know it. I didn't understand all that yet. I was in love, we'd bought a nice apartment that we felt special in, and so I had a double whammy of love. Years would go by before I started to feel our place was a bit cramped and the kitchen the only good room and wanted the yard to be mine exclusively and, in fact, to have a whole house instead of only part of one. Years before I would convince Andy we needed a bridging loan so we could get a former schoolhouse which needed tons of work, years before I would sit in a bad market worrying about interest rates and thinking that no one would ever, *ever* buy the apartment which was once my dream home and was now the lump of sand I wished to sell in a desert full of sand. And many years before I would find myself literally sitting in what I now considered a really rather inadequate apartment feeling particularly hateful toward the fireplace because it made me remember the whole Eloise argument, which made me think of all the other arguments Andy and I have had, which brought me inevitably back to the most recent argument, about the coming baby that Andy had made it obvious he did not want.

Which should I be more upset about? I pondered. Which of the many horrible failing aspects of my dreary life?

1. *The inevitable breakdown of my marriage—I guess you can call it a breakdown when the man literally abandons you.*
2. *The two different mortgages we had on two proper-ties, one of which was uninhabited and the other of*

> which was only half inhabited, that is, I was living in
> it and Andy was not.

3. *The baby who, for all practical purposes, was now fa-*
   therless.

Really, it was a toss-up. And where was Andy
anyhow? He was responsible for all this and where
was he? On a train looking for another Adrian? Probably. Or not looking but finding anyway. Men
stumble upon women while women race around
frantically looking for men. That's one of the many
great inequities of being female. When Eve bit the
apple—one bite of a food that any good doctor rec-
ommends on a daily basis!—God condemned her,
condemned her to a life of trying to seek a mate
while Adam, apparently, got to sit in the garden eating the rest of the tree bare, and picking up women
who were on their way to the stream to bathe. Which
is why, though we don't know much about God, we
know that God is not a woman.

The baby started kicking and I counted the kicks,
one, two, three, the way you are meant to do in the
later stages of pregnancy. It gave me something to do
other than contemplate my fate as a single mother
with a double mortgage. I rather dreaded the moment
when the baby stopped kicking because then I would
have to find something else for a distraction. When
Andy was with me, that is before he left me, the days
always seemed so full. We were always, but *always*
busy. We were searching for the correct hand-painted
French tile, or figuring out how much reworking was

needed on the window casements. We were getting roofing quotes, we were interviewing architects to see if they had some good ideas for how to remodel the second floor of the new house (the original renovation was terribly inadequate and we needed another bedroom and a completely new bathroom). So how come at eleven o'clock in the morning on the first day without him the day seemed to stretch out enormously beyond proportion, like the day of the Rose Bowl always does? Because the new house was no longer the new house; it was the house that was probably going to be sold, well under value, in order to divide our assets evenly. It was the dead house.

The doorbell rang. I hardly recognized it because the doorbell never rings. Everyone I know just taps the door and comes strutting in, there is no reason to ring. The baby gave a tremendous leap inside me and I rose up and looked through the glass to see James, as in Carla's James, standing at the door, his hands filled with flowers.

"Meggy, this is too awful," he said, taking me into his arms and hugging me. James is tall and prematurely gray—really white—with a beard and round blue eyes and a slightly English accent from having spent the first fifteen years of his life in an English village in Kent before moving to America. He is awesome and charming and looks a lot like Hemingway. He has a small paunch from all the food and wine—he is a restaurant critic for several national magazines—but it only makes him more charming and accessible. Carla says he's wonderful in every way and that their love deepens each year—a statement I would never believe except Carla is emphatically truthful and they live in the same house, a nice enough colonial but nothing special, and have never once done any major remodeling to it or talked about a second home. They are content, they are happy. But they must also be gifted with second sight because how would James know, know already without my having made a single call, that Andy had left me?

"He phoned Carla this morning. He told us to look after you."

"He phoned *you*." I was dumbfounded. "That brat husband of mine took off and phoned *you*. He might have phoned *me*."

"He is too ashamed of himself."

"Is that what he told you?"

"He told Carla."

That really made me mad. He was always telling Carla things he didn't tell me. And while I am not proprietary about my friends, I did feel that Carla was my friend first, my friend by a long shot, and if anyone was going to do a lot of phoning her up to tell her mean truths about their inner worlds it ought to be me, not him.

I threw up my hands. "She probably knew he was going to leave me before I did!"

"No," said James, taking both my hands in his. "It came as a terrible shock to her. She's very upset. She would have come this morning herself but she has patients all day."

"But why would he phone her instead of me?

That's not a normal thing to do: leave your wife and call her best friend and tell the best friend you've left."

"This is Andy we are talking about."

"What else did he tell her?"

"I don't know."

"You don't know?"

"It was her conversation."

"And you didn't make her repeat it verbatim?"

"We don't do things like that."

Which is why they are happily married, I assumed, but it made me so mad to think he had to enact another of their principles, that of giving each other space to be a whole person unto themselves, when my marriage was the subject. Had it been James calling Andy to say he'd left Carla I would have made Andy come off the phone and repeat into a tape recorder not just every word but every syllable and inflection of every word. But that was me and I was no longer with a husband, I reminded myself. And then I burst into tears.

"He's a bastard!" I sobbed, clutching James.

"He's a fool," James murmured into my ear.

"He's ruined my life."

"He has ruined his own life."

"He's ruined our baby's life."

"He's squandering his chance to be a father."

"I hope he gets mugged, wandering the streets at night with his wretched insomnia."

"I hope he finds peace in whatever way he can."

"You aren't helping, James, let's go back to the bastard part. He's a *bastard*!"

"He's a fool . . ."

James stayed with me. That was nice of him. He stayed the whole day and I told him the complete history of me and Andy. James is a little shrinklike, having lived with Carla all these years, but while Carla is forever seeking more genuine motives for people's behavior, James subscribes to the theory that everyone is slightly crackers and it has to do with no one thing you can pinpoint. I once asked him why he and Carla lived together eight years before getting married—why they waited the eight years and then why, after all that, they decided to get married—and he shrugged and said, "Who knows? We had a clear month on the calendar?" Carla would have had some explanation. She'd have said something about their "connection" and the balance of their relationship and made all sorts of other really rather banal but perhaps quite accurate observations about the nature of their lives, but not James. He giggled. "Who knows?" he said, and I loved him for that. I loved him for being so smart—they are both so horrifically smart— and being willing to chuck all that aside.

"Don't ask me what I'm going to do," I said to him as we sat on the couch together in my living room, holding hands like a couple of children, or like a father holding his daughter's hand before she goes into a doctor's office for a painful inoculation.

"Why would I ask that?"

"Because Carla will. She always does. Doesn't she ask you what you're going to do when you have a problem?"

He looked at me blankly.

"Oh well," I sighed. "Perhaps she just saves it for her pathetic and hopeless friends."

James squeezed my hand.

"You think I'm pathetic and hopeless, don't you?"

"No, not hopeless."

"But pathetic."

"No, not pathetic."

"Then why did you squeeze my hand?"

"I don't know. It seemed the right thing to do."

"It was because you agreed with me when I said I was pathetic and hopeless."

"I just said I did not."

"You said that, but you do—" I stopped myself. How was I capable not only of getting into arguments with my own husband but getting into arguments with other people's husbands as well? I changed the subject. "You wouldn't leave Carla if she were pregnant, would you?"

He looked at me. He had lovely blue sorrowful eyes. "You want me to say something painful for you to hear because you need to cry," he said. "So I'll say it: no, I would not leave Carla if she were pregnant. Nor if she were not pregnant."

Oh, he was so right. So right that I fell against him in a burst of convulsive tears.

"But if I were married to you, I wouldn't leave you either," he said, and for a moment I felt a little better.

C H A P T E R

F O U R

MET ANDY WHILE SPIRALING DOWN A BOTTOM-less pit of depression following the departure of the previous great love of my life, Theo Clarkson. If it hadn't been for Theo I might never have met Andy. When things were good with Andy I used to think, Okay, Theo was very bad news, but he did ultimately show me the path toward true happiness in the form of Andy. Then I didn't think about Theo, except during those infrequent times I happened to see his name in the book review section of the *New York Times*. Then, when Andy went wrong, I thought about Theo again and I thought, Theo was very bad news and, wait, it's getting worse.

I cannot tell you how in love with Theo Clarkson I was—no, I can tell you—I was so in love with Theo Clarkson that I used to ride my bicycle to where he lived on campus and stare up at the hall to the third-floor window which was his room and wait to see a sign of him, a fluttering of light, a glimpse of his shirt, or perhaps some larger part of his torso if I was lucky. I was consistently lucky and I got to see a great deal of him naked even before I'd ever had a conversation of more than four sentences with him. And for many months I felt I had a closer relationship to his appendicitis scar than I did to anyone or anything else.

He was in my creative writing class, and he used to gaze down at the various manuscripts we scrutinized twice weekly with an intense vision that I felt indicated true genius. He was very smart and treated fiction with the utmost seriousness. He would talk about an "ear" for dialogue and the "cadence" of a sentence and the "arc" of a narrative and I watched him, awed and cowed, practically drooling on myself, matching up his aggressive intellect with the powerful, muscular torso I saw through his window. Had he not had the appendicitis scar, which was really a very dramatic scar, as it turned out the operation was performed under emergency circumstances, I don't think I would ever, ever have breathed a single word to him, but the scar softened him somehow, made him seem vulnerable, approachable, or at least operable. I allowed my crush to continue and occasionally, drunk with love, I stumbled toward him and made some vague comment that I hoped sounded insightful, but actually sounded absurd.

"Boy, that title," I'd say of one of my classmate's efforts.

"What? You liked it or didn't like it?"

"Well . . ." I hedged.

"It was stolen—" he accused.

"Yes, I thought I'd read it before—"

"—off a jazz album."

"—or, you know, *heard* it."

This crush on Theo was an all-consuming passion. I almost failed the class. I would have failed had it not been for the kindness of the teacher, a dreamy, soft-spoken woman named Marilyn Brown whom we were all crazy about because she wrote so well and because her stories showed up not infrequently in *Esquire* and *The Paris Review, Story,* and the one we all desperately sought, the showcase for American fiction, *The New Yorker,* yes, *The New Yorker.* She was also a beauty, with lovely swimming green eyes and a long, elegant nose. I was half in love with her myself, which is the only thing I shared in common with Theo, who was totally besotted and desperately in love with her. He never looked at anyone in the class, just at her. He laughed only when she laughed and on those rare occasions when his opinion of a story clashed with hers, he charmingly deferred to her better judgment. He was chatty with her, he was sweet, he was not this way with any of the rest of the class, who he seemed to regard with a measure of hostility for taking up space in the same room with him and Marilyn, whom you felt he'd rather be alone with.

If he initiated conversation with me it was always with one, lone sentence. And when he deigned to utter this, it was usually without even bothering to look at me. He spoke out of one side of his mouth while handling his books and papers before him in an obsessive way, as though polishing a stone. "Was that your story we read in Marilyn's class last week?" he'd ask.

We never knew whose story was whose because the manuscripts were anonymously presented, with the name of the writer scratched out. Eventually we all got familiar enough with each other's computer typefaces that there was no mystery at all about whose story we were beating the hell out of. Later in the semester he didn't need to ask if it were my story, which meant he never talked to me at all—but in those early months it was common practice to ask such a question, always in a casual, offhand way, though with secret bloodthirsty curiosity.

"No, not mine," I'd said. In fact I didn't write a single story until the end of the first semester, and then I wrote four in a hurry.

"Good," Theo'd say, and then he'd make some comment like, "because I thought the narrative was pedestrian."

I always agreed with him, nodding furiously. I was in love with Theo exactly because he said things like "the narrative was pedestrian" and I had no idea what he meant. Theo, himself, was a marvelous writer. He'd taken a class with Marilyn before and was on a first-name basis with her. He often showed up to her office hours and disappeared behind her closed door for twenty minutes at a time. There were rumors (complete, bald lies) they were having an affair, rumors that Theo did nothing whatsoever to dispel. Another rumor, this one true as it turned out, was that he'd had a short story accepted by a literary magazine. We were all jealous of Theo, but only I was so crazy as to bicycle to his dorm to pay homage to his appendicitis scar.

As I say, he had no interest in me, none at all. I dressed in ways that I thought would turn his head. He, himself, was very much an artist, given to black jackets and black high-top basketball shoes and jeans with frayed patches around the knee and crotch. I tried my best, discarding my Fairisle sweaters and cream corduroys for Lycra leggings and a pair of sneakers like his. He paid no attention to this. That's not quite right, when I first got the sneakers he looked down at my feet and said, "New chucks," and I realized, first, that you never call them basketball shoes, you call them "chucks" after Chuck Taylor who endorsed them along with the NBA, and second, that you never wear them new. I don't know how you avoid that second thing—do you wear them in the privacy of your home until they are old enough to present to the public or do you buy them already used, in which case what stratum of society wears them new? Anyway, he disapproved. I tried various other outfits, a Spandex all-in-one with loafers and a man's blazer, a velvet dress with paddock shoes and a hat, several shawls and scarves I hoped made me look mysterious, and none of it to any effect.

The end of the semester arrived and I'd turned in nothing, not a single word. How could I, knowing as I did that Theo Clarkson, with a Calvin Klein ad torso and a story that had been paid money for, was waiting like a hungry crocodile to say something absolutely correct and damning that would end my writing career before it had even started? Marilyn took me aside and said in her kind, nonthreatening manner, that she'd loved to read some of my work (as though I had any work) and I told her I was just dotting the i's and crossing the t's on a very promising draft. She nodded and smiled in her thoroughly dazzling way. She was so beautiful. Theo was so beautiful. They were made for each other, I thought.

I went back to my dorm, to the suite I shared with Carla and Beth and Nona, the one none of us talk to, and I told them about Theo (they already knew about Theo, but I told them again, for the hundred and nineteenth time, about Theo) and mentioned, too, that I was going to fail the class unless I got a short story written very quickly indeed.

"He must have some kind of sex karma," Beth said.

Carla looked up from her Lévi-Strauss and said, "So what are you going to do?" She was like that from the beginning. Her double degree in psychology and philosophy was a cinch for her, and she'd already started psychobabbling like a pro.

"Fail the class," I said.

"Get him in bed!" Beth said.

Carla sighed. She looked straight at me. "What are you going to *do*?"

"Write a story?"

"That would by my vote," Nona said. She was sitting half naked on the carpet in one corner of the room preparing to wax her long, extremely shapely legs, legs that the rest of us were very jealous of. Even Carla, who wrote her junior essay on why jealousy isn't really an emotion, was jealous of those legs. In front of Nona was a copy of *Vogue* and a single-burner electric stove, the kind that plugs into the wall and is illegal in every campus in the nation, and she was melting wax in a tiny saucepan she used exclusively for this ritual. It brought tears to my eyes every time she stripped that wax off her long, pink, painful-looking legs, and I absolutely cringed when she got to her bikini line, but she insisted it was not a big deal. All part of being a woman, she used to say. And I suppose that if you consider that women in China used to have their feet bound until they bled, leg waxing wasn't so bad in the scheme of things.

"It would be a good idea to write a story," said Carla.

"Okay, I'll do it. I'll do it now."

"That's the spirit," Beth said. "Write a sex story that really turns him on."

Carla put her hand over Beth's mouth. "Don't worry what turns him on. Ignore Theo Clarkson."

"Personally, I could never ignore the man I loved," Nona said, patting her leg with a dollop of honey-colored wax. "Or what he thought of my creation, especially a story or poem, which never fail to reveal so much of oneself."

"Nona, shut up," Carla said.

"—because my poetry *is* me."

"No, it's not. Your poetry *was* Sylvia Plath, then you stole it and reconstituted it as you."

"That is *so* unfair. And I'll tell you something, Carla de Soto, Sylvia Plath hardly benefited from psychoanalysis. If you are thinking that someday you can actually help people by trotting yourself out as a doctor, my advice is that your patients save their money and stick their heads in the oven *now*—"

And with that, I exited for the library and wrote a story.

Theo liked the story. Theo liked the story so much that he started sitting next to me in class and regarding my opinion with a measure of respect. I wrote another story. He liked that one more, he asked me to dinner. I wrote another story and we went on a skiing weekend together. We lay in bed and he quoted back my work to me. I became even more familiar with his appendix scar. It was only a matter of a few more stories before we were living together.

I will say this for Theo, he was a very good reader. He was the sort of reader that writers dream of, remembering every character's name and background and demeanor. After we made love he would sometimes seem to be thinking something really deep and emotional and important and when I asked him he'd say, "I just wondered if you might rework the opening dialogue in the third chapter to include Miranda's lover."

Sometimes I'd get out of bed and edit the work right then, while he hovered behind my left shoulder in his skivvies. Sometimes, he'd decide he needed to work, too, and he'd switch on his word processor and we'd write in tandem. Very unconventional, very weird. I'm not sure if we had a love affair or a four-year writers' conference. What I do know is that he worked very secretly on a novel that he barely let me read and continued to get his short stories published in literary magazines. I worked openly on a novel that simply could not be finished, mostly because he always had some very good suggestion to make that required rewriting from page fifteen forward.

The first time he threatened to leave me was when he'd finished his own novel and I had writer's block so bad I couldn't even think about mine, which I'd nicknamed *Mission Impossible*. I really couldn't write a single word. Our pillow talk, which had mostly consisted of editorial commentary, went down the road toward extinction and sex soon followed the same path. By the time he actually left me I'd more or less given up on the novel and was devoting most of my time to working night shifts at the all-night convenience store below our apartment in Kenmore Square. Theo was making frequent trips to

New York to go to book launches and publishing parties and to talk up his own novel. Among the many things I didn't know about Theo was that he was fed up with being paid .0001 cents per word and wanted the big money. His novel was a four-hundred-page semi-thriller called *Swear* which was mostly about a very cold, masculine man with a square jaw and a talent for pool, entering into and then discarding various relationships with extremely thin women—"her impossibly thin waist" was one of his descriptions— which he'd almost finished but hadn't yet. He was guarding it fiercely, schmoozing crazily among New York's *literati* (at least whatever segment of it he'd managed to wheedle his way into, which might have been none of it for all I knew) and deciding between three endings. He was staying on Nona's couch—on the couch, he claimed—though of course he was having sex with her and talking about her poetry— she still thought she was a poet—and about her career as a publicist with HarperCollins.

"This really is your fault," he accused one day late in summer while packing a pair of jeans into a knapsack on his final excursion to New York, from which he did not return. "It isn't healthy for me as a writer to live with someone who's got a bad case of writer's block."

"Theo, I love you," I said. "And I think you love me, too—"

"I'm leaving you *as a writer*. As a person, I'll be there for you if you ever stop having block."

Isn't that wonderful? Four years and he was leaving me as a writer, but not as a person. As a writer he took off for the train station, as a writer he went to Nona's second floor walk-up near Washington Square, as a writer he didn't want anything more to do with me. If I ever stopped having writer's block and finished the novel he'd made it impossible to write by constantly editing it even as I was typing out sentences, he might have me back—as a writer or a person, I really couldn't tell you.

I called Carla.

"Don't ask me what I'm going to do," I said, "or else I might do something desperate like throw myself off a bridge."

"I know what to do," she said. It took me aback to hear her speak like this. It was so unlike Carla to tell someone else what to do, what exactly. "We go to Nona's apartment and we steal that sexist thriller book of his. We make it look like a break-in."

"You mean we *actually* break in," I said, "and then get arrested? And then have to give back *Swear* and probably pay damages to Nona? That's your good advice?"

"I have a key," Carla said.

We went to New York. We stole *Swear,* and we stole all the diskettes. We made it look like we were trying to steal other stuff and that we got interrupted. It was a total success and to this day I mark it as a triumph. Theo and Nona continued to live together but a "terrible" thing happened. Theo got writer's block. Since the loss of *Swear* and his lead character, Crash

Jenkins, a kind of male folk hero who sleeps with every female character except one, a dwarf who he allows to follow him mascotlike on his various escapades, he simply could not muster up the momentum to start again.

"Listen to this," Carla said, when we were safely back in Boston. We were reading *Swear,* marking with a yellow highlight pen all the really fiercely objectionable paragraphs. He could write, Theo, but he could not help but write in a way that demonstrated his true character. Even his good fiction was sexist but his bad fiction was really downright hateful. Carla quoted, "*Crash liked her and wanted her, but thought perhaps she was that menacing kind of woman who would take more than it was worth. He'd woken up too many times to the smell of bacon and perfume, a lethal smell that meant she wasn't parting any time soon, and found it hard to extricate himself without the sound of crying. 'If we do this,' he said, brushing his hand over her nipple—he'd kiss her later if it was good— 'it's your idea, right? You understand? Your idea.' She nodded. She unbuttoned her dress.*" Carla looked up. "God, Meg! You lived with him?"

"I didn't know Crash was such a bastard. I only read up to page eighty, when he first loses his virginity to the sociopath who tries to strangle him in his sleep."

"That wasn't a sociopath, that was a woman of judgment."

"Well, I had no idea that he was so, you know, horrible. Now that I do I am glad Theo's gone, and even more glad that he's with Nona, who I've always thought was a slut, though I didn't want to say that because I thought that really I was just jealous of her."

"I never trusted her—that tiny voice, that lisp. She is very physically attractive, okay, but if you close your eyes while she is talking she sounds like she's just swallowed a vat of helium," Carla said.

"Why was she in our rooming group anyway if I never liked her and you never liked her?"

"You want to know why? Because Beth thought that she was pretty enough to attract great hoards of men to our room, and from there Beth would be able to exercise her charm and steal them her way."

"She is so practical."

So I had *Swear* and most of Theo's clothes, and a great adrenaline rush—I think it lasted three months—from having burgled an apartment in New York. I looked at myself in the mirror: Meg the writer thief, Meg the thief of writing. I was proud. I was so proud I didn't mind that Theo was gone. I forgot that I had writer's block and I returned to an early draft of *Mission Impossible* and finished it, retitling it along the way. Then the adrenaline wore off and Theo was still gone and I realized that just because you've finished a novel your life does not change. I worked at the convenience store, I lived in the apartment I'd once shared with my first love. I was standing behind the counter serving enormous coffees in travel mugs to a group of construction workers when a nice-looking blond-haired man in a suit asked me if I could help him. He thought he had the right address for Theo Clarkson but it turned out to be the convenience store, he explained. He was endearingly muddled about how Theo's address could be a convenience store. I didn't know it at the time but it was how Andy manages to get people to help him, by appearing muddled, and totally in need of guidance, which I now am beginning to believe is not an act at all but perhaps a real condition.

"He used to live above this store," I said soberly. "But he hasn't for about four months."

"Do you have his new address?"

I gave him Nona's address. I wrote it on the back of a doughnut bag. He looked down at the bag and said, "Oh, he's in New York now."

"Yeah, he had a sudden change of plan."

"You know Theo?"

"I knew him briefly," I said. I could not hold back the sarcasm.

"I promised I'd look at a novel of his. I forgot about it until I ran across one of his stories in *Harper's* on the train from New York this morning."

"He had a story in *Harper's*?"

"'The Writing Class.' It's wonderful; it's about a guy—a student—who falls in love with another student in his writing class and . . ."

"He had a story in *Harper's*!"

"Yeah, and the girl is very talented but also a little strange, changing her dress style in dramatic ways to attract the main character, who is an 'I' narrator—"

"That little bastard!" I yelled. "He had a story in *Harper's* after writing about goddamned Crash, the hard-dick, I could just shoot his—"

I got fired.

I got fired and Andy and I were asked to leave at once. We left, me having come to my senses and feeling sheepish and humiliated, and I told Andy he could have *Swear*—what did I care? Theo was going to be a star no matter what I did. He was living with a publicist, for one thing, and he could write well for another. He could write well enough to appear in *Harper's* and badly enough to probably make the *New York Times* bestseller list. He was a sure bet, a winner. I brought Andy up to the apartment and had him wait by the door while I fished *Swear* out of the bottom drawer of my desk.

"He was my boyfriend," I said. "I was the one in his writing class. I stole this manuscript from him months ago. He'll be pretty surprised to see it again," I said, and grunted out a laugh without smiling.

"I see."

"We lived here and did nothing but write. There's no TV; there's no stereo. We had books, our own and the ones we bought and read and tried to learn from. We had each other."

"I'm sorry. If it makes you feel any better the girl in 'The Writing Class' was described as talented and very attractive."

"Oh, ha ha."

"And I'm sure you are both of those. I mean, I can see you are attractive, but I bet you are talented, too."

"Oh *sure.*"

"Well, thanks for *Swear.* If you ever have a novel of your own, I'd be happy to put it under an editor's nose. I'm not an editor myself, I'm a sales rep, but I do know a number of them."

"Oh, *please.*"

"I mean it."

"Look, you have fucking Theo's fucking book, now *scoot,* okay?"

"Okay," he said, but he didn't move.

"Go!"

"Just one piece of advice," he said, raising a finger. "If you are going to live alone, I'd get a television if I were you. I live alone and I really find TV makes it a lot easier."

I slammed the door in his face. I slammed the door and turned away and thought he was probably right about the TV. Now, I ask you, how is it that I have driven Andy away *now,* at this late date? How could a man who has witnessed such a scene from the very onset of knowing a person (me) and has loved her anyway be driven away by, well, anything really? I thought about this and I wanted to know, if only for curiosity's sake. I had slammed the door right in his face, nearly clipping his nose, and he didn't even flinch.

Of course, much later I found the business card he slipped under the door and sent him a note apologizing for my behavior along with a copy of my novel. The novel was accepted by Bill, who worked in the same house as Andy (Bill is also Theo's editor, as I may have mentioned). I went to New York to meet my new agent, the one who was magically interested the minute an editor wanted to tender cash for my novel, and I saw Andy on my way to Bill's office.

"You were right about the TV," I told him. I used part of the advance on my novel to buy a Panasonic with a twenty-four-inch screen. "I even have cable now. It does make a difference."

He raised an eyebrow. "Home shopping?" he asked.

"Of course."

"You'll be fine."

I saw him again on the way back from Bill's office. He was waiting near the elevators, a big smile on his face.

"I liked your book," he told me. "I liked the main character."

"Bill said she was a little passive."

"That's because Bill lives in a world of main characters, and main characters are not supposed to be passive. But I'm in sales, and anyone in sales not only knows that people are passive, but really rather relies on that fact. The novel sounded true. I loved it."

"Well, thanks," I said.

"You might try the cooking shows. A lot of viewers are put off by them because they think they have to cook to enjoy them, but I've found that isn't the case."

"There's that cooking game show thing. I've seen that."

"*Cooking for Dollars?* Yeah, it's good. But try *The Gay Gourmet.*"

I rode the train back to Boston and I thought how Andy was very cute and how now I had to suffer the heartbreak of Theo along with a pang of affection for Andy. I decided he was probably gay. I told myself that any really cute man who is sensitive and likes cooking shows and passive main characters is probably gay. I was lying on my bed dialing a toll-free number to give my opinion on violence on television for a viewer poll that one of the cable channels was conducting when the call-waiting buzzer on my phone indicated that someone was trying to call me. I half expected it was Theo or his lawyer, threatening to sue me for delaying his great fame by temporarily stealing *Swear.* But it was Andy.

"It's on now, *The Gay Gourmet.* He's doing a dish he invented called quattro chocolatto and you have to see it."

"Channel?" I punched the button and there was the gay gourmet. He was a beautiful man in a skimpy dress and frilly lap apron. He wore a lot of eyebrow pencil and a lot of hairspray and looked a little like what you would get if you crossed David Bowie with Wilma Flintstone. He was whisking furiously into a lovely crystal bowl, his lips pursed, his eyes cast down on his mission, to make his own cream for the quattro chocolatto. *Even amounts of whole milk and unsalted butter,* he was saying. *A few ten-second whizzes in the blender and, baby, you have cream.*

"I love him," I said.

"Afterward is an alternative home fix-it program. They do all their housing repairs using natural materials. I've been tempted to burst pipes in my own bathroom just to try out their techniques, except I don't know where in Manhattan I'd find hemp."

"What's he doing to that orange?" I asked.

"That's his method for getting the most flavor out of the rind. He says you have to roll it around like that before grating it. He has his own restaurant here in town. It's called Methuselah's. The health department closes it down once in a while because he is a great believer in raw food but it's really very good. I'll take you there one night if you want."

That's how it started. I rode four hours on the train to New York to go to a restaurant whose owner and main chef refused to cook his food and I didn't come back for two weeks, and then it was only to collect my mail and clean out my refrigerator. Andy and I were an item right away, we were in love.

He took me roller skating in Central Park. It was autumn, leaves littered the crowded sidewalks. Andy skated beside me, cocked his heel, and was suddenly skating backward, facing me.

"If you married me we would have two televisions. Think of the opulence. Think of the luxury!"

"We could videotape on one and watch on the other," I said.

"Well, would you?"

"Only if there were two movies I really desperately wanted to watch on two different networks—"

"I mean marry me."

"Yeah," I said, and realized that it never occurred to me that we wouldn't marry. That first night we had taken a taxi from Methuselah's twenty blocks uptown and decided which block we would like to live on. You see, we went straight into talking about real estate—I knew we'd get married. But while he popped the question in that bold, confident way, the follow-through on actually getting married was very slow indeed. I should have realized then that there was something essential passive resistant about Andy, an aspect of his character that meant he had a difficult time with commitment and responsibility. He asked me to marry him when I was twenty-eight years old. We set the date for June 25th and I ordered a white satin dress with capped sleeves and a deep, sweetheart neckline and lace everywhere I could think of. But did we actually get married on June 25th? No way. We set a date for May 9th of the following year, by which time I'd come to my senses a bit and removed a great deal of the lace, had the neckline brought up a half inch, and concentrated on which veil to wear. May 9th came and went and still I wasn't married. I had the sleeves changed (what was I thinking, capped sleeves?) and the dress went into a box for another year. In the end, it took *five years* for us to actually get married, by which time I'd ditched the satin dress, the train, the veil, and gone for an ivory-colored silk to be worn with a bolero jacket and a hat. In a way it makes total sense that Andy would run out the minute I got pregnant (or at least seven months into the minute I got pregnant); there was no possibility for taking a raincheck on the birth. Given his track record he was likely to face up to the role of fatherhood—something he had sworn he desperately wanted—in time to take the child to start his first semester at college.

Why was he like this? I don't know. Carla would say it stemmed from his father, who was a weak role model and given to bouts of psychosis. James would throw up his hands and say, "We're all that little bit crazy!" Beth would suspect sexual problems. But if you ask my opinion it's because he has a really bad time imagining anything that isn't actually there. Marriage, before it occurs, is impossible really to contemplate. A baby, before it is born, remains an abstract concept. His inability to imagine anything that wasn't actually, physically in front of him was demonstrated every time we looked at a house. In each case, Andy simply could not accept that a house might look different than it already was. He is a man who understands different architectural styles, who has traveled to New Orleans to see the Cabildo and the Louis XV prison, to Jamestown to see the first state house with its serried gables and to Acoma, New Mexico, to see how big a place you can build using mud, but if the hallway of an ordinary house of the sort we looked at to buy was printed with raised velveteen paisley paper, he simply assumed it must *always* be printed with raised velveteen paisley. I'd say to him, "Honey, haven't you ever heard of a wallpaper steamer? Haven't you ever heard of a decorator?" and he would agree theoretically but, still, when it came to bidding he simply would not pay anything near the asking price, "anything near" being anything within 70 percent of the asking price, so we never got the house. This happened time after time. A four-bedroom colonial on a private road, but sadly also with shag carpeting throughout the first floor, a cape-style house with an enchanting wooded garden but also with a crumbling garage addition that never should have been erected in the first place, an 1892 clapboard house with a wraparound porch but, unfortunately, an interior that had been gutted of its original features. He couldn't imagine recarpeting, hauling away the addition, refitting the interior. I'd explain to him, I'd go through painstaking efforts with the use of visual aids—design magazines, actual architects' blueprints, interviews with builders and joiners. But nothing worked. We were too late or outbid every time. We lost house after house. It was the same problem with our new house, the former schoolhouse. He said, "But Meggy, it's got no upstairs to speak of."

"That's because it used to a be a school. We'll build an upstairs."

"How?"

"With builders."

"But what will it look like?"

"It will look fantastic."

The house is set on a quarter acre of wonderful overgrown garden complete with a pergola and a few leftover apple trees from a long-ago orchard. It joins a section of parkland protected by the State of Massachusetts. It has a gravel driveway and a wooden barn.

The renovation to the downstairs was done with great respect for the origin of the building and every detail, from the polished boards in the living room to the Welsh cupboard in the kitchen—not a "fitted" kitchen with boring, matching units but one which was cobbled together with pieces from architectural salvage yards and featured a wonderful larder as well—just worked somehow perfectly, incidentally, uniquely. The second owners had added the loft, which was serving as a second story, but it was a slapdash effort involving a staircase little better than a stepladder and a lot of false walls. The best bid I got was $42,000 to complete the second floor, and another $10,000 if we wanted the upstairs bathroom remodeled (we did—it was only a kindergarten toilet under a sloping roof that you had to back into in a crouch position). I thought, given the beauty of the location and the uniqueness of the house, we ought to bid.

"Two hundred thirty-five," I said. "We can swing that."

"One hundred seventy-five," Andy said. "That's as high as I'll go."

The asking price was two seventy-five, and given the location even that was a steal. "Are you crazy?"

"Not crazy enough to build a second story into a house that is going to go up in flames if anyone drops a match."

"Once that second story is completed it will be worth a hundred thousand more. And we're only going forty-two thousand deep."

"Ha! We'll be bleeding money into the thing. Dry

rot, woodworm, rotten beams and plumbing, beneath that beautiful exterior is something akin to Boston's sewage system."

"It's worth it."

"You wait, the actual cost will be three times what they've quoted. One seventy-five is as high as we go."

"Two twenty," I reasoned.

"Two ten," he countered.

"God, *all right*." I stomped off to call the realty agent.

The agent made the bid. Andy went back to his newspaper, confident we'd never get the house. But Andy hadn't counted on one thing: two ten bought the house. It was fate, I decided, it was meant to be. I guess I should have known that if you go around underbidding on houses long enough someone will one day take you up on your meager offer. That night we celebrated. We'd gotten the schoolhouse, our dream house, which even Andy had to agree was a pretty solid investment, perhaps the best investment we'd ever made. Or the worst, if you consider that neither of us is likely to ever live in it, given our most recent history.

WEDNESDAY ARRIVED AND STILL NO ANDY. That is, he did not call and he did not return home. I might have been inclined to tell the police except that Andy was spotted by my neighbor, Mrs. Martin Martin. Clearly I cannot go on at this point without remarking on Mrs. Martin Martin's name, though it is easily explained by pointing out that she is married to a man whose parents, Doll and Jerome Martin, thought to name their son Martin the way that some people name a child John Johnson or Robert Robertson, forgetting that their name was Martin, not Martinson, so that the whole thing sounded just a little too much like Humbert Humbert. It was a ridiculous name, ridiculous to everybody except Mrs. Martin, who proudly called herself Mrs. Martin Martin, in the habit of women of her day. If anyone commented, she paid no attention. She was too busy upsetting everyone within her reach anyway and with much bigger issues than her name.

I remember the day we met her, which was the day after we'd moved in. She brought a casserole and used it as an excuse to push her way past the door so she could get a good look at all of our belongings. I could almost hear her making mental notes—messily packed boxes, chipped china, tatty furniture with not a single collectible. Right away I didn't like her. Andy said I was being unkind and after all she was an old lady, but I didn't like the way she stood back and stared at us, clearly in a state of indecision as to whether we were bringing the neighborhood down. The casserole she brought was covered in tinfoil with a little Post-it note telling us to reheat at 350 degrees for forty minutes and serve with potatoes. That was very nice, the casserole, but it seemed a little nervy to me, *serve with potatoes,* what if I wanted to serve with rice? Would she come over and sweep the casserole under her arm, raise her voice to a soprano, and announce that no casserole of hers was going to be served with rice? Or would she hear about it through the local gossip network and confide in the rest of the neighborhood that she was really very disappointed at our choice of accompanying carbohydrate?

A few things about Mrs. Martin. First, her cooking. She cooks incessantly and is forever talking about recipes and dishes she's made—morning coffee cakes and hors d'oeuvres—food I don't have time to eat, let alone cook, and she cooks from really bland and unimaginative recipes that call for ingredients that are not in themselves food but what the industry calls euphemistically "food products," Crisco or cream of mushroom soup or Bacon Bits or Kraft cheese. Also, she wears aprons almost all the time, as does her husband, Martin, and the aprons usually have some sort of supposedly witty phrase or picture on them, "Beef Cakes" is one of Martin's, which is more than slightly ironic as Martin is five foot six and weighs about 240 pounds. And Mrs. Martin has a Christmas apron on which there is an enormous Christmas tree the top of which reaches just below Mrs. Martin's neck so that her head serves as the star. They are retired and sixty-ish and I should be a lot more generous than I am about them, but I can't help myself because Mrs. Martin is always stirring up trouble one way or another.

Typical: She came over a few months ago to tell me about one of the neighbor's cats—one that she believes belongs to number 14—which she claimed was defecating in all of the area's rosebushes. I said to her, "You mean the cat systematically goes to yard after yard, bush after bush, making sure that not one patch of enticing mulch is left undefiled? You know this?"

She narrowed her eyes. "It is a nuisance!"

"How many bushes does it get to in a day, Mrs. Martin? I'm just curious."

She laughed politely and continued, "I really think we should put a stop to it. It isn't fair to the rest of us to have that cat around."

After some questioning it was revealed that "Put a stop" meant have the cat put to sleep.

"You want the cat killed?" I asked her.

"Not killed, heavens!" she said. "Perhaps sent to the country."

Over the past five years she has wanted three dogs, two cats, and one small child "sent to the country." She also thought that number 21's rather invasive bluebells "ought really to belong in the country." Number 3 bought their teenage son a pickup truck when he graduated from high school (a typical over-privileged Newton gesture, I'm afraid) and it bothered Mrs. Martin to no end to see it parked outside the house, not because it was outrageous to buy your kid a twenty-thousand-dollar graduation present when a decent watch would probably do instead, but because she objected to the notion of a truck on her street. "As though we were living in the country!" she cried. I don't know where she thinks the country is, other than obviously the place where badly behaved pets and people go to stay with their unsightly vehicles, but I suspect that if Mrs. Martin had her way we'd all be living in the country and Newton would be hers exclusively.

Mrs. Martin came over on Wednesday and said to me, "Was that your Andy I saw at the laundromat?"

So that was where he was, at the laundromat. Somehow you don't expect a roving husband to end up at the laundromat. You expect eventually he might surface long enough to be glimpsed drinking his troubles away in a dark bar, or perhaps parked along the street asleep in the backseat, or maybe alone in a coffeehouse listening to some stringy-haired girl with a guitar sing shakily about love, but what you don't expect is for him to be mixing color brighteners and softening additives, for him to be folding and creasing, perhaps even ironing, for him to be taking care of himself in such a way. I was furious.

"No, that was not Andy," I said.

"I'm sure it *was*. He was wearing that plaid woodsmen shirt he wears to rake leaves."

So, he was wearing the L. L. Bean hair shirt I bought for his last birthday. He was so unsentimental as to be able to put on that shirt. I was even more furious. I had to close my eyes to pee in my own toilet because the sight of his razors over the sink made me fall weeping to the floor but he could stand dry-eyed in the local landromat in last year's birthday present from his loving wife—last year when we were a couple in love and together and happy—and cheerfully shake the wrinkles out of his jeans. How dare he! And then another thought came to me. How did Mrs. Martin know he wore that shirt to rake leaves? I had the sudden image of Mrs. Martin casting a spyglass over all the houses within a quarter mile of her own. If she were able to look four houses over to our yard to see what Andy was wearing to do his gardening, then certainly she knew much more than I cared to imagine about what he was doing in the laundromat. She would have discerned that he was only washing his own clothes, for example, and from there concluded that, as we no longer shared a laundry basket, we obviously no longer shared a life. Anyway, what was he doing at a laundromat, she would ask herself, when they had their own washing machine and tumble drier? Mrs. Martin knew, or was pretty sure she knew, that Andy had left me.

This I could not bear. The idea that Mrs. Martin had lifted her fat self out of her armchair and come to confirm her data really made me mad. The thought that now she would know—now she would know and she would waddle away on her Rockport shoes and her water-retaining ankles to tell the world about how Andy had left his pregnant wife, she would stand at the gates of houses all over the street, sucking her teeth and speaking in low tones as though she were only letting out this confidence with great reluctance, just so they were aware in case *I* should need something—the thought of this filled me with a terrible darkness. I've always wanted to say that, "filled me with a terrible darkness," it sounds so dramatic, but until I was indeed filled with a terrible darkness I never knew just how terrible it was. It was really terrible, and I had no choice but to pull the ace card.

"Andy is in bed with a dreadful case of flu," I told Mrs. Martin, slowly and succinctly so she didn't miss the meaning of my statement. I do not know much about old people, but I know that the flu puts the fear of God into them. If you mention flu to a group of senior citizens it's like pointing out a pride of lions to a herd of gazelles. "He's been down with it for days."

Mrs. Martin looked perplexed. "But I'm sure I saw him just now in—"

"Asiatic flu," I said. "Good thing he's such a young man."

Her chin dropped and the line of red which is meant to demarcate her lips drooped in a half moon. "Asiatic, oh I had no idea—"

"Have you had your flu shot, Mrs. Martin?"

"Well, no I haven't."

"I really think you ought to get one. Andy has been delirious with this virus. He keeps thrashing in bed yelling, 'Beat the Pirates.'"

"Oh dear—"

"And Mrs. Martin, he has never even been a base-ball fan."

She shook—she visibly shook—and she shrank away from me back to her miserable house, her spy-glass and her Cheez Whiz, to sort out what to do with this new bit of information: Influenza in the Neighborhood.

Did I feel guilty? No. I half expected she'd come around again, insisting Andy be sent to the country.

The fact was I had even bigger problems than Mrs. Martin. Wednesday, you might remember, was our childbirth class night. I was faced with the prospect of going to my childbirth class without him and I felt I really did have to go.

Why did I have to go? Because at the last session we were each sent home with one of the life-sized illustrations of the uterus in labor so that we could talk as a couple, in the privacy of our own home, about what we might be feeling at this stage of our own labors, and we were meant to report back our conclusions. This notion of "we" remained absurd to me. What *we* might be feeling as the cervix cranks open millimeter by millimeter? What *we* might be feeling as the head descends the vaginal canal? Wait, wait, I felt like shouting, are there *two* cervixes in this room? Does my husband have a secret vaginal canal of which, until now, I was uninformed? The fact is that no matter how intimate and shared an experience birth might be (a debatable point in itself) each parent retains his or her own individual nervous system. And from that it follows that the woman will be feeling searing pain, the likes of which she has never felt before, while the man might be feeling a little anxious, assuming he is present at the birth to begin with.

But back to the point. The point is that I did not want to go, I did not have to go, but Andy and I had been given the illustration of when the baby actually comes out, arriving into the world. We had the final birth picture. I imagined how the group would progress that night without me, the uterus stretching and contracting in first stage, the cervix opening with pressure from the baby's head, the transition stage between first and second stage, the baby fully within the vaginal canal, the baby's head about to be born, and then, just as everyone is getting excited, nothing. No baby. Baby being born is not able to be discussed because Meg and Andy Howe had failed to turn up. Somehow it seemed a cruel blow, not to mention a particularly bad omen, not to bring the baby being born illustration.

"You cannot go to a childbirth class alone," Beth said. "It is simply not the done thing."

"I have to go," I said. I held the telephone in one hand and the illustration in the other. At the bottom corner of the picture was its title, *The Uterus in Triumph*. "I've got to return the picture of when the baby actually emerges."

"Can't you send it by courier or something? Can't you fax it?"

"*The Uterus in Triumph*," I said. "It's too late to send it."

"I'll go with you," Beth said.

"The decor will make you sick," I warned her. "You will forever associate pregnancy with cheap sofas upholstered in animal prints."

"That's better than what I associate it with now," she said.

"Which is?

"Labor."

I picked Beth up at her house, or actually since I don't ever remember which of the two identical houses is hers and which is Mark's, I parked the car in the middle of both and honked the horn. After several minutes I saw her—she'd been at Mark's house as it happened. She came out with smeared lipstick, torn panty hose, and a missing earring.

"Busy afternoon?" I asked when she got in the car.

"Isn't new love grand?" she said. "I'm an inch away from an emerald, and probably not very far from a diamond."

"But is it love? Are you really in love with Mark Ponghurst? Can anyone be in love with Mark Ponghurst?"

"We've been looking at furniture lately, and we found the most wonderful Italianate lantern in gold leaf. I think this means something. I think we're going to be sharing a single house *very soon.*"

"If that's what you want," I said. I might have continued, If that's what you want, I'll try to begin to like Mark. But the fact is I had very fond memories of David, who was still her husband by law. Obviously, he had his shortcomings—having an affair with short, fat Diana didn't exactly qualify him for best husband of the year—but whenever they came to our house for dinner he always brought both Andy and me a present. He'd get Andy a bottle of something and bring me flowers, or chocolate or a book. At Christmastime he would find some beautiful sterling ornament for the tree. He loves giving gifts—which is in part of course why Beth married him in the first place, she loves receiving them. It was Beth's idea that they actually divorce over the Diana thing, and I did understand why, but I still missed him. "Well," I said, not daring to say any of this to Beth, "you can't put a lantern like that in a ranch house. Anyway, do you love him?"

Beth made a face like she'd just taken a bite of lemon. Then she said, "We have so much in common. I love Portuguese tile, he loves Portuguese tile. I love Spanish revival, he loves Spanish revival. Do you know how hard it is to find a man in Massachusetts who doesn't want a period home? David was always going on about exposed brick and 'interesting recesses.' Now I ask you, what is interesting about a recess? I've had it up to here with period houses, all those dark little rooms. And they smell, too. Have you ever noticed? They smell like old things."

"Some people like old things. They call them antiques."

"Yuk."

What I could smell was aftershave, Mark's aftershave. It smelled nice and I realized painfully how much I missed that sort of thing. Aftershave, men's shirts, neckties left carelessly hanging over the back of a chair. Only a week had gone by but already I felt as though that whole part of life, the male part, had receded forever beyond my reach.

"Givenchy Ultramarine?" I asked.

"What? The cologne? No, no," she said. "Kouros. It's pure pheromone. Mark wears it all the time now—he's such a slut. So what are we going to learn tonight about babies?"

"Probably very little. The group is dominated by Elaine and she treats it as a therapy session. She'll probably tell us a great deal about being heavily pregnant, more specifically about how when you get pregnant, I mean when you get this pregnant, you have to have sex on all fours."

Beth looked at my blankly. "So who doesn't do it on all fours anyway?"

"I mean all the time. Apparently when you're heavily pregnant it is uncomfortable to do it any other way—"

"Oh, I get it," she said. "*Pas de variation.*"

"—that is, if you are foolish enough to have sex at all, which I never bothered with. When you are already pregnant sex, it seems to me, is a little redundant."

"Oh, this childbirth class stuff *does* sound interesting."

I introduced Beth to the group as casually as you can imagine, as though it were perfectly normal to bring your best friend to such an event in lieu of your husband. She sat on the faded chintz couch, I took a straight chair with a cushion in Aztec design.

"Hi everybody," Beth said.

"I'm not sure I like the idea of Beth being here," Elaine said. "We are a group. We trust each other and confide only in each other."

"Elaine, we don't *know* each other," Donna said. I was beginning to like Donna. Her many hours on the Internet made her a walking dictionary of medical terms and she regarded advice from our group leader, Gail, with a certain amount of doubt. Gail would talk about the unnecessary use of the cesarean section and

Donna would mention, as though it didn't really matter, that in many cases cerebral palsy in newborns is a result of delaying until too late a quite necessary cesarean section. Then she'd say, "If you're worried about that kind of thing" while we sat perched in awe at the edge of our seats worrying about exactly that sort of thing.

"We *do* know each other," Elaine insisted. "I know you are a computer analyst, for instance. I know your husband is Paul."

Donna turned to Beth. "By the way, I'm a computer analyst. This is Paul." She turned back to Elaine. "There, now we're all even."

"I think there's something going on," Stewart said. "I think there's something Meg isn't telling us."

"Were you in group therapy, too?" I asked.

"Yes, that's how we met, Elaine and myself."

"Of course," I said. "I should have known."

The group went very quiet and I knew they were all wondering—now that it had been suggested by Stewart—what great secret I was harboring. Why would Andy fail to show and I bring my friend Beth instead? Gail intervened.

"It's fine for you to bring Beth. I want all of you to know that you can have as many people as you wish—within a reasonable number—present at the birth. Lots of people have a friend in addition to their partner or husband. Multiple labor partners are perfectly normal. Beth is welcome here."

Multiple labor partners, a disturbing thought.

That out of the way, Gail picked up the first illustration, a cross-section of the internal workings of a pregnant woman, the baby looking a little like a squashed pumpkin. "Right," she said, "whose card was *The Dawn of Labor*?"

"That was ours," John said. "We thought probably we'd be feeling very excited. I might cook a little something—an omelette, perhaps, to tide me through the long hours ahead. I'd also make all the necessary phone calls to work, letting them know that zero hour had arrived and I was going to need a few days off. Of course, I might be at work in which case I'd let them know in person, perhaps faxing some of my larger clients so they don't think I just disappeared unwarranted. And Valerie, what did you say you'd be feeling?"

"Pain," she said.

"Right, Valerie says she'd be in some pain. But not much pain, right, honey? Not with those teeny-weeny early contractions?"

"I still think there is something funny going on with Meg," Stewart said. "Even if Beth is welcome here why not bring Andy, too?"

"Andy is at the dentist's," I said.

"At eight at night?"

"It was the only appointment he could get."

"Why are you going to rush around cooking omelettes when Valerie is in pain?" Greg Brady asked John.

"I hope you aren't hurt by my earlier comment,"

Elaine said to Beth. "It must have sounded really hostile for me to say that you didn't fit in with our group."

"Oh no," Beth said. "Anyway, I like it here. I feel so thin."

The class concluded—finally—with my own card, the illustration of *The Uterus in Triumph.*

"What do you think you'll be feeling at this time?" Gail asked me.

"Um, triumphant? I think I'll be greatly relieved." I didn't know quite what else to say. Are you still in pain after you give birth? Do the contractions stop immediately? I had no idea. One thing, I was pretty sure that I would be upset that after eight or twelve or twenty-four hours of labor I would not be able to show Andy our child. I would have no husband to sit with, no father who joins me in smugly admiring our new perfect baby.

Gail said, "What do you think you'd be feeling at this time, Beth?"

"Me? Gosh, I don't know. I'd be very proud of Meg. I'd think, Meg, you made this baby. And you did it all yourself even though Andy is such a schmuck he ran out on you, I think you're fantastic."

"That's it!" Steward shouted. "I knew there was something going on!"

"Beth, how could you!" I yelled.

"It's okay," Elaine said. "We're all friends here."

"I'm so sorry," Donna said.

"Beth, you bitch!" I said.

"I am," she said. "I'm a total bitch. Me and my big mouth."

We left soon afterward. We walked to the car and I handed Beth the keys.

"I'm too pissed off to drive."

"Meg, I am so, so sorry."

"Now that Elaine is going to talk all night about me. She's going to discuss it with her 'life partner.'"

"You mean Stewart isn't her husband?"

"No."

Beth unlocked the car. "So where is her husband?"

An interesting question. I hadn't thought about where Elaine's husband was. I had just assumed that Elaine went around quite happily with her life partner and didn't worry about her husband. In fact, I really hadn't envisioned a husband, if indeed there were one to begin with. "Maybe it's not unusual for husbands to leave their pregnant wives," I said. "If that's the case then you can bet there is a support group somewhere and that Elaine is a full-up paid member. Anyway, it doesn't matter where her husband is, if she ever had one, she's got Stewart now. It's amazing how a new man cancels out the old, bad one. This time last year you and David were organizing a Christmas party, now you're looking at light fixtures with Mark."

"Not all light fixtures, not light fixtures generally. It's just that we ran into this particular Italianate lantern in gold gilt. You should see it, Meg, the detail is fantastic."

"Still, you're doing it with Mark."

"I'd rather do it with David. But he hates gilt anything."

"You'd rather be with David?"

"Yes and no. I'd rather be with someone and not no one. I'd rather not be alone."

Whatever anger I had toward Beth dissolved instantly. There we were, not much different from each other. Okay, I was deeply into the third trimester of my pregnancy and Andy had only just walked out, Beth was skinny and sexy and with a man—albeit Mark—who could assuage some of the hurt that David left behind when they split up last spring, but we were essentially very much in the same situation.

"Well, I think I'd rather be with no one," I said. I carefully maneuvered myself into the passenger seat and put a protective hand over the great bump of my stomach, my baby. *My* baby, now, as opposed to Andy's and my baby. Perhaps that was a better thing, to have total possession of one's child, perhaps that was worth quite a bit in the long run. "I was sick of Andy anyway, he was such a complainer. He'd ask, 'How are you?' and use that question as a launching pad for all his various ills and complaints. If I said I was tired—tired and with muscle spasms in my legs— he'd say 'God, I'm *exhausted!*' and talk about his insomnia. I'd say my back aches and he'd say, 'My head is *killing* me.' I'd say I think I better lie down for a while and he'd say, 'If I don't sleep soon I'll have a *heart attack.*' Finally, I would say, 'Look, I am the pregnant one here, not you.' And do you know what he'd say? He'd say, 'Yeah, after the baby is born you'll be feeling better but I'll still feel like shit.' Can you believe it? That was the man I married. That is the man I vowed to love through better and worse, and worse and worse and worse."

"Meg—"

"If I'd only known how much worse it would get. The tiniest physical complaint—a hangnail, a cold sore—he'd wail about endlessly. '*I can hardly eat with this welt in my mouth!*' Never mind that a welt is the opposite of a cold sore—God, that's exactly the kind of exaggeration *cum* incorrect word usage that really pisses me off—you'd think he had to go to the emergency room—"

"Meg, I think you should know—"

"What a pain in the ass he was! What a loser. Beth, why aren't we going anywhere?"

"Because Andy is in the backseat of the car."

"What?"

And there he was, his face popping out from between the bucket seats like it was being poked at me from the end of a stick. "Hi, Meg," he said.

"What are you doing here?"

"I knew it was our childbirth class night, but then when I got here I couldn't figure out which number house it was. Seventy-six? Seventy-nine? Sorry I missed the class. I still want to be at the birth, you know."

"Oh, you do?"

"Yes, I always planned to be at the birth."

"You planned to be at the birth. Well, how nice."

"I mean, you'll have to let me know when it is."

"Andy," I said, sighing heavily, "I don't know when it is. Sometime in the middle of December, the baby hasn't been more specific than that."

"I have a phone number for you."

"Who would you like me to call? The baby? Shall I call the baby and ask it when it is planning to arrive so we can have the bed ready? Beth, let's not sit here with the engine running, let's drive somewhere."

"I want you to call me when you go into labor."

"I don't want to call you when I go into labor!" I yelled. "Beth, would you *go!*"

"Where? Give me a house number, there's a possibility of three different destinations here."

"I want you to be with me when I go into labor, do you understand that, Andy? I want you to be next to me in bed, or across from me at the dinner table, or beside me as we're drying the dishes, I want you to be there—"

"I know," Andy said. "I know—"

"I'll go to my house," Beth said.

"No, you do not! You do not know! Beth, stop the car! Stop the car now!"

She pulled over on Harvard Street in front of that glass-encased fast food place that sells roast beef sandwiches. It wasn't a great place to be at ten o'clock at night with no car, but I kicked Andy out anyway.

"Get out!" I told Andy. He protested, he objected, but knowing as he did that there reaches a point with me from which there is no return, he stepped out onto the street.

"Drive forward," I told Beth.

"You're going to leave him there?"

"Why not?"

"On the street like that?"

"Sure."

She drove away and we spent five minutes on Storrow Drive in total silence. To our left ran the Charles River, reflecting the moon in its dark water, a few chunks of ice floating at the edges. Cambridge spread out over its banks, lit with white lights. The sky was shot through with stars.

"You think he has a subway token?" Beth said. She said it seriously, with the same tone one might use to ask whether a hospital patient was likely to live or die. For some reason I found it funny. Then we started to laugh—I have no idea why because nothing that had transpired that night was in the least bit funny—but we started to laugh and soon we were on the turnpike, going home.

C H A P T E R

S I X

Before Andy left, before we'd bought the schoolhouse, before I'd gotten pregnant, we'd spent a great number of hours looking through property listings and calling for the details on houses all over the Boston metropolitan area. A chore to younger couples who are much more interested in each other than any house—even a house with an atrium or ocean frontage or a self-contained annex suitable for an office or artist's workspace—this endless searching for the perfect home is to couples further down the road in their marriage a kind of ceremony of love. If I am honest with myself I will admit that this ceremony pretty much replaced the more traditional method of showing love and, looking back on it, I wonder if we might have been making a mistake by underestimating the power of sex.

In all the articles about sex you read that married people have sex two or three times a week on average. I always thought this number was a little—okay, *very*—high, and that people lie on these surveys—but then why shouldn't you lie if someone has the audacity to ask you how many times a week you have sex? I'd be tempted to answer a hundred and two times, just to strike up the numbers and raise a ripple of shock and worry through the survey conductors. It is true, however, that new couples have sex a lot more than couples who have been together a number of years, and much more than married couples. Married couples have a lot of good alibis for why they have less sex but don't mind so much. They tell you they have more meaningful sex, or better quality sex, or that sex is just one aspect of a marriage and that it isn't even all that important (these are the people who are really in trouble). They might be slightly more honest and confess that it is just one of the many compromises one makes for the constancy of marriage. Or that their passion for their partner has waned a little, but that their friendship has increased much more, and there is so much sex on TV and in movies that you feel like you are having it all the time anyway.

I don't quite believe any of this, or, I do believe it but I think we all—and here I mean married couples—want sex back. We want that passion and that dare and that desire we remember all too well and that pains us to remember. We want it so much that some of us leave our spouses to seek it elsewhere. We want it so much that some of us stay with our spouses and fight about things as irrelevant as who does the dishes and who puts the laundry away.

I thought this when Andy left me: I'll never have sex again. As pregnant as I was, as much as I didn't want to have sex, as seldom as I'd even thought about sex in, say, the past eight months, I thought with great despair that I was washed up in the sex department. Can I tell you that even with a belly swollen out to the next county, and stretch marks in places I didn't even think you could get them, and all sorts of blue, bulging veins and hair that lay flat against my head and skin that showed a mask of hormones, and feet that had swollen into the next size, I thought how I would miss sex. And this made me realize that no matter how gone to hell your body is, you still want it, which meant a fact of life I was until this time denying unconsciously, was now brought to the surface: old people want sex. I don't mind that old people want sex, I'm thrilled for them, but it made me very upset at this particularly difficult time in my life, because the fact that you still want sex when you are old meant that I'd be suffering even longer into my life than I had until then really bargained for. I was going to want sex and be old and alone; I was going to want sex and be incapacitated. What was I going to do with all that desire? What was I going to do with all that wasted passion?

I stomped around the house thinking about this. And I thought, if you don't have sex for ten or twenty years does it feel different when you finally do have it? Would styles have changed so that you might not even know the current trend for how to have it? Not that it changes all that much, but I might point out that making love in bright light or daylight used to be thought of as very risqué. In my stompings and wonderings, my thoughts diverted—would I ever get so desperate that I went to a sex shop and bought one of those really frightening vibrators? *No* was the answer. I was in the dining room now, which is, *was*, Andy's study. Hundreds of old books were stacked in piles on the table or put away in shelves under a system of library management that only he understands. The fact that he hadn't come to collect all his books I took as a good sign, an indication that perhaps he wasn't as completely out of this marriage as his absence would suggest. On one of the bookcases, gazing down with eyes that lacked pupils, was a bust of Robert Burns, a wedding present from his father.

So it was me and Robert, he was the man in my life. When we'd first gotten the bust, I'd hated it. Then I found it funny. Now I saw it as odd and collectible, if not actually useful as a dinner party companion for myself. The bust loomed large in the room, which was not difficult because the room was a cozy square, some would call it poky. It occurred to me that we really should have knocked down a wall and combined it with the living room, which would have opened up the downstairs into something bright and rather grand. Why had we been here five years ignoring the living room for being rather dark and small itself, and relegating the dining room to a workhouse for rehabilitating antiquated books? In my mind, I knocked down the wall, floods of light came tumbling in, our living room was at once a solved problem. More importantly, almost miraculously, the mental adjustment I'd done to the structure of our apartment got me right off the the subject of sex and onto the subject of houses, just as it had reliably done for years.

Having sorted out the living room, at least mentally, I decided I needed to sort out a few other loose threads in my life. After all, December had arrived. We were three and a half weeks from Christmas and two weeks from the baby's due date. It was time to think of practical things. If I was going to be without husband, if I was going to be eight and a half months pregnant without a husband, I needed a mobile phone. I needed to be able to call a taxi or an ambulance if I went into sudden, advanced labor (I didn't realize then that women seldom go into labor for the first time in any sudden fashion. You can have twenty-four hours of buildup before they even consider that you are starting labor). Also, I needed to be able to answer the phone before the caller rang off, and lately I'd found it difficult to move fast enough to get there before five or six rings had elapsed. I'd be out of my armchair by the fourth ring and just about have reached the phone by the time the caller hung up. Then I stood with a phone at my ear, the line dead, the baby kicking in furious protest at having been roused from sleep by my sudden movements, and fantasize at length about it having been Andy—Andy in a state of apology and heart-wrenching confession begging me to take him back. I'd already constructed my response, "I never told you to leave in the first place, of course I'll take you back." At these times I wondered whether I should call him just in case it had been him on the line, presuming that I was simply not home. This went on several times a day and it was beginning to drive me nuts. I needed to know who was calling me and I needed to stop thinking about Andy all the time.

A mobile phone was the obvious choice. I went to Phone City and asked for the most deluxe and advanced of their line. I was given phone after phone to examine, a dark red slimline model hardly bigger than the palm of your hand, a white one that came with free voice-mail, a chunky yellow one like the kind the AT&T repairmen have, a sleek black specimen with a mouthpiece that reminded me of what the astronauts used. I modeled for the salesman.

"Am I more the sunny yellow sort or do you think this little black number is really me?" I asked. "Does the white one make me look fat?"

He laughed. He was pretty cute, with slick black hair and freckles over his nose. His eyes were so light blue it was hard to believe he could use them to see. I flirted with him—I amazed myself by this—and he flirted back—which amazed me even more. "I like a woman in black," he said. "Timeless, classic, irresistible."

He was about twenty-one.

"So you would go for the TF700 with the speed dial and advanced audio enhancements?"

"If it were my choice," he said.

I wore it in a holster on my hip.

So I had the telephone, that was an improvement. I sounded very efficient answering as I did now on the first ring. The downside was that I was suddenly really very angry at Andy because I now realized that it had never been him calling me all those times I thought perhaps it had been. He hadn't called me, he hadn't called me in three weeks! Therefore, I concluded, I would divorce him. For this, I would need a lawyer—being hopelessly bourgeois, of course, I knew no end of lawyers—and I chose George Lambrick. I chose George Lambrick, but a few minutes into the initial discussion with him I realized what a foolish decision that had been.

"Are you sure you want to divorce him?" he said. "Can't you find it in your heart to forgive Andy? He's so nice, he's so sweet. And funny, too, the guy makes me laugh. We all love Andy."

"Can we just remember that *he* left *me*? How sweet was that?"

"A temporary break from the marriage. How long has be been gone, three or four weeks? That's nothing, that's just a little comma in the great tome of your marriage."

"I thought the term was *abandonment*—"

"An ugly word. You need to give him time, he'll come around."

"George, this is not the aggressive stance I expect my legal representative to take. I need to protect my assets, not that I have any. He's left me with an apartment that is apparently unsaleable, and a house which at the moment doesn't even have central heating. Both are mortgaged, one of them is uninhabitable. The baby is due any minute so I can't even sit up in a chair properly to write, which means the novel is a long way from finished, not that I'll make much on it anyway."

"That's just it," George said. "You can't afford to get a divorce."

"Can't afford?" This thought had never occurred to me. I hadn't realized that divorce was a luxury item, that you had to budget for one. I thought it was just something you got, like illness or a bad rash.

"I'm sorry. I didn't want to tell you, it makes you sound so poor." He paused and I heard his secretary speaking through his phone intercom—I knew it was that, because I'd seen one at Phone City. Then he said, "Andy is a nice guy. Women should be more forgiving."

More forgiving? Women should be *more forgiving*? This was my lawyer talking, about *forgiveness*? I was about to say to George that he didn't end up owning a four-story Beacon Hill brownstone with a superb elevated position, two roof terraces, and a walled back garden by managing to forgive the very people his clients wished to sue. He didn't forgive his way into his newly remodeled kitchen with its Firestone sink and its Lacanche range with solid brass castings and trim, and he wasn't likely to be doing a lot of forgiving if he wanted to finish the loft conversion that Lori and he had started that autumn.

Then I knew.

"You're having an affair, aren't you, George?"

"Good heavens, no," he said. "Ha ha, an affair. I would never have an affair."

"You had an affair with that Claire person."

"That was ten years ago."

"George, you can't lie to me—"

"All right," he said. He threw out a sigh and then said, "It's Lori who's having an affair. I'm trying to see it as a temporary problem. Unfortunately, the temporary problem seems to think he's in love with my wife. Since she came out in the open with it he's taken to calling me and trying to persuade me to give her a divorce."

"Which you obviously don't want to do. Lori, being a most wonderful person, a great friend, a marvelous mother, and a devoted wife . . . well," I hesitated, "devoted up until this most recent gaffe."

"Now you understand why I told you how sweet Andy is?"

"I *suppose*. But Lori really is a special person, besides being an excellent surgeon. How many people could, if necessary, receive bypass surgery from their spouse? At your age you don't want to divorce a woman with those hands."

"She's a damned good golfer, too," he said. "More to the point, she doesn't want a divorce. Since we started that loft conversion she's too busy for the affair. She's completely consumed by the house."

"George," I said, "you are a wise man. Still, I think I need a different lawyer."

"I'm telling you, Meg, you can't afford a divorce. And I know Andy, he'll come to his senses soon. Once you get on the divorce track there's no going back. My advice is leave him be, go have your baby, don't worry too much about the house situation. *Do not* start legal proceedings."

"Really, that's your advice?"

"Listen to me, Meg. Forget about divorce. Install central heating."

I thought that sounded right, at least for the moment. Then I thought about what it meant exactly to install central heating. I thought about pulling up floorboards and going through bad plaster and putting in pipes and hoping it all worked without some terrible leak occurring which ruined the original beams, which was the whole reason for buying the damned house in the first place, and I knew I could not install central heating. I could not install central heating because when you get as pregnant as I was you can't imagine doing anything more strenuous than taking a bath and even though I'd never planned to *personally* install the central heating system, that is to actually

take hammer in hand and go at it myself, even over-
seeing a contractor seemed too much work for me
just then.

So I phoned my real estate agent.

It was time I took charge of my life and I was beginning to like this feeling. Snapping my TF700 out
of its buckskin holster and speed-dialling my real estate agent I felt thrusting and powerful.

"Marianne Poupopolis," I said in an authoritative
tone, well, as authoritative as you can sound while
getting your tongue around the name Poupopolis.
When Marianne came on the line I didn't even give
her a chance to speak. "Marianne, I've been thinking
about it. Maybe we should sell the schoolhouse and
keep the apartment. After all, I'm used to it here and
the schoolhouse needs a lot of work. I know we'll
lose money on the deal, we've lost a lot already just in
mortgage payments, but to be honest with you I just
can't face the prospect of renovating right now. My
life has become all too disjointed for renovation."

"I don't think that would be wise, Meg darling,"
she said in her kittenish voice. Marianne used to work
in a talent agency, only as a receptionist but she
picked up a lot of pointers. Calling people "darling"
for one, and purring into the phone when male
clients were on the line for another. She had a reputa-
tion for being able to sell even in the deadest market,
even when the house had been empty since 1960, or
had a railway track running through the backyard, or
was so embarrassingly primitive inside that you dared
not ask to use the toilet. When we first put the apart-

ment on the market we had underestimated the necessity of someone like Marianne and, for a year, enlisted another real estate agent to no effect. Then, when I was complaining to Sarah one day about how the market was dead and the only people who'd come to see the place were the types who went to every open house regardless, she sighed her here-is-the-answer-sigh and suggested Marianne. Marianne Poupopolis, I said to Andy, wasn't that the one whom we bought from? It turned out she'd sold us our apartment and she'd sold it to the people whom we bought from (the Andersons, you will remember). Perhaps the only property that gets sold in Boston during a market slump is sold by Marianne Poupopolis because she had apparently sold our apartment again. "The buyer who I showed it to last week wants the place," she said.

"You showed the apartment last week?"

"Of course, I show it all the time. I tried calling you but you don't answer your phone."

So it had been Marianne who'd been ringing me all those times I'd thought it was Andy. Want to know how crazily I was thinking? I was thinking so crazily that I could not entirely take in that Marianne might actually have sold the apartment, which meant it was truly make-up-your-mind time about whether I wanted to sell it. (Of course I did want to sell it, but I only wanted to sell it if Andy and I were going to do up the schoolhouse together and I did not have to oversee the central heating installation.) But I didn't think about selling or not selling. All I could think about was how not one of those phone calls had been from Andy. Even after I'd gotten the mobile phone and never missed a call, I had still thought that the previous calls had been Andy. In my deluded lonesome confusion I'd made up that whenever the phone rang it was Andy. When it rang and I was not home it was Andy and when it rang and I hadn't gotten to it in time, it was Andy. Not just Andy, but Andy on his hands and knees praying I would take him back. Now, in a flash I had to recognize that none of this was true. It had never been Andy—it had been Marianne.

I didn't know what to say, so I said, "I have a new phone now; it is with me at all times."

"Good, because this fellow is coming around with an architect on Thursday."

"With an architect? This is all happening too fast."

"You've been on the market a year and three months, now you're complaining it's too fast?"

"What's he planning to do in this little place that would require an architect?"

"Knock it through to the rest of the house. He's buying the whole thing."

"He can't buy the whole house," I laughed. I felt better now. Knowing that the buyer could not have the whole house had somehow translated into my mind that he couldn't have our apartment either, which meant I did not have to install central heating in the schoolhouse, which I suddenly, desperately, did not want. In fact, I'd decided that the schoolhouse must be avoided at all costs. The last place on earth I wanted to live was in that crumbling old schoolhouse. "An old woman lives in the rest of the house," I said cheerfully. I was already considering what the asking price of the schoolhouse should be—was it possible that we could get more than we paid for it? Or at least recover the money we'd already put into the not-so-simple transaction that it took to acquire it? There was a silence from Marianne, which I took to mean she was waiting for an explanation about why the rest of the house was not for sale. I explained. "She's never going to sell. Mrs. Russell was *born* in this house. She gave up just enough for our apartment because she couldn't handle too many stairs anymore, but she always said she was born here and she would die here, too."

"Yes, well—" Marianne said, "she got her wish."

It took a moment for this to sink in. "Are you telling me Mrs. Russell *is dead*?"

"Died weeks ago. I'm surprised you didn't know."

Well, that just summarized it all, I thought to myself. I'd been so involved with my life, with the disappearance of Andy and the ever-growing pregnancy and buying my telephone and wondering whether to sell the apartment quick so I could start work on the schoolhouse or sell the schoolhouse instead and hang on to the apartment, that I hadn't even noticed that our neighbor—our housemate, really, if you consider that we all lived in the same structure—had died. Died *weeks* ago. I went into the breakfast room and looked out the window at the back garden, which Mrs. Russell always kept so well. Because it was wintertime not much was growing. Little had changed since she died. But now that I knew what had happened I could see all the telltale signs. The tarpaulin that normally hung over the iron garden furniture had come away at one edge and no one had placed it back into position. Her watering can, a handpainted one that was one of her favorites, had been left out and there was a pair of clay pots into which she'd obviously meant to plant something, but had never gotten to it. The greenhouse lacked its usual array of forced bulbs and there was no feed in the birdhouse.

"I'm so sorry," I said.

"Her kids want to sell the place. They're letting it go cheap. I'd say you should buy it, except you already have that adorable schoolhouse—"

"Don't remind me."

"—and a buyer for your property."

I see in all this I have sort of lost track of Andy. This is because at this point in my life I really had lost track of Andy. I knew from the supermarket incident that he was living in Brighton within easy shopping distance of the Eco-Save. I knew he was unhappy with the Eco-Save, and that he had a phone number—but if you remember, that night he gave me the number he didn't say he wanted me to call him, he said he wanted me to call him *when I went into labor.* To my way of thinking, this translated into what he was really saying, which is do not call me *unless* you are in labor. In other words, do not call me. So I felt I could not call him. I could not call him at work, where he spent ten or so hours a day compulsively reshelving books and deciding which new titles should go closest to the door and which smart paperbacks should be positioned by the register, and I could not call him at home, at his new home somewhere in Brighton, unless I was in labor.

"Hello, Carla, I'm calling you because I cannot call Andy. I'm not allowed to call Andy unless I am in labor."

"What? You're in labor?"

It was one o'clock in the morning. I'd woken them. I could hear James whispering, "Has she had it yet? Is it a boy or a girl?"

"Tell James I don't know yet. I'm still pregnant."

"She's still pregnant, James, now shut up so I can hear."

"I'm sorry, Carla," I said. "It's very late."

"Who told you that you couldn't call him? He did? Forget what he says and do what you want."

"You think I should call him?"

"I think you should do whatever you want."

I could hear James in the background. He was saying, "What? *He isn't back yet?*"

"Do you think I should divorce him? George says I can't afford a divorce."

I heard the swift scratch of a match being struck and then the draw of Carla's cigarette. Carla, bless her, is the only smoker friend I still have. We all used to smoke—I personally was only a ten-a-day smoker, but I loved every minute of those ten cigarettes—but over the years the health campaigns got to us and we became convinced that being a smoker is about as close to being aligned with the devil as you can get without actually joining a cult. So we gave up, all of us except for Carla. She was sitting up in bed now— I could picture her perfectly—with the phone in one hand and a cigarette in the other, pushing her long hair away from her face with the lit end of the cigarette bent well away to avoid singeing her hair. She said, "George is full of shit. He means he doesn't want to do your divorce for you because he'd have to do it for nothing because he's a friend. He means *he* can't afford your divorce."

"How do you know this, Carla?"

"I'm trained to look behind the apparent truth for hidden motives. It's a rather useful skill."

"So you think I should divorce Andy?"

"I can't answer that. But may I remind you of one thing: the weddings. All the weddings you planned and never had and then the actual one that did occur."

"Oh yeah, those." For awhile there we celebrated the anniversary of each date that was canceled, but it all got too confusing and we ran out of gift ideas.

"June twenty-fifth," she said.

I could hear James in the background. "Black Saturday," he said.

June 25th was the first day Andy and I didn't get married. It was perhaps the worst of the various non-weddings. I'd been woken by my mother—I'd been so consumed by all the old-fashioned notions of weddings that I'd insisted on spending a few days at my mother's and not allowing Andy to steal even a glance at me for at least twenty-four hours prior to the wedding day. Mother woke me up, not with a gentle nudge and a whisper in my ear, "Today's the day," but with a great shake, shouting "The goats! The goats!" I hauled myself out of bed, pulled on my jeans without even a glance at my wedding dress, which was hanging from the wardrobe, swaddled in plastic like a cocooned butterfly, and went charging out after my mother, who in her hysteria had led me to believe that the barn was burning with all the goats in it. What had actually happened was that the goats, who were not kept in a barn in summer anyway——I might have remembered that if it weren't six in the morning——had broken through the post-and-wire fencing and were eagerly assaulting Mother's vegetable garden. I dashed outside the farmhouse to a sky blackened with threatening, ominous rain clouds and my mother darting and feinting in an effort to dissuade twenty or so goats from her hard-earned produce. I saw Carla—Carla who was born and bred in Philadelphia and who considered farm life to be a quaint anachronistic lifestyle that survived only among Mennonites—in one of her Mary Quant summer dresses and desert boots shooing a nanny goat away from a tomato plant. James had taken a more aggressive stance, raising his arms up like the wings of an aircraft and running at them in full cry. Beth and David were not there, having had the foresight to realize that Mother's house was full of animals and therefore not particularly comfortable for humans. They had the excuse of David's asthma and were happily tucked up in a nearby bed and breakfast, probably just about to take long hot baths before sitting down to a breakfast of scrambled eggs and French toast.

I will tell you something about goats. Goats do not easily give up their food. Also, goats have horns. And if they are Mother's goats they have no fear of people. Try as we might, we could not get them off that stretch of ground through sheer threat. We ran around as the sky opened, pouring out dollops of rain and then hail, sharp and biting against our exposed summer-loving skin, and smashed with our shoes as many vegetables as we purported to be saving. Finally Mother got an idea and raced off to the feed room to get three buckets of oats. By allowing the goats to attempt to wrestle each of us to the ground in an effort to separate us from those oats, we managed finally to move them into a holding pen long enough to fix the fence.

By nine o'clock that morning, covered in mud and exploded tomato and goat spit, I went back to the bedroom where I'd hoped to begin the morning, sitting for long, dreamy hours in front of the vanity table deciding how to wear my hair, only to discover that my cocooned dress had fallen from the wardrobe (I'd hooked the hanger over the top edge of the wardrobe and it hadn't been very secure) and was now being used as a bed by one of Mother's innumerable cats. That wouldn't have been much of a problem, the plastic was ample protection against cat hair and fleas, but this particular cat was still enough of a kitten to find irresistible the netting of my veil, which was not in plastic, and to have torn much of it as well as eaten a number of its silk flowers.

"Oh, Percy!" my mother said, shaking her head as though at a naughty child. "A whole farmyard of mice out there and you have to concentrate your efforts on Meg's clothes!"

"Not my clothes, Mother, my wedding veil! That cat has destroyed my veil!"

"Oh well, you don't have to wear a veil. I didn't have a veil."

"But I wanted a veil!"

"Well, we could try to piece this one together, or perhaps do a quick job on some net curtains."

"Mother!"

"I'm sorry, honey, what do you want me to do?" Mother asked, and then dashed out of the room after her Labrador, Bruno, who had gotten ahold of her own wedding hat.

The rain and hail had made a mud slick out of Mother's driveway so that the vintage limousine that was meant to escort us to my place of matrimony would have to completely ruin its shining, waxed exterior in order to get to us. Carla pointed this out— good, smart Carla—and we telephoned the company just in time for the driver to be instructed to pick us up at the end of the driveway. James had to carry me in my dress out of the farmhouse and into the car—

while I earnestly clutched my train—and we all piled into Mother's Buick and rode out the muddy quarter mile to the main road. There, amid a long line of rural route mailboxes we waited for half an hour or more for the limousine. The rain had stopped—this I mistakenly took as a good sign—but now the sun was penetrating the air with an intense heat that meant we could not sit there like sausages in the car. Certainly, I could not, as I was layered in white satin. I was roasting. I thought how stupid we'd been to set a wedding date for the end of June—a thought I bore in mind a year later when I got to go through it all again. As I've mentioned, the next one was for early May, a much more temperate month.

Mother, James, and Carla very sweetly got out of the car in hope that if I were allowed some space it would make it cooler for me in there. Finally, however, I had to give up my hiding place in the backseat and stand with them at the side of the road, providing great spectacle to the passing vehicles. Cars, trucks, a bulldozer, a tractor, a horse box, a load of sheep, all went by at regular intervals, staring and smiling and some even honking their horns. By the time the limousine showed up I felt I'd been subjected to a cruel rite of passage from some ancient and hideous culture and that wherever the shining black vintage limousine was taking me I was surely on my way to be further harassed by chieftains in body paint and spellbound warriors with hot pokers speaking a dialect foreign to me and plucking out my hair until it matched their own mohawks.

What happened instead of this was little better. I ended up at the whitewashed Methodist church in the village five miles from Mother's farm where I sat now on my own in the back of the limousine until twenty minutes past the hour I was meant to be married and finally, when it became apparent that Andy was not going to show up, I instructed the driver in as controlled a manner as I could to take me back to the farm. He drove efficiently to the spot from which he'd collected me only an hour before and this time I had him go all the way up to the farmhouse. I flipped off my silk slippers and held my train over the mud, and went back into the house where the whole horrible day had begun to change into my jeans and find electric wire for the goat-pasture fence.

All of this I remembered in an instant when Carla said, "June twenty-fifth." The look on the driver's face, my own mortification at realizing I'd been left at the altar—or not the altar exactly, but only because I refused to get out of the car if indeed Andy were not showing. Andy's father, Sam Howe, was there. I'd seen him through the window looking skinny and disheveled even in his morning suit, making leggy strides with that endless psychotic energy of his around the churchyard as though he were searching for his son behind hedges and graves. His socks were red, though I noted that at least they matched, and he was carrying his flute, an instrument he does not actually know how to play, and for a moment I was glad Andy had failed to show because I knew that had we taken our vows that morning I'd actually have been related to this man.

"I see the connection," I said to Carla. "But I don't know what you are driving at. Are you saying that Andy has disappointed me before and is likely to disappoint me again? Or are you saying that June twenty-fifth was a good example of how something can start terribly, so terribly that you can be sure there is no hope of a future at all, and then it all turns right in the end? Or are you saying that the whole marriage started out badly, even though we eventually did manage to appear in front of a preacher at the same time and *do the thing*, and that it only makes sense that it would teeter to this final alarming precipice and be hurled to its death, by Andy, of course? Carla? Carla?"

I heard some noises and then James's deep, slightly English voice. "I'm afraid Carla has fallen asleep, dear."

CHAPTER SEVEN

MARIANNE SOLD THE APARTMENT. GOOD OLD Marianne, she's so efficient that she managed to put a pregnant woman out of a home. The schoolhouse, which until now had remained firmly in the dream house stage, even though we held title to it, was suddenly no longer the dream house at all, but the only house. The contract was being drawn up, lawyers had been called. The buyer was moving right away into the part of the house that poor Mrs. Russell had occupied. If I dragged my feet a little I had three months to move out, if I wasn't before then driven out by all the building work that the buyer was apparently employing right away.

Mrs. Martin Martin came over, teetering on her thick, water-retaining ankles, shrouded in black and carrying a clipboard, her reading glasses on a chain around her neck.

"It is so sad about Mrs. Russell," she said. "You must be devastated."

It was sad about Mrs. Russell, I thought. But to receive "devastated" status at this particular time in my life, this particular homeless, pregnant, left-by-husband time, was beyond the reaches of poor Mrs. Russell, who after all had done the thing—had died—on her own, without actually involving me.

"It's very sad," I agreed. I looked quickly at my watch, "Oh, look at the time. Sorry to leave you so abruptly, Mrs. Martin, but I was just on my way out!"

Mrs. Martin's mouth gaped. She has an uneven mouth, the result of a minor stroke some years ago, and it dipped like a half moon. "On your way out?" she said incredulously. "But you haven't got on any shoes!"

"I was just putting them on." There was a pair of Andy's green rubber rain boots just inside the hallway. I slipped them on over my naked feet. They rose up well above the knee, making me look a little like the Jolly Green Giant. "Preparing for the weather!" I said.

"Mrs. Russell was the last decent neighbor we had!" she cried. "To think that her life was stopped short by flu."

"Is that what she died of, flu?" I said. I honestly didn't know. To imagine that Mrs. Russell's life was stopped short was a bit of an exaggeration—I mean she was in her eighties—though I found myself in the uncomfortable and unique situation of agreeing with Mrs. Martin that it was a tragedy nonetheless.

"Now, don't pretend you didn't know," Mrs. Martin said, bowing her head in a tsk-tsking way. "Of course you are upset that your husband gave her the illness which caused her untimely death, but you must own up to it!"

"My husband?" I had no idea what she was talking about. Then I remembered how I'd told her Andy was suffering from flu. "Mrs. Martin, I really doubt that—"

"You mustn't deny it! The Lord forgives those who truly repent. We know perfectly well that it was his flu that killed her. Now, some of the neighborhood has gotten together a little petition," she said.

"A petition—?"

"It is the neighborhood's opinion that you ought to send the Russell family a donation for the headstone. As it was your fault that she died, I think this is the least you could do—"

"A headstone? You want me to give them a headstone?"

"The neighborhood wants it. I'm just delivering the message. Now, we've found a very good stone-smith in Cambridge—did you know that Cambridge has the highest number of funeral homes per capita in the United States?—anyway, we've found a perfectly lovely polished marble stone that would be just marvelous for Mrs. Russell. We'd need to have it shipped to the family seat in Rhode Island, and of course you would be expected to pay delivery charges as well, but

I've done absolutely all of the paperwork for you already, so you needn't worry about that—"

"No, I said. "The answer is no."

"We all agree that it is the appropriate first step—"

"Absolutely not."

"—really the least you can do, considering."

"Mrs. Russell is not getting any goddamned headstone from me, do you understand that?"

"Really, dear, it's not so expensive as all that. The whole thing for just over a thousand dollars, which considering that you killed her—"

I grabbed my car keys and shot past Mrs. Martin.

"I did not kill her," I said, clomping toward the car in Andy's boots.

"Of course not, dear," Mrs. Martin said, following me. "I meant your husband."

I got in the car. Just as I was seated a copy of Mrs. Martin's petition floated onto my lap.

Mrs. Martin said, "Nobody is taking legal action, but not every wrongdoing is actionable. A headstone would be a civilized gesture."

I wadded up the petition, threw it on the lawn, and closed the car door, locking it immediately.

"We should talk further about this!" Mrs. Martin said, speaking loudly into the glass of my car door window.

I drove quickly through the neighborhood streets, then out onto the turnpike heading into town.

My plan was to go to Saks to buy maternity bras. My plan was Saks, but somehow I ended up driving to Andy's bookstore, Between the Covers, which is a medium-sized shop, partly given over to a café that sells coffee from around the world. The tables were set up outside on the sidewalk, their blue-and-white parasols sheltering those who gathered beneath them to drink coffee and eat frozen yogurt while thumbing through magazines and paperbacks, not necessarily purchased at Andy's store. I drove back and forth, knowing as I did that Andy was inside, and thought how any member of the public—anyone except me—could walk through the open glass doors of Between the Covers with nothing more complicated in mind than an eight-dollar puchase.

I double-parked outside, clomped out of the car in Andy's rubber boots, and edged my way into the store, looking frantically from left to right, scanning the small crowd of shoppers for Andy. I ducked behind a bookcase of computer manuals just as Andy and his store manager, Isaac Slater, appeared from somewhere within the stockroom and marched together to the front door. Andy looked awful, he was wearing a very old linen suit which was frayed at the elbows and knees and crumpled well past the casual lived-in look that linen is supposed to give you. It hung from his thin frame like a tattered scarecrow jacket, making him look more or less like a beggar, or like a younger version of his poor demented father, while Isaac, in a perfectly crisp Oxford cloth shirt and chinos stood beside him with a notebook, the paragon of efficiency.

They were deep into a discussion about which should be near the door, erotic fiction or travel. Andy's argument was that it ought to be travel; erotic fiction gave the wrong impression of the store and might offend some of his more delicate customers.

"I've never felt good about erotic fiction," he said, thumbing through a copy of something called *Sweet Dreams*. "I mean what exactly is erotic fiction other than a bound version of *Penthouse Forums*?"

"What is it?" said Isaac patiently. "Think of it as a magnet that attracts customers into the store."

"But what kind of customer? We want readers, not . . ." here Andy was stuck for words. "Not voyeurs."

Isaac smiled, balancing on his heels. "Think of it as money on the more desirable side of the balance sheet."

"I don't know, I've never felt great about this kind of thing."

"Think of it as fiction with an R rating. You go to R movies, don't you?"

"Yes, but I cringe during the sex parts. I'm more comfortable with video rentals."

"Aha," Isaac said, raising a finger, "you are ashamed but curious. You'd be even more comfortable with books if you tried them."

"Well, I admit I *have* read Henry Miller," Andy said.

"Bingo!" said Isaac. "And let me tell you, there's not a whole lot of difference between Miller and—" he lifted a title from a carton, "and Anonymous here.

Anonymous is a kind of alternative Miller. For the guy who likes sex and books, and likes them in combination, too."

"Oh, I don't know. Still, maybe I should give it a try."

"You should! You see, Andy, now how can I say this? You are the erotic book audience. You typify our ideal reader and customer. Trust me on this, put erotic fiction by the door."

Issac won, erotic fiction got the prime position. This is why Andy's store is successful, because Isaac runs it. Truth be known, Andy would prefer to own an antiquarian bookshop in which he didn't actually have to bring himself to part with any of his stock. But Isaac had business sense, Isaac knew how to move product. And he knew how to bring Andy to the correct decision, despite Andy's natural inclinations. Now why couldn't I be so persuasive? Think of the baby sleeping soundly as we sip champagne in the bath together. Think of the baby singing nursery rhymes in the back of the car as we travel up the coast. Think of family holidays, buying our child his first bicycle, a bright red wagon. Would any of these images bring him home to me, to the soon-to-be us?

I went to Saks to buy maternity bras. These are the horrible zippered bras that you wear in order to breast-feed discreetly (of course, there is no way really to breast-feed discreetly) and that you come to know more intimately than any other part of your wardrobe because you are in them all the time. In the early days of motherhood, when your breasts are pumped up to basketball size, you even sleep in them. I went to Saks because I was trying to make what is a not very pleasant experience—being measured for a bra—as positive as I could. The last time I'd been measured for a bra was when I was fourteen years old and I remember standing nervous and half naked on one side of a curtained partition at Hecht Company while a salesgirl with very big breasts and a lot of makeup whispered to one of her salesgirl pals that I didn't really need a bra anyway. I went away with a single Maidenform A cup and the beginnings of a complex about my body and its design inadequacies. I'd chosen Saks because it had been recommended by Sarah and because I knew that even if the bra buying was a lesson in humiliation—I should say a *further* lesson in humiliation because really everything about those last few weeks of pregnancy and then, even worse, labor, is a continual assault on one's dignity. When people talk about having a positive birth experience they are *not* saying that you go in, have a great time, and write postcards to all your friends saying "Wish you were here." What positive means in this context is that after the whole thing you are still about your person enough to be able to locate and gather the shards of self-respect you left strewn about the labor ward and move in the general direction of a bed. At any rate, I was told Saks was a good place to go. So I went. I went and stood half naked on one side of a door, taking into perspective the enormity of my pregnant self from three different, rather unkind angles, until an efficient, rather matronly woman arrived with a measuring tape and informed me that there was no choice in the matter, I was a Robinson's 38DD.

I bought four of them. They were fifty-two dollars each. I came out with over two hundred dollars' worth of industrial-strength bras and took the escalator down to women's accessories to look at all the things I would rather have bought for my two hundred dollars. The usual Christmas garb was all over the place. Stacks of holly-laden boxed sets of perfume and aftershave, chocolate in various shining foil wrappings. There was a festive-looking decorative Christmas train, uplit from its setting on three blocks of clear glass that had been swept with wax chips that were meant to look like snow. The train was ordinary enough, creeping around a circle of track, but the land through which it traveled was apparently some sort of anthill, dozens of little ant figures dressed in mufflers and boots skated in the mirror pond and waved as the train passed by. A tall, thin woman in black with a pair of bauble earrings, one red, one green, passed by the ant train with her equally tall and thin friend.

"You want to know how thin I want to be?" she said to the friend. She gestured at the insects beside her. "I want to be *that* thin."

I was thinking of leather gloves and a beautiful silk scarf, or maybe a tidy little leather notebook with a gold pen that I could keep in my pocket for when a great sentence pops into my head and I don't want to forget it, things I never would buy but that I could have possibly bought if I hadn't had to buy all those zippered bras. I passed a few cases of watches—I could have gotten a watch for two hundred dollars—and then hair accessories, velvet headbands, and tortoiseshell combs, and on to ladies' hats. I'm always trying on hats. I don't own a single one but trying them on is an easy form of amusement. Saks had a great variety of outrageous models for Christmas, ranging from a jaunty black number with a single dyed-black ostrich plume to a thing the size and scope of a sombrero encrusted with a pictorial of New York's skyline in ersatz stones. I found a cashmere beret with a cluster of colorful stones and arranged it on my head at various angles. It was a pretty little hat in a pleasing shade of pink, so soft and light you hardly noticed it on your head. I thought I could have bought this hat with the two hundred dollars I'd just spent on underwear with the texture and attractiveness of building scaffolding. I must have lingered too long because an oval-faced saleswoman with skin as white as that of a Chinese doll and black hair slicked back into a skilfully executed chignon lighted on me.

"Pretty," she said and wrinkled her nose at me as though there were a private joke between us. "Something like that would draw attention away from your bump and to your face."

I didn't want to buy the hat and was about to explain to the dainty saleswoman that, at any rate, unless the hat was capable of emitting a sound and light show from its small island of colorful stones, it was very doubtful indeed that it could draw attention away from my pregnancy, when I spotted David—as in Beth's David—twenty yards away in ladies' handbags.

He was with Diana, I recognized her from her calves, which are those very short, square calves of tiny women who gain weight uniformly throughout their bodies, ending with chubby toes and necks and wrists. She was wearing black stockings, a good choice for fat calves, and an alpaca cardigan in festive green, which made her look a bit like a small hedge. When she turned to exclaim to David how very dear, "how very, very dear" were her exact words—I could hear her quite well as I'd advanced at speed in their direction—she found the Judith Leiber panda bag she was admiring, I noticed that she was wearing a red holly leaf on her green sweater and I realized that what they were doing was Christmas shopping. As I edged over—I was pretty sure that David would not recognize me, pregnant as I was, unless he got a good look at my face—I realized further that David was about one credit card swipe away from buying her a three-thousand-dollar designer handbag in the shape of a panda for Christmas. The saleswoman had placed the bag on a scrap of satin where the light from the track of spot lamps above was reflected in the myriad of black and white rhinestones to blinding effect. Diana was enamored, moved almost spiritually by the thought that the panda could be hers, and there was no graceful way at this point for David to step out of the deal, if indeed that was what he wished to do.

In case you are not familiar with Judith Leiber bags, let me explain that they are small, rhinestone-encrusted satin-lined bags in the shape of animals or eggs or, occasionally, an insect. They are cute, if you like that sort of thing, and they are useless. Some people don't ever use their bags, who can blame them, but instead stow them away in acid-free paper in their closets. I haven't yet grasped the reason why a certain segment of society finds them irresistible. I've heard them described as "witty" but how can something be witty that is as absurd as a handbag shaped as a pig, hinged at the haunches, and covered in pink rhinestones? But apparently they are witty, they are wonderful, everyone agrees, but like colonic irrigation, the pleasure of a Leiber bag has somehow always escaped me.

Diana loved the panda. "Oh, look at his little face!" she cooed.

Now what is a friend to do? I couldn't just stand there and let David hand over his Amex card to the saleswoman and buy Diana that panda. On the other hand, I didn't have a lot to say that might persuade him otherwise if the price tag hadn't already done so. There was no question of minding my own business, I knew David too well, I knew David so well that there had been times late at night after David and Beth and Andy and I had finished off another of our millions of dinner parties that, at the door, we really weren't sure who went home with whom. I'd known David for as long as Beth had known him; and Beth had chosen him out of a crowd of dental students at a dental school party she duped me into going to with her when we were about twenty-two years old. Our connection to the school was tenuous at best, Beth's cousin was a recent graduate and she'd persuaded him to take her as a guest and then to allow me to come, too; she'd guessed correctly that she'd have to spend the night talking about porcelain molar implants and periodontal disease if she tagged around after her cousin and so I was there to keep her company while she combed the various male dental students for signs of maritability. We were easily spotted as nondental students, and spent a great part of the evening looking foolish, until David came along and Beth convinced him she had the best teeth he'd ever seen (this might be true) and that he really ought to take a look inside her mouth. That was fourteen years ago. Beth has done a lot of crazy things since but the sight of her parting her lips to show David her perfectly orthodontized and beautifully maintained teeth, and even better, his reaction to them, which was visible and enthusiastic, sticks with me as perhaps the most poignant and evocative moment that typifies Beth's anything-goes policy to hooking men.

"When in Rome," she said to me, when David disappeared to find us drinks.

So what would Beth do if she saw her husband parting with three thousand dollars of their yet undivided cash to procure a Leiber bag for another woman? To be fair, Beth had done a lot more than buy an evening bag when David and she separated, she'd bought a whole new house. Still, there was something about the scene here that set me on edge. Partly it was a demonstration of how very wayward we all had gone—Andy and me, David and Beth— and partly it was the rather predatorial stance that Diana had taken with regard to this purchase. Diana in her Christmas garments, her tidy black hose and Italian shoes, holding on to David's elbow and urging him to buy the ridiculous bag. David, who is notoriously generous, who used to bring a bottle of champagne and a bottle of Calvados and a bouquet of roses just to have lunch with us, who could be persuaded to buy anything, even if he didn't have the money to do so, was putty in her hands. Also, I was Beth's best friend; there were a lot of years behind us. I could not sit back and allow David to spend three thousand dollars in front of my eyes without consulting her. I ducked behind a rack of mufflers and unholstered my TF700 from its trim little resting place at my left hip, dialing Beth's number from memory as I had done for over a dozen years.

"Beth," I said. "David is at Saks with Diana and she's persuading him to get her a Judith Leiber bag."

"Which one? Not the egg? I've always wanted the egg."

"The panda."

"Oh, a stupid one. Well, I guess it's better than the lips."

"What do you want me to do?"

"What can you do?" she sighed. "Go up and give them both a big smile and ruin the moment for them. That's all anyone can do in these circumstances."

So I did. I moved along quickly from wallets to Filofaxes to cigarette cases to jeweled lipstick holders and finally to evening bags. I got to them just after Diana had handed the panda to the saleswoman and given David a big thank-you kiss.

"David!" I piped up. "What a surprise!"

"Oh, Meg," he said, and ran a hand through his hair. He was breathing quite hard and his hair, he didn't have much of it, was wet with perspiration. I guess the panda purchase was already costing him, he looked nervous and shifty and, if I was not mistaken, slightly ashamed. Whether he was ashamed because he was buying an expensive gift for a woman who was not his wife, or ashamed because I'd caught him at it, or ashamed because nobody should spend three thousand dollars on a handbag in the first place, it was hard to tell. "It's great to see you. Gosh, it's been a long time. Oh, here, let me . . ."

He took a half step and then leaned forward over my bump and kissed me dryly on the cheek. It was an awkward gesture from start to finish, and a far cry from the enormous bear hugs I was used to from him, back when he was my best friend's husband.

"I didn't think you were the evening bag type," I said to him.

"Oh it's not for me, the bag. We're getting a panda. Or, Diana, I mean, she is getting a panda."

"Oh," I said, pretending I had not until just that

second noticed Diana, who stood beside David with a look on her face as though someone had just shoved a tray of ice up her back. "Oh, I *am* sorry. How do you do."

"You know Meg, don't you, Diana? You met once before."

"You were considerably thinner," Diana said. "Is that a baby you are expecting?"

I could do any number of things with that insanely stupid remark, but I decided to be kind. It was important that I ruin the moment for them, that I really ruin the moment, which meant I had to bait and switch a little.

"What? A baby!" I looked down at my belly as though it had just suddenly popped out like that, big as a pillow in front of me. "Oh God, well, it certainly appears that way."

She smiled, the twit, and I smiled back.

The saleswoman returned to the counter now with David's credit card and the wrapped panda gingerly placed in a Saks bag for Diana.

"So, what did you say you bought?"

"Oh, the cutest evening bag," Diana said, embracing anew the pleasure she got from her new status handbag. "It's a panda, it has these big panda eyes."

"Oh, the panda, yes," I said, addressing David. "I remember that one."

David gave me a puzzled look. Diana scowled. I became *faux* flustered and ran through my words, as though backtracking in a hurry. "Perhaps I'm mistaken. Beth has so many of them. You know how she is, bags of bags, ha ha." I kept smiling, I don't know how I did this, it was really quite cruel. I looked from David to Diana, then back to David, making it seem as though I was a blunderer who didn't mean any harm. "But, hey, the panda was always a winner. I mean, who wants an owl or egg or . . ." I looked over her shoulder at a rectangle of perfect glass under which several Leiber bags glistened like so many diamonds, "or a butterfly. Really, you got the best one, Diana."

"Oh great," Diana said, looking up at David as though he were a criminal, as though he'd spent the three thousand just to make her look like shit. "She has the butterfly. You bought me this knowing that she has the butterfly and half a dozen others."

"Oh, they aren't all bags, some are just pillboxes," I pretended to be pedaling backward in a desperate attempt to save us all. "Little trinkets, hardly worth a mention."

"I just can't believe this," Diana said.

David stood, dumbfounded, his mouth opening and closing again but failing to utter a single sound.

"I don't even want the thing now," she said, dropping the bag, literally right onto the floor.

"But, Diana," David said, "Beth doesn't have a . . ."

Diana took off at speed through a crowded sales floor. David scooped up the bag and looked in the direction Diana had gone. The word "panda" rose softly from his lips. But it was too late, she was consumed by a crowd of women similarly dressed in

Christmas red and green, all of them going so many opposing directions that it was anyone's guess as to where Diana had fled. It was either chase after her or see what had become of the three-thousand-dollar evening bag, dropped so unceremoniously onto the floor.

"I can't stand to look," David said, handing me the parcel.

Swaddled in parchment and set upon a cozy nest of shredded paper, the panda was intact as far as I could tell. Held in one's hands it was a much more beautiful object than I had expected, bewitching, almost frightening, like an amulet, a lucky charm. For a moment we both stood, marveling at the abandoned panda. David was the first to speak.

"Why did you do that?" he asked gently.

"I don't know. Malice, I suppose. I still can't get used to it, you and Beth with different people. You were married too long to start this kind of stuff. You were married so long you even began to look like each other."

"Don't tell me that, I like to remember Beth as an attractive woman."

"It was dumb of you to have an affair with Diana and dumb of Beth to kick you out because of it. I don't blame either one of you—I'm like Switzerland here—but I simply can't stand having Mark around instead of you, and Diana instead of Beth."

"Beth told me Andy walked out on you."

"Don't try and change the subject."

"I'm sorry."

I took him home. He was still living in the house he'd formerly shared with Beth, mostly because they'd already converted the cellar and garage into a dental office and it would be just too much trouble after all that for him to move. We drove to Newton, floating on a familiarity that felt nostalgic and warm, and served for the moment as a tonic that soothed us both. He sat close to me in the front seat, his hand on my shoulder, and pitched the quarter into the turnpike toll with an underhand swing that showed how very often he'd made that same perfect toss.

"Oh, Meggy," he said, when I pulled up to his house. He was one of the only people, other than Andy, who called me by that rather silly diminutive. "Do you want me to talk to him?"

"No, no," I said.

David said, "Okay, I will."

"But don't make him come back for the baby's sake," I said quickly. "I want him to come back for my sake and his sake, for all of our sakes."

"Okay."

"David, was I really mean to him? Did he leave me because I'm such a bitch?"

"Of course not."

"Was it because I insisted that we bid for the schoolhouse?"

"Don't be silly."

"Then why?" I asked him. "Why would Andy leave me six weeks before our first baby is due?"

He shook his head. "When I was in high school I went out with a girl named Bernice. I went with her from tenth grade all the way to senior year and we were a sure bet for Best Couple at the prom. She bought a prom dress and I rented a tux, all the school was buzzing with the upcoming prom and Bernice was so excited you sensed she was already there, at the prom, dancing amid the shadows of teenagers clutching each other in the dark." He paused now and looked at me, a long look that I'd never quite seen from David before. "I'm a nice guy, right? I'm not so handsome or tall but you'd say I was nice."

I nodded. "You bought that panda."

"Right. Bernice, I was sleeping with this girl, I'd been sleeping with her for two years and going with her for three. But you know what I did to her? I broke up with her two nights before the prom. Don't ask me why. I could have stuck it out two more nights and let her have the prom she always dreamed of. But I couldn't do it. Something about being at the senior prom with Bernice, dancing beneath that rotating silver ball, I'm telling you a freight train couldn't carry me into that gymnasium. Prom night came and I went to the movies with my brothers and got rowdy and threw popcorn at the screen. A week later I called Bernice. We got back together and shuffled along until it was time to start our freshman year at two different colleges. She went to Barnard and me to BC. We never saw each other again and all that summer we never once discussed the prom."

"So Bernice sucked it up and had you back, you bastard."

"The last night before she went off to Barnard she

took my class ring and held it in her hand and said, 'You won't have this back,' and I didn't dare say a word."

left David at his house and drove home. I almost expected Mrs. Martin to be sitting half frozen on my doorstep (or wholly frozen, I'd be more than happy to contribute the headstone for that one) but instead I spied Marianne's pristine BMW 5-series parked on the curb. Marianne is the type of real estate agent who considers all her listings to fall under the aegis of her own private ownership. She will do anything whatsoever to sell a house. She's been known to take a perfectly ordinary 1970s apartment, add a few ceiling roses, a dado rail, a picture rail, and some cornicing around the door, paint the whole thing with four layers of yellow paint in varying shades so that it looked like thirty years of different paint, and convince the prospective buyers that they were getting a deal on this charming period apartment which, given just a few decorative improvements, would be any couple's dream. There were rumors that she employed her own mother as a cleaning lady to tidy up messy houses and she was known to send over cans of paint to clients with instructions on which walls to paint what color penned in her own florid handwriting. She had a theory that citrus colors showed best and was a big fan of matte paint. Curtains, she will tell you, are unnecessary impediments to sale houses, serving only to block out light and make windows seem smaller than they are, and she regularly gathered them up and whisked them away from her listings with a conviction and efficiency that left you speechless.

God knew what she was up to now, but I entered the apartment with trepidation and found her in the middle of the kitchen, a blueprint laid out across one countertop, one heeled shoe cocked, toe upward, as though she'd just completed the final twirl of a complicated dance step. Beside her was a man I instantly recognized. He was wearing a white cotton shirt, crisp as a freshly minted dollar bill, with his tie loose at the collar and his jacket tossed over one shoulder like the bookbag of a schoolboy. I recognized those narrow hips and his long torso, the broad, hunched shoulders like those of a swimmer. He'd changed his hair so that it swept back from his face, and tamed the curls so that they were not as girlish as I remember, and he'd swapped the silver rectangles of his former eyeglasses for a pair of owlish tortoiseshell ovals, but it was still Theo Clarkson, handsome in a reckless and unfriendly way.

He and Marianne had been studying a blueprint and it was clear from the polite unfamiliarity of his initial hello that he did not at once recognize me. How could he have? When last he'd seen me I had long wavy hair and an athletic frame. All of that final summer we'd lived together, ten years ago I hasten to add, I'd worn, almost exclusively, a tight pink T-shirt beneath a billowy denim-cloth shirt, and a pair of khaki shorts that fell to my knees. It had been a hot summer with a lot of sun, we'd sunbathed together from the rooftop of our shabby building, and there, for several months prior to the heartbreak that he would bestow upon me like the mighty punch of a fist descending from the sky, I became accustomed to seeing my skin in the flattering glow of a rosy tan. Now I had short, badly styled hair and a figure suitable for Father Christmas. My maternity leggings were so beaten to hell that the corduroy had been rubbed off from the entire length of the inside thigh and I had a variable complexion that ranged from oatmeal to rust.

Theo did not recognize me, and frankly I did not want him to. What I wanted was to turn and run. I might have, too, but the baby took this moment to try out a few of its exercises and suddenly my stomach began jiggling visibly and I got kicked so firmly inside the ribs that it caused me to take in a breath. The baby was often given to grand flights of movement—even though they tell you that during the last few weeks they settle down and hardly move—and in the Richter scale of babyquakes, this one was firmly up in the 9s.

"Never mind this," I said, pointing at my belly, "It's only if my head starts spinning around and I talk about Satan that you have to worry."

"Meg Mackenzie," Theo said, calling me by my maiden name, also my pen name, the only name that Theo knew me by.

"You two know each other? Good," Marianne

said, glancing from Theo to me then back to Theo again, "because you're going to get to know each other a whole lot better real soon."

"Oh, I don't know," I said in an ordinary bantering manner, smiling as the baby did yet another loop-the-loop.

"Mr. Clarkson is going to be living in the main house until you've vacated the annex," Marianne continued. *Annex?* That was the current word for what Marianne had previously described in her house listings as a charming, lovingly restored two-bedroom period apartment in an idyllic setting? I might have objected to her calling my home "the annex," except that I was too overwhelmed by Theo, alive and breathing inside my very home. I remembered him as a furtive, darting, melodramatic young man, an obsessive watcher of everything around him, who carried in the hip pocket of his frayed jeans a quarter-page-size memo book into which he scrawled descriptions of ordinary life, unpoetic and mean. His feeling about metaphor was that it obviated what was real and he thought, like many writers before and since, that the truth of a sentence was found in its simplicity.

"You've changed so much," Theo said. He smiled his straight flash of white teeth; a glint came into his eyes. There was a moment of utter silence, an awkward five seconds beaten out in time by the pulse at his throat, and it occurred to me that he might be sizing me up before striking for the kill with some really hateful comment, the likes of which I could only imagine. Then he did something I would never have expected from Theo, who I didn't remember being the sort of person to be moved to show warmth for a fellow human, who I didn't remember seeming a regular human being himself, but more like some creature that had emanated from darkness and who rode out the daylight hours by squinting a lot and keeping to corners and shadows, he came toward me and placed the flat of his palm against the pit of my lurching stomach just as the baby was completing a circuit of assaults on all my inner organs.

"That's so beautiful," he said.

CHAPTER EIGHT

THERE'S A LITTLE TIME WARP HERE—WHAT
ought to have been six months' worth of happenings crammed themselves into the space of one week,
but it all revolved around one extraordinary event,
which was that Theo moved into Mrs. Russell's
house. I looked out the front door of my "annex" and
saw a moving van the size of a brontosaurus parked
outside. Three men with padded gloves and canvas
overalls were moving what looked to be the inherited
contents of Theo's grandmother's barn—Theo's
grandmother is a collector of antiques, an obsessive
woman who has bought so many antiques she cannot

house them in her own gothic Victorian and so stuffs them from floor to ceiling in each of the four stalls and the whole of the hayloft of her stone barn in Salem, Massachusetts. The movers worked with efficiency and care, handling a horsehair sofa, a grandfather clock, a dresser, a set of shutters, curtain poles with a fleur-de-lis decoration, as though these were ordinary items the likes of which you might find in Kmart.

I was jealous, of course, why do only a handful of people have *all* the antiques? But I was terribly curious. If he had oak refectory chairs and a fifteen-foot refectory table, a stained glass art-deco table lamp, and a three-panel gothic screen, what *else* did he have?

That night the power failed, an act of God that can be interpreted many ways. Some might say that it was meant to break the ice between Theo and myself, ice that had formed over the past twelve years, but I saw it as an omen that he was never meant to occupy Mrs. Russell's house. She'd always sworn that the one thing she would not do was sell to one of the "yuppie house hunters" who cruise Newton in their big German cars looking for exactly her sort of house. I never pointed out to her that Andy and I were exactly the species she purported to despise, without the car, of course. We were kind of want-to-be yuppie house hunters, although what I have always really wanted (because in this respect I am completely irrational, if not actually dangerous to myself) is not a house in Newton that you could drive to and look at, but an ancient oak-framed building that I could *re-erect*. Re-erection is what you do to a building that has been painstakingly drawn, measured, sketched, numbered, and photographed before being dismantled, sold, and then hauled to another site to be built all over again. Re-erection is for crazy people who get weepy to the point of crisis over old buildings and are willing to do anything to acquire one, even sort through numbered oak staves. I would love to re-erect, perhaps in another lifetime I will. There is, however, an equal and opposing side to my personality that feels the way that Mrs. Russell does and I think that there is a need in my case for a little self-censorship.

Anyway, Theo came to my door at about nine at night asking if I had any extra candles. There is no such thing as *extra* candles when the power has failed, I informed him, but I relinquished two of the six I had and threw a penlight into the bargain so at least he could read. Theo, like me, is a compulsive reader. People like us go through printed pages like elephants grazing and the biggest problem for us is that there just isn't enough out there that is sufficiently interesting to consume. Or I should say, we find plenty that is interesting, but it is all nonfiction, it's about the real world, which is okay for our vital rations of printed thought, but the great and mysterious one-eyed inner *thing* that lurks within us and forces us to waste years of our lives searching the dusty shelves of secondhand shops and making mad dashes to the library as though it were a breathing hole in a dense and uninhabitable atmosphere, yearns for fiction. Good fiction, and that was much more difficult to come by.

"Thank you!" he said when I gave him the penlight. "I'm halfway through an Alice Munro story. It is such a relief whenever I get a hold of one of hers."

I nodded dumbly and pushed the candles into his hands. Alice Munro is my favorite, too. He knows that, or he used to know that, back when we were a couple.

He returned an hour later.

"I don't have matches," he said.

"It took you an hour to realize that?"

"I didn't want to admit it. I made do with the penlight."

I got him some matches and he looked at them as though a little disappointed. "Why don't you come over?" he said. "The place is so big. I'm used to a two-bedroom co-op in a building where you can feel the buzz of other people twenty-four hours a day. Now I'm in this big ghoulish house with no electricity. It's weird."

We went into his house; the hallway smelled of furniture wax and old paint. I tripped, he took my hand. He led me to a Venetian wing chair upholstered in cut velvet and I sat, squinting into the darkness trying to make out the other antiques, a Knoll sofa, a walnut desk clock. Although I admire antiques I also kind of hate them, mostly because they are so much *the thing* these days and, besides that, there is a part of me, in direct opposition to the part of me that yearns to re-erect, that would rather live in a brand new house with skylights and carpeting and furniture that you didn't have to worry about having woodworm.

"My grandmother gave me all this stuff," Theo said. "She had to give up her house a few months ago and live in a smaller place with no stairs. She didn't want to sell it and she worried it would be damaged in a storage unit. She practically begged me to take it. The truth is I didn't even want it at first. I went up to Salem planning to organize some kind of specialized storage house, but when I walked into my grand-mother's house and saw it all, saw how beautifully she'd kept it, how hard she'd worked to maintain its condition, I just couldn't do it. I told her I'd keep the furniture and she was very pleased. But then I didn't know where I was going to put it. One thing led to another and here I am. Do you think I'll make it in a suburb? I thought you have to be married with chil-dren to live in a suburb."

"Getting married shouldn't be a problem," I told him. "Just hang a sign out the window saying 'Man with Aga.'"

We talked about Andy and I was open and honest and unashamed. I explained that he was on an ex-tended business trip. Then I went into a lengthy ex-planation about this business trip, how important it was, and how Andy couldn't wait to get back. I guessed he bought it.

"A woman came by this evening looking for you. Something about Andy owing another woman a headstone," Theo said. "That seems a strange item to be owing somebody."

"Oh no, Andy is not responsible for anyone's

headstone. I mean, how could he be? He isn't even here."

"She said he gave her a disease."

"Andy has never given any woman a disease," I said. "As far as I know."

He talked about his past love, a woman he'd fallen for and who'd broken his heart. I told him he had probably deserved it and asked if it was anyone famous (it wasn't). We were just getting into a light discussion about what a shithead he'd been for most of his life and how (he says) he has changed over the years when *presto* the lights went on.

"It's the ghost of Mrs. Russell," I said. "She sensed that you were enjoying the blackout. Her spirit has returned to make your life a misery. I'm sorry, Theo, but that's the way it is. You should think about moving before it's too late."

"Ghosts," Theo said, and laughed a single ha. "Wouldn't that be something if there were ghosts in this house?"

"Nothing like a ghost to distinguish your property from all the others when it comes time to sell. You might even get more for it," I told him.

You see, I resisted an impulse we all have when confronted with the very person who has previously taken a cheese grater to our young hearts and then run off to become rich and celebrated. I did not try to win favor with him, I did not try to look good in his eyes.

One Sunday, while cooking a morning feast for

myself, one of those never-ending meals that starts with cold cereal, moves on to French toast with maple syrup, and then culminates in scoops of ice cream with great lashings of chocolate sauce (those of you who've been pregnant know exactly what I mean), I burned toast and set off the fire alarm. Five minutes later Theo was at the door.

"Are you okay?" he asked.

"Of course."

He was in sweatpants, no shirt or socks. His appendectomy scar, that old friend, was faint but visible lurking at the top of his waistband. "I worry about you, being all alone."

"I'm not alone," I lied.

"Oh, good, well, I won't disturb you."

He'd become polite. He'd become concerned. I reminded myself that he was the same man who'd trotted off to my former college roommate's bed after declaring that living with me was poisoning his creative process. I reminded myself that he'd been selfish in bed (I think he averaged two orgasms for every one of mine, and he was usually so impatient that we started it all too soon and I ended up sore), and that he had actually stolen parts of my writing style, if not whole segments of various rough drafts of my first novel, to incorporate into his own. Okay, he was very young when we were together, which explains the bedroom business, and this last bit about literary thievery might have been my own invention, but his second novel carried my sensibility, my humor, and my structural methods. I had never known Theo to tell a joke or say anything even remotely funny, his forte was being serious and smart and having that particular look that women around the world go for, but his novel, *Branded New York,* was full of humor, my humor, and when he hit the bestseller list I couldn't even sue him for it. I'd considered sending firebombs, disguised as royalty checks, to his fancy uptown address, but in the end simply vowed to hurt him in any way I could personally and professionally in the future. But he'd asked for candles during a blackout, come over to check on me when the smoke alarm sounded. He'd even brought in some groceries from my car when he'd seen the open door and all those bags. And he'd left me a first edition copy of Alice Munro's latest book. Just the book, no soppy card. The book was enough, he knew, and said everything. I was not hurting him as I had vowed to do. Instead, here I was liking him again.

Carla called me. I didn't have time to tell her about Theo Clarkson, who I was acutely aware was just a few feet of plaster and plywood away from me, or about seeing David and Diana at Saks, or about the quotes for central heating I'd been going through that afternoon, all of which I thought were a little high. She called me and she began speaking as though we'd begun the conversation several minutes previous to the moment I answered the phone. It took a few minor mental adjustments for me to figure out that it was, indeed, Carla, and that the person she was talking about was my wayward husband.

"He was here, he's a mess. He arrived just after

eleven at night, James was out, I was asleep. I thought at first he'd been drinking he looked so bad, but it turns out that he isn't sleeping, when I say he isn't sleeping what I mean is the last night he slept, he *thinks*, was Tuesday." She spoke in rushed, bulleted sentences, as though she were reading them from a page. "He'd been to visit his parents, and his father blames himself for being a bad influence and thinks that it has been genetically determined that Andy will never live a useful life. This, Andy *believed*. I took him upstairs to my very bedroom—I didn't dare put him in the spare room because it has an exterior door and I thought he might disappear—and gave him a couple of Xanax and he slept there for about an hour before James came home. Then he woke up, I don't know how because these Xanax are like horse pills, and told James that he wanted to kill himself but was afraid, due to some further comment that his father made and that I could not understand because, with all the barbiturates I'd given him, he was slurring his words. But I believe that he said he'd kill himself if he thought that he would do it effectively and wouldn't end up a vegetable for life."

"He said he wanted to *kill* himself?"

"I *think* so, but I can't be sure, you know how vague Andy can be even at the best of times, and this certainly was not the best of times. I wrote down what he said." There was some shuffling of paper and then Carla's voice once again through the receiver. She spoke in a serious, professional shrink manner, as though consulting with one of her many gray-bearded psychoanalytical buddies. "His exact words were 'I'd put an end to it today except I'd probably dick it up and end up like Mr. Potato Head.' Does that sound like a suicide threat to you?"

"Yes," I sighed, "did you tell him that he could end up like Mr. Potato Head *or* he could simply come home?"

"I mentioned to him that he had a wife who loved him."

"But you didn't tell him to come home?"

"Not directly, no. He was in a lot of pain, he needed to talk. He has a lot of stuff to unload about his father and he sat up all this morning telling us the most sad tales about how his father used to fill the car with all his possessions and just leave them—"

"Yes, yes, I know about all that." His dad was into dramatic exits, always taking off in his tiny Fiat until he clocked up fifteen hundred miles or so and had a change of heart. Some kind of chemical fired off in his brain, sending him into madness and back within the space of a few state lines. He clocked up a lot of miles but he always came home, usually with a new touring map of the Midwest. "But why didn't you tell Andy to come home?"

"He needed to talk—he sat in our kitchen and cried."

"But *you* didn't tell him to come home. The first thing you should have said when you opened the front door to him at eleven at night was 'Andy, go home, go home to Meg *now*.'"

"He was reaching out—"

"Anybody else would have had the common sense to put him in a taxi." I said, and then gulped. One of the contractions that I'd had recently, Braxton-Hicks contractions, named after the (male) physicians who "discovered" them, as though millions of women hadn't already discovered them, took hold of me and silenced me for a moment. They were "practice contractions" my OB had told me, and though they were more uncomfortable than painful they could stop you in your tracks.

I took puffy breaths, the best I could do with my stomach being pushed up into my lungs. Carla said, "Meg, don't be angry at me. I've just had a very late night and a lot of emotional stress—"

"You could have told him to come home. He'd listen to you."

"You know I don't do that."

"That *what*?"

"That telling business!"

We paused now, each sucking our breath through clenched teeth. I find her infuriating when she refuses to make direct statements or give even a smattering bit of advice. She finds me positively Neanderthal in my approach to human relations.

"Okay, thank you for that information about Andy, about which I can do *nothing*, due to the fact that you refuse to give him direct and sound advice. Now, Dr. Freud, I have a little further ingredient to add to the pot. Theo Clarkson has just moved into Mrs. Russell's house."

"Mrs. Russell who died?"

"The very one."

There was a pause. I could almost hear Carla's enormous and highly organized brain clicking through the various possibilities for why Theo was in Mrs. Russell's house and, after opening and closing various avenues of thought, plus executing a random search for hidden meanings, coming up with an empty set. "Why?" she uttered finally, as though I'd asked her a trick question.

"Because Theo has bought it, and bought our apartment, and he intends to knock the two into one. Apparently, he's decided that the rich New York literary life has taken him too far from his origins as a writer and from now on he's forgoing nightly book launches and literary parties and all the publicity he's enjoyed for the past ten years while I've been hoping for an invitation even to join PEN and go for a clean way of living up here in quaint old New England. Besides, he needed somewhere to house all his grandmother's antiques."

"And he's moved in already?"

"Why not? It's his. Mrs. Russell's relatives were only too happy to sell him the place before it was empty for too long to insure."

"So," she said cagily, "what's that like for you?"

What had it been like to have Theo as a direct wall-sharing neighbor? A good question. All the little noises I used to hear from Mrs. Russell, and which I ignored automatically, screening them out in that unconscious way that urban dwellers do, suddenly had become like deafening echoes in my psyche. I knew when he rose from bed—eight-thirty—and how long he took to shower and what radio station he listened to and how long he spent watching television (about ten minutes, I gathered, which seemed to me an admirably small fragment of one's day). I took deep breaths every time he cooked, trying to figure out what exactly he'd made. Chicken cacciatore? Grilled salmon? French onion soup? (He was quite an adventuresome cook now; when we'd been living together all he ate was Burger Chef hamburgers and something called Atomic Peanuts which made his breath like gunpowder.) The phone would ring—his phone—and I'd count the rings and then wonder who it was who'd telephoned him. Was it his agent? Was it his/my editor? Was it the *New York Times* asking him to do a review? Was it a lover? If so, what did she look like? I was even ridiculous enough to wonder if she were prettier than me, which given my appearance at that time, she would have had to be.

It wasn't as though it was so easy to hear all these things. I could not hear the shower, for example, but I had a fair knowledge of the various bangs and hisses of the arcane plumbing system, that tangle of leaden arms that encircled both the late Mrs. Russell's and my own premises, and so could tell that water was being emitted from a pipe at great speed somewhere in the house, which meant Theo was running it. He showered for an average of eight minutes and then the pipes would bang in a series of dying echoes signaling that the shower had finished. The cooking thing was even more difficult to pinpoint, sometimes

I think what I was smelling was my own imperfectly cleaned oven. But certainly I could hear when he went out the front door. Mrs. Russell had an interior door and a screen door and a heavy double-fronted main door, and so there was quite a din when Theo went out for his daily constitutional—sometime within the past ten years he'd acquired the ordinary but charming practice of a daily walk—and besides all the opening of doors and squeaking of hinges, there were a great number of ancient, iron keys to find and insert into equally ancient, tricky latches that had a tendency to whine and scrape just before lurching into place with a sudden snap like a guillotine dropping. What it had been like to live with Theo next door was what it must be like for one previously in a coma to suddenly spring awake and rediscover all the trivial, taken-for-granted aspects of our daily world, its sounds and smells and colors. Not that I derived any pleasure from this newly awakened sensibility, but the word self-conscious applied to nearly every action of my waking life.

"Well," I said to Carla, "it would appear he is still single."

"Okay, you want some direct advice? Direct, from-the-hip commentary from a qualified doctor and longtime friend?" she said. "Leave now. Leave in the dead of night under cover with a gun. *Get out.* Do not speak to him, do not see him, do not tell him where you are going. Is that direct enough for you? Is that putting my message across in a way that suits your conversational habit?"

"That pretty much transmits," I said. "But I can't go until the central heating is installed in the new house and then I can't go because I need a functioning upstairs bathroom and then I can't go because I will be at Beth Israel Hospital having a baby."

"Oh, right, the baby. That might keep him at bay for a little while."

"Him, who?"

"Theo."

I laughed at Carla's foolishness and then a thought struck me and the laugh stuttered and was left unfinished. "There's nothing between me and Theo," I said firmly.

"Yes, there is, my pet, there is exactly one wall between you and Theo."

The heavy stuff with Theo started one morning after I'd been out having my wedding ring sawed off my finger. I should say now that this was an act of necessity rather than sentiment or hostility, because my fingers were really quite swollen and the ring was rubbing in a way that irritated and inflamed the skin surrounding it. For many months I'd been applying Vaseline and hoping gangrene didn't set in, but lately a sinister rash had spread down the back of my hand and I knew it was time to get rid of the ring. I'd gone to my local doctor to have him remove it, but he said I'd have to either go to a hospital, where someone in orthopedics would probably manage the task with a plaster saw, or I could try a jeweler. As I wasn't sure how exactly to present myself at the hospital—it didn't seem right to go through the emergency room—I went to a jeweler in town, a tiny Chinese man who squinted through the glass door in his dollhouse-sized shop and buzzed in people whom he assessed on sight as unlikely to rob him at gunpoint. I didn't even have to explain. He took one look at me, one look at my finger, which was raw and shining from all the liberally applied, ineffective Vaseline, and got out a minuscule jeweler's saw from beneath a counter.

"Dis take us hoo-one meeneet," he said. He had me sit with my left hand placed firmly across a sheet of velvet and applied himself to the task of ridding me of my wedding ring. He was careful and very thorough, rolling my fleshy skin back away from the gold band and taking tiny swipes at the ring. The band was fourteen carat, we'd bought it together one warm, foggy spring day, and I remember feeling so sentimental about it that I would not allow myself to wear it for more than the shortest fraction of a time it took to determine that it was the right size for my hand, before slipping it off and placing it into the gray velveteen box with a satin lining that it came in, and where it stayed for several years before finally having it placed by Andy on the third finger of my left hand. It had been a hard-won moment and I'd not removed the ring since.

Perhaps the jeweler read my thoughts. "We feex latah," he said. "You don't worwee."

Just then a couple came to the front door and he

looked up, correctly guessing them as a couple seeking the same kind of ring he was right now working his knife through. He buzzed them in and they fell forward into the tiny store, smiling and gripping each other and marveling at the glass cases of precious stones. They were after an engagement ring, it was obvious, and they pointed and gasped at the ones before them, their breath making patches of steam against the immaculate glass of the Chinaman's display.

"Are any of these under four hundred dollars? We only have four hundred dollars," the girl said. She was only a girl, too, just past the twenty mark to my reckoning.

"You see I busy?" the jeweler growled. "You wait, den I talk to you."

"So there are some under four hundred dollars?" she said hopefully.

"We might be able to manage five hundred," the boy said.

"I gotta layaway pran. You affraud anything," he said. "Now you be quiet. I concentrating."

He looked down at my finger, squeezed either side of the incision he'd made across the ring, and let out a satisfied breath as the metal popped in two.

"Wow, did you hear that?" the girl said. "A layaway plan."

My ring was dead. My old, tarnished, scratched ring with tiny dents from five years of constant wear. Now this young couple was investing in one of the pristine models from inside the jeweler's vast cases.

"Kids," the jeweler said, handing me the broken ring.

I put it in the breast pocket of my blouse and returned home, feeling as though my marriage was now truly over. I hadn't wanted to kill my ring, I told myself, it had been a medically necessary procedure, the symbolism of which was not valid. But I'd spent too many years reading Hawthorne not to feel as though the split ring was the portentous act that signaled Andy's and my final matrimonial doom and that, considering the scene that had just taken place, at any moment the skies would grow dark as black horses and issue forth a torrent of angry thunderous roars, the trees would bend down and lash out with their branches, and somewhere within my journey a deadly snake would stalk about my path. Instead I drove the cedar-lined streets of Newton on a perfectly ordinary winter morning, with winter sun and a crisp but not cold breeze. I parked outside the lovely, sunflower yellow Victorian house that was now Theo Clarkson's, but never mind, and entered my apartment without incident or further emblematic detail that would serve as a metaphor for my ailing marriage.

I was there for about thirty minutes before Theo came to the door.

"Hey," he said, as though we'd often visited like this. "The contract has gone through. I brought a bottle of champagne to celebrate."

There it was, my additional symbol. If Hawthorne had been a late-twentieth-century writer, he'd have written it just like that. Forget tempests or hailstorms or savage accidents in horse carriages, the legal world provided all the meaning we needed. There was no turning back. Andy's and my apartment was now officially Theo's.

"Congratulations. I think it's great what you're doing, this old house will be nice restored to its original dimensions," I said to him with the enthusiasm of a automatic teller machine that says "Have a happy day" to its customers. "I take it that our part was once the servant's quarters."

"Marianne said you bought a nineteenth-century school house, a fixer-upper, but classy. Hey, aren't you going to invite me in?"

"Do I have to?" I laughed, noting the disappointment in his face. "I mean, you own it now."

"Oh, right," he said, perking up. "Well, technically. I don't take possession until the fifth of February."

I let him in. I found some glasses. It isn't considered good practice to drink champagne late in a pregnancy, but I thought perhaps the baby would rather have a nice, relaxed mother instead of the nervous wreck I was becoming by the second. Theo and I sat in the living room, Theo looking dashing in an English Jermyn Street dress shirt, denim jeans, and a pair of Italian loafers, and me rubbing my raw finger and hoping that the support hose I was wearing hadn't run.

What did we talk about? Well, we didn't talk about our long-ago romance, nor reminisce about the days we'd shared a studio with a sofa bed and a galley kitchen and bookshelves made out of planks and bricks. We didn't talk about how I stole *Swear* and how I was still plugging away at literary novels, exactly the sort that didn't sell more than five or ten thousand copies in hardback, while he'd managed to find every hotspot in American publishing and hit the best-seller list on a regular basis with novels as junky and diverse as *Branded New York,* his comic novel about a down-and-out Manhattanite who makes a spring for a new life on the rodeo circuit and ends up broken-hearted by a cowgirl, the very novel in which he stole great chunks of funny bits I'd made up and discarded for my own first work, and *Big Sky,* a western version of *Wuthering Heights* in which the Heathcliff character (a handsome brooding cowboy named Grayson Flack, who matches his inventor in every possible way except that Flack could ride a horse) sleeps with Cathy and everyone else before his final tragic end. *Big Sky* was actually a decent book, perhaps because its model was a work of genius, but the next one, *Cannonbury Tales,* which was a westernized version of Chaucer's work, and I think you know which one, was a recognizable disgrace, even to the literary world that hailed Theo as a hero. He'd never come near the best-seller list with that one. It was printed on a grand scale and went straight into the remainder piles.

But we didn't talk about that. Or about how we used to love each other. Or about how we'd come to hate one another and then later to forget that hate. He was remodeling Mrs. Russell's bathroom. He wanted to know where to find a bath renovator. How was it that two people with the sort of history we had behind us could sit on a winter's afternoon and talk about whether to go for original bathroom products or reproductions and do it with a straight face?

The power of the home and interiors market never ceases to amaze me.

"I love the cast iron bath—it's got a rolled top and those funny feet—" Theo said.

"Claw-footed," I corrected.

"Yeah, but there's all these yellow patches and—I think—rust. I've scrubbed and scrubbed but it still looks kind of gross. I've been taking showers."

"I know," I said. He raised an eyebrow. "I mean, I know what you need. Re-enameling."

"Right!"

"You can go for vitreous enameling, but only if the cast has no cracks, or you could try cold spraying, but usually the top coat is a polyurethane, not that it matters so much."

"Is there a kit you can buy?"

"No, no," I said. This last remark showed just what an amateur he was in period restoration and I had a sudden premonition that Theo's next novel would be about a New Yorker who moves from the Trump Tower to a farmhouse in Vermont where he manages to fuck up every period feature in the place before retreating back to the world of high-rises and building porters. "You need to have it coated and then dried with infrared heaters. It's a professional job."

He looked as though someone had just reached into his bank account with a long arm and begun grabbing at wads of his cash, which is pretty much what builders do, and I cheered him up by telling him about the schoolhouse and how, right now, men in blue overalls were unceremoniously pulling up the wide oak planks of its polished floors, crashing them about as they fitted extensive gray tubes at great personal cost to me. How they were filling the house full of dust, dropping nails everywhere, and peeing without accuracy into the toilet. They were banging its precious walls and scratching everything with their boots and ladders and how I dared not even visit until the heating system was installed because I would probably have a nervous breakdown or start going at them with knives for having driven right up onto the lawn and killed all the grass. I was just drunk enough to feel dreamy about the schoolhouse, remembering fondly its rough wooden porch, the array of windows, each with their ornamental shutters, the brilliant vaulted ceiling. I told him how the day I first saw it, a thrush flew onto the stone birdbath in the backyard and started making the most blessed sounds and I took it as an invitation to buy the place.

"I love your enthusiasm," he said, looking into my eyes with those beautiful pale eyes of his own. "I always loved that about you, even when I didn't show it."

"Trouble is that not only thrushes but whole swarms of other birds have made the schoolhouse their home, including a pair of nesting barn owls which are now occupying the chimney. I can't even use the fireplace because of these stupid owls. Not that it is properly lined anyway."

"Can't you convince the owls to nest elsewhere?"

"They are under protection, they can nest anywhere they want in the whole of the state," I said. "The bastards."

"You'll sort it out. It will be fantastic. Though I'll miss having you next door."

"You won't. Not when the baby is born and starts howling in the middle of the night. You won't miss us then."

"A family," he said, as though I'd spoken of something rare and precious and burdensome, which I suppose is exactly what a family is. "He better get back from his business trip soon or he'll miss the big event," he said, and I could tell he'd figured out I'd lied and that Andy was away for his own reasons. Then he said, "My girlfriend wants a baby."

"Oh?"

"She's still in New York. She doesn't like Boston, says it's too small-town. This, from a kid from North Carolina!"

He laughed and I laughed, and I thought probably his girlfriend was about nineteen.

"She's just young," he said.

"I bet."

"A former student of mine,"

"Uh-huh."

"Okay, actually she is still a student of mine. I'm

lecturing once a week at NYU for another couple of terms, not for the money or anything, it's just that it makes me feel part of things."

"And Boston is so small-town."

He opened his mouth and then, smiling, let out a breath. He filled my glass for the third time (I vowed not to drink anymore, but took dainty pretend sips to make it look as though I were) and slumped into the couch in a fetching way that told of his guilt at being the greedy oversexed writer/professor he apparently was, which you could tell he was not altogether displeased about.

"I like your short hair," he said to get himself back in my good graces.

Finally, and I don't know exactly how, we ended up back at the subject of Theo's bathtub, and whether he should re-enamel it or just get a new one.

"What would you do?" he wanted to know.

I told him I couldn't tell without looking at it and we'd drunk enough champagne to feel that it was important I come and inspect his bathroom that very moment. I entered Mrs. Russell's house for the second time ever—I'd only ever spoken to her while she was out in the garden tending to her string beans in summer or, during the winter, in her greenhouse where she forced narcissus and tinkered with a few irritable orchids—and I felt like a trespasser or a thief. I felt exactly the way I had years ago when Carla and I had let ourselves into Nona's Greenwich Village walk-up, stepping quietly around the array of underwear and nail varnish and tossed books and condom wrappers until we uncovered *Swear,* beneath one of Nona's filmy black negligees.

"The stairs creak," he said, as though to a doctor. "Is that a bad sign?"

We reached the top of the stairs, took a few steps into the wide, airy landing with its polished floors and picture window, and Theo led me into the bathroom. An intimate room, no matter what the circumstances, I noticed his array of soap bars and dental floss, a marble-handled razor, a badger-hair brush, all neatly arranged on a glass shelf with gold finish. His towels were thick terry, navy in color, and he'd draped one over the radiator. The sink was certainly antique, with four-point taps and a stopper that had long ago gone missing, but the basin was chipped and I thought a little precariously balanced on its pedestal. Above the modern glass shelf on which he'd placed most of his toiletries, was an edged mirror that pivoted on two brass back plates shaped like heraldic roses that fastened the mirror to the wall. The toilet was new, probably brand-new from what I could tell—a good thing even for the antique buff. The bath sat in the very middle of the room, its feet, which were not really claws at all, but griffin feet, resting on four bricks so as not to damage the floor. Water marks formed from beneath two globe taps, a lovely pair of chrome taps with ceramic buttons indicating hot and cold, and formed in various degrees all the way up the sides of the tub. There were greenish marks at various points and the drainage area was stained a saffron color. Still, it was a nice bath, so deep you wondered how Mrs. Russell got in and out of the thing, and I thought it could probably be saved. A nickel bath bridge rested over its top—from the soap and water marks on it I gathered it had been used for decades along with this bath—and it occurred to me, looking at the thing, that it might not even be a reproduction.

Time to check for cracks. I bent over to inspect the surface of the bath's enamel—it was old and scratched in places but I didn't see any obvious cracks or chips. I ran my hand under the rolled rim and then turned on the water to check its color. As big as I was, and as tipsy, I felt a little unsteady on my feet. Sure enough I stubbed my toe on one of the bricks that supported the thing and slipped, my wedding ring falling out of my pocket and straight down the drain.

"What was that?" Theo asked.

I couldn't speak. Part of me knew that the ring was recoverable—Theo had said he didn't even use the bath at present and I'm sure there was plenty of time to get a plumber out. But the thought of my wedding ring, already broken and now somewhere within the bowels of Theo's bathroom, made me grimace and choke and, finally, sit cross-legged on Theo's bathroom floor and cry. I cried and my belly shook and the baby started to kick. I held onto my stomach to quiet down the tiny life inside me, and sobbed further, which made my belly shake even more.

"Are you in pain?" Theo asked.

"Yes," I said. "Yes, I'm in a lot of pain."

"My sister had a baby. She said to blow like you're trying to blow out a candle."

"That's for labor pain."

"So, you're not in labor?"

"No. No, Theo, I am not in labor."

I heard some footsteps and the voice of Theo's maid, formerly Mrs. Russell's maid, whom he'd wisely kept on after the house changed hands. She was a Salvadoran woman named Amelia, whose tiny body shot through that house, cleaning madly and singing love songs in Spanish. I'd seen her regularly once or twice a week over the past several years and occasionally managed to coax her into expending some of her enormous Latin energy on Andy's and my few rooms. Hearing sobs, she came into the bathroom, knocking softly outside the door as she entered.

"Meeses Howe!" she said, surprised to see me. "Don't cry there. That where Meeses Russell pass over!"

I didn't understand right away what she meant. Theo was patting my shoulder and telling me it would be all right. He'd gathered now that it was my wedding ring that went down his drain and he was promising to have it found and returned in good order. Meanwhile, I was thinking how it was unlikely I'd ever wear it again in any case, and crying liberally onto my distended belly.

"Meeses Howe, you not stay there! Bad omen for *mujeres embarazadas . . .*" and then she brought her hands together, stood over Theo and me, and started praying in Spanish. "*Dios mio, escucheme bien,*" she began, as though God were a naughty schoolboy who might not be paying sufficient attention. She prayed for a long time, her voice rising in pitch and gaining momentum as she went through half a dozen saints, and Theo wiped my tears with his fingers and touched the short hair he apparently admired, and I thought how nice it was to be touched by a man, and then I thought how crazy this was. Theo's face was inches from my own and I had to remind myself that not very long ago I'd hated Theo. Furthermore I was married, furthermore I was going to have a baby.

"Goddamnit," I said.

"Aaahh!" screeched Amelia, and started praying all over again.

The phone rang. Not Theo's phone but the little one I carried with me now.

"*Gracias a Dios,*" Amelia said. She'd been directing her discussion with God to Theo's bathroom's cracked ceiling, but when the phone rang she thought she'd finally had an answer and looked down, in the general direction of the telephone, which was hidden behind my left hip.

I answered it. It was Andy.

"David came to see me," he said. "God, his life is a mess. Diana hates his guts and they're not sleeping together—already and they aren't even married—so you tell me what *that* says about their future. I told him he ought to go back to Beth, I mean if you're going to be not sleeping with someone it might as well be your wife. And then I thought maybe I ought to do the same, not that your and my circumstances are anything like David's and Beth's. Maybe I better come home. I mean, that's what David says. What do you think? Would you want me to come home?"

No great apology, no *I must have been crazy*, no *I hope you can forgive me*, I took the phone from my ear and stared at it, my mouth opening and closing in silence. I was amazed, not because he had, finally, offered to do the sane thing and return home, but because he'd come upon this obvious notion only because David told him to.

"You little shit," I hissed at him. "Not word one in six weeks and now you call me up and tell me that David says to come home—"

"But he said you *told* him to tell me."

He told him I told him! Can you believe it? Any woman would have the good sense to make it look like an act of their own volition given out of the goodness of their hearts for the welfare of those they love, but a *man* just blurts out that he was instructed by the wife to intervene. Which defeats the purpose. Or ought to. Worse than that, Andy didn't even have the sense, Andy and David *together* didn't have the sense, to agree not to disclose all this to me, which put me in the irrecoverable position of having to get mad at Andy for doing exactly what I wanted him to do.

"So, David says you should come home and you think you better, well—" I was about to tell him a great deal more about how I wouldn't have him back if he were the proverbial last man on earth, this after my hoping beyond hope that he would do exactly as he was now promising, but I was suddenly visited by one of the gripping Braxton-Hicks contractions that had been seizing me with increasing fury over the past few weeks. I had to wait as my uterus froze tightly around my guts, pushing my lungs up into my throat and then, with tortuous graduation, released me from its hold. "What I have to say is—" I began again, but I couldn't finish this one either. A new Braxton-Hicks came on—they tend to get you when you are stressed or overactive or, in my case, raging in anger—and I had to breathe through this one it was so strong. Sometime during the peak of this particular practice contraction, I found myself holding—squeezing—Theo's hand.

Andy was saying, "Look, Meg, you know how I am. It's not my fault."

"Of course it's your fault!" I said.

"Okay, it is my fault but I can't help it. I love you. You know I love you." With the warmth of a food processor he said that. *I love you,* as though it were an instruction like "Take a right at the end of the block." *You know I love you,* as though I ought to know already to take that right.

"Go to hell, you and your love!" I raged. I still had my wits about me long enough to catch the look in Theo's face, which was something close to wonder and terror, as though he were witnessing the eruption of a volcano.

"Just remember May the ninth," Andy said.

May the ninth was the date of our second never-to-be wedding. This one was meant to take place at the chapel near his parent's home in Rockford, Illinois, where Andy was raised. His father, who I have mentioned is unbalanced, rose at 5 A.M. to discover that his son had done what he, himself, had done innumerable times in the past. He'd loaded up the car with his possessions (in Andy's case, this was only a leather valise and the suit bag in which his wedding clothes were encased) and taken off for the highway. Sam Howe spent the morning walking in circles, mumbling to himself and twirling the patch of hair that covers his pointy skull, while Andy's mother called police stations as far afield as Madison, Wisconsin, giving them a description of Andy's car. I showed up, once again, at a church in which there was no groom. This time I waited inside, and when Andy didn't show I invited everyone back to the house for a drink anyway. I was relaxed about it, I didn't really even care. Andy would come home, I knew, and I knew further that he would marry me. I thought I knew one thing in my life, which was that Andy would be my husband.

"Don't worry!" I told all our friends, who had made great efforts to fly or drive or train it to Rockford. "He'll be back by the time we've finished the champagne and are on to the hard stuff."

His reappearance was not as quick as that, I must say, but the show went on without him and we all had a pretty good time. I discarded my wedding dress in favor of the going-away outfit I'd selected, a jazzy cocktail dress that was meant to get a laugh, and danced the cha-cha and the rumba and the Charleston, none of them dances that I know, but one of Andy's cousins was a dance instructor and so I took the opportunity to learn a little. Why not? It was my wedding day. Carla smoked liberally through the whole event and I stole drags off her cigarette just as though I were a teenager and she told me I was pretty incredible, which is unlike Carla, who usually says things like "You're acting out" when you do anything unusual. Later, when Andy did indeed rejoin me at his parents' home, I informed him that he'd missed a damned good party. And as we were not yet legally wedded I gained great satisfaction in having charged the whole thing to Andy's Amex, an act he never dared once complain about or even mention. "Next time, I *swear*," he said to me earnestly.

"Oh, why bother actually getting married? Let's just have a grand party every year or two instead," I'd suggested. I was happy, life was fun. Life was not so fun now.

"May the ninth," I said just as another Braxton–Hicks started, "is not now. Now is December the tenth and I am sitting on the bathroom floor of Theo Clarkson's new house and I think I might be going into labor."

Which I was.

C H A P T E R

N I N E

T HE NEXT PART IS NOT ANDY'S FAULT. YOU SEE, we'd planned to have the baby at Beth Israel Hospital. My doctor, a highly acclaimed OB/GYN, doctor to the doctors, a woman who had been recommended by all my friends who, I noticed, had live babies, worked out of Beth Israel. I hung up on Andy fully expecting to load myself into a car and head toward that very hospital and into the skilled and expensive hands of Dr. Gilda Stevenson, but that isn't how it turned out. How it turned out was that I moved with great difficulty from Theo's floor to Theo's bed (as bad a state as I was in I did note that it was a large caned bed, a nifty item that fit neatly into the dormer window space) where I kneeled on the mattress and, by focusing on the silently rotating hands of his brass Tiffany clock, timed the length of the contractions, then the length between contractions, with Amelia shouting all the while about hot towels (what exactly are you supposed to do with hot towels anyway?) and Theo now praying. "Please, God, let me call you an ambulance," he said.

The reason I wouldn't let him call an ambulance was because of those stupid childbirth classes. In Gail's class, which I later wished I'd never stepped foot in— no, that's not quite true, I wished I'd never stepped foot into them right from the beginning—I'd been persuaded that I should not have the knockout shot that had guided my own mother through all three of her labors, that such a shot no longer existed, and that labor was something that our bodies just did, naturally and efficiently and without *undue* pain. The word "undue" was always stressed, and it occurred to me now that I was beginning to experience such pain that the reason for this was that there is no such thing as *undue* pain when it came to giving birth. I mean what kind of pain was not undue when it came to stretching your body wide enough to pass a baby through it? We'd also been told that labor was neatly divided into three parts and that the first part gave you short contractions interspersed by longish periods of relief. I got the contractions all right but I was lying on Theo's bed waiting for that relief that was promised. When it didn't come I thought perhaps I just wasn't doing it right. I actually believed that. Hey, I asked myself, I'm in constant pain, what am I doing wrong? Had I never been to Gail's class I would simply have phoned the ambulance, an action Theo was begging me to take, figuring that at any moment I was going to give birth, and would probably have received a nice dollop of analgesic in the spinal column, thus numbing the pain to a small whisper. But no. I was educated. I was doomed. I lay down and called Dr. Stevenson's number and told her answering service that I was in labor, serious agonizing near-birth labor and that if she wanted to see me alive she better see me immediately.

"Dr. Stevenson has been called on emergency to Massachusetts General," the voice told me. "She's due back at Beth Israel sometime after supper."

"But this is an emergency! Vital organs are shutting down even as we speak!"

"Stay where you are and I'll page the doctor."

Stay where I was, that was the great advice from Dr. Stevenson's office. What, stay right here instead of go to the mall and finish my Christmas shopping?

"You mean I shouldn't put on a Liz Sport jogger and do a few laps around the block!" I yelled into the phone. But it was no use, I'd been hung up on. Me, the pregnant one, the in labor one, the one who had paid great sums for this particular doctor, had been hung up on.

"Rub my back," I told Theo. Then I thought about what I was doing: I was asking my ex-lover whom I vowed years ago to kill or, even worse, to review critically if I ever got the chance, to soothe my ailing body. I was asking my perfectly formed, really quite beautiful ex-lover to hike up my blouse and lay his hands on my vast, bluish white body with its Pillsbury Doughboy shape, a body so bloated it might have been dredged up from the Charles River, and push on my lower back with all his might. "Please," I added, as another pain came on.

What was happening, I found out later, was that the baby was turned the wrong way around and so I was having what they call a "back labor," which is an extra special painful kind of labor which, though completely harmless for the baby, is a little like being stretched on a torture table for the mother.

The phone rang. It rang five times.

"Should I answer it?" Theo asked. "It's for you," he said, pushing the phone to my ear.

"What's happening?" Andy asked, then a stream of sentences I could hardly take in. My stomach was doing flip-flops (another thing they don't tell you about labor, you vomit a lot. Ask ten women and you'll find eight of them vomited. All those exercises, what a waste of time. Guess what? You can't breath or count backward or enlist the help of all those relaxation techniques they tell you to do when you're vomiting). Andy was saying something, I recognized a few words, ". . . terrified . . . worried . . . miss you . . . excited!"

"I'm going to the hospital," I told him.

"I'm on my way," he said, and hung up.

A question we spent many years sorting out later

was whether it was my fault for failing to tell him I was going to Mass General because that is where Dr. Stevenson had been called on emergency, or whether it was his fault for hanging up before I might have told him. I suppose we could spend most of the next forty years debating the issue, I'm pretty sure it was my fault, but so much had been Andy's fault up until that point that it only seems fitting to pin that one on him as well.

I would like to say that I don't remember very much about the labor. I'd like to say that, I'd like that to be the truth. But sadly, I remember all too much. I remember Theo driving me to the hospital, me in the backseat, turned away from him and digging my teeth into the upholstery. I remember the long wait in the hallway of the maternity ward, me squatting on the floor doing a duck walk and clutching Theo's calves, swearing in various formations throughout. I remember nurses coming by, seeing me squatting and waddling on the floor and asking, from what seemed to me a great height, what I was doing there. "I'm having a baby," I yelled up to them. "God, don't they train you people!"

I remember thinking they were finally doing something when they gave me an internal examination—and I'm telling you the sensation was enough to send me levitating from that table—and then being told I was only a centimeter dilated and that they couldn't administer any painkillers until I was three centimeters.

"Why not!" I screamed.

"Because it might stop your labor."

"Good!"

I remember calling out for Dr. Stevenson and being told she was busy in O.R. and Theo whispering in my ear that I was doing fine. I remember being sent back out into the hallway because they needed the labor room for one of the other women and feeling slighted by this.

"You've got some time yet," they said.

"I am imminent!"

"We really need the room."

"*I* need the room!"

"Don't worry, honey," a black maternity nurse with the auspicious name of Patience said to me. "Your time ain't too far off. Now scoot."

"Fine! I'm going now! Out into the hall to give birth on my own! Labor and birth right out here, out of the way! On my own!"

Back in the hallway I crouched and scampered and whined and swore. I did the duck walk again, with Theo behind me, following me. He pulled me away as I made a grab at the anesthesiologist's legs when I saw him dart by in his blue frock, wheeling a tray of various antidotes to pain, which to me was a bit like a starving man watching a banquet table flying by.

Finally in the labor room again I was given a black mask from which I breathed nitrous oxide, which soothed me for a half hour or so until it started making me sick. The pain was on the increase and had shifted from my back to my front. "That's the right kind of pain," Patience said on one of her many fly-by jaunts through my room and out again to another, and I wondered if all that pain before was of no use because it was the "wrong" kind of pain. By now I was in a T-shirt—and nothing else—trying to pee into a kidney-shaped metal bowl which reflected my private parts with unsettling accuracy. I desperately had to pee but it didn't seem to happen. Theo ran water and told me to think of the ocean. Still nothing. Then some. Then none.

You might wonder if I felt self-conscious about Theo. The answer is that some small part of my brain was still intact enough to realize that I was *mortified* by my display in front of Theo, but a much larger part of my psyche did not care. Patience came back into the room as I was squatting over the bedpan and frowned at Theo in that certain, wise way that only black women can do and said, "You the husband?"

"No," he said.

"You the father?"

"No he's not," I said.

"Don't you tell nobody," she warned. "Else you be put back downstairs."

Then she came toward us and swiped the bedpan from Theo's and my hands. "You don't need to pee," she told me. "I tell you when you need to pee."

It might sound an assault on my person, having a separate individual inform me of my functions, but she was right. I stopped trying to pee, resumed duck position, had nitrous oxide, vomited, had more. Patience came back an hour later.

"When do I get painkiller!" I yelled.

"You have to pee now."

"I want painkiller!"

"What you want? Injection?"

"A complete spinal block!"

"I see if I can find a doctor," she said. She said this as though finding a doctor was as unlikely as catching a wild horse.

"Why is finding a doctor so bloody difficult!" I yelled at her. She was walking out of the room again and this last comment was directed to her back. "I mean this is a hospital, right? This is where doctors congregate, presumably to treat sick people!"

She turned and gave me a look, the sort of look you might get from a chef whose dish you've just insulted. I panicked, realizing that my big mouth may have cost me a great deal in terms of pain relief. "I mean, yes, please," I said. "Please if you would be so kind as to find a doctor."

She handed me a bedpan and I peed into it. It came out in a perfect golden stream.

"Terrific!" said Theo.

He was good, I'm telling you. He was so good that I didn't at once miss Andy. In my delirium I had half convinced myself that Theo was my husband and that this was his baby anyway. And I had no concept of time, of course. I could not have realized that hours had gone by without Andy showing, let alone made the mental leap and realized that the man was lost. He'd gone to the hospital that he had every reason to think was the correct one—Beth Israel—and he had no way of finding me now. I'd left my TF700 at Theo's house and the only person other than me and Theo who knew of my whereabouts was Amelia, who had no doubt gone rushing to church to pray for me.

By the time Dr. Stevenson arrived I was on the floor, squatting on all fours by the foot of the bed in a T-shirt drenched in sweat, my hair standing on end, my veins bulging at my throat, my skin flushed and my stomach clenching around me like a vice. She walked in, took my chart from the hook above my head, and started reading it. She conferred with Patience, raised an eyebrow at Theo, and then glanced my way. I was screaming through each contraction, I was kicking my feet, I was writhing, my naked bottom in the air, wondering who I could sue. Patience and Dr. Stevenson seemed totally unmoved by this. I was reduced to a screaming, writhing, kicking, vomiting animal, pulling itself along the floor, and they showed no apparent concern. Do you know what Dr. Stevenson said, seeing me like this on the pine-scented black-and-white linoleum where no doubt countless women had gone through the same agonizing procedure? "She's doing great," she said.

"When do I get the painkiller!" I screamed.

And just then, like an angel of mercy, the anesthesiologist entered the room.

I loved him. I loved him the way Christ's disciples loved the Lord and I would gladly have given him anything, even the baby inside me who in my panic and pain I'd forgotten all about anyway, if he could relieve me of the hell that was my labor. He came in, put his tray of magical solutions beside the bed, and informed me that I would need to keep perfectly still as he injected the needle into my spinal column.

"Get on the bed," he instructed. "Do not move."

Can I tell you I'd have done anything he said, hung from a chandelier, gnawed off my own arm, just to get that needle? I was relieved and happy for the first time in hours. Theo was delighted. He was kissing my forehead and telling me that now everything would be great, and I believed him, I believed him and I smiled and I pulled my legs as far up to my chin as I could—which wasn't all that far because of my stomach—and promised the anesthesiologist, my angel in blue, that I would not move a muscle.

And then what happened? The obstetrician whom I had sought out and held council with, who had graduated with honors from Harvard, who had come with the highest recommendations from all my childbearing friends, and who was *costing me a fortune,* interrupted the proceedings.

"I think I better check how far along she is first," Dr. Stevenson—that bitch—said.

"Why! Why!"

"A quick look," was her response as she and Patience rolled me over on my back.

Nine centimeters. Nine out of a necessary ten. They would not give me my epidural. Whereas previously when I'd screamed for it I had been assessed as not being far enough along, now I was apparently too far along.

I cried.

"Poor you," Theo said. "Poor, poor Meg."

"That baby'll be here in forty minutes," Patience said, the first kind words she'd issued thus far, and they were a lie.

I t was actually two hours later and by then I was hysterical, really hysterical. I was so hysterical that it made my previous shouting seem no more than the harmless yaps of a toy poodle. Theo continued to be great. He held my hand and wiped my brow and told me, endlessly, how terrific I was doing, how much he admired me, how incredible I was, as though I were the first woman ever on this earth to give birth.

"You want to touch your baby's head?" Dr. Stevenson asked as the baby did what they call "crowning," which is what happens when it doesn't come out easily, but lingers between birth and not birth in an excruciating manner.

"NO!"

"There's a lot of hair," Patience said. "You want to look?" she asked Theo.

"NO HE DOES NOT WANT TO LOOK!" I yelled.

"Ready, steady," Dr. Stevenson said. "Here comes a baby!"

"NOOooooooo!"

She was so beautiful. I'd been prepared to see a

wizened, red hunk of human, shriveled as though it had been shrunken by headhunters but instead I was shown Frances. Mothers always tell you how beautiful their newborn is, but in my case it is really true. They showed her to me and I saw her face, a color of pink I'd never seen before, a white pink like a carnation but with a luminous quality as though she were from another world. I did not at first know that she was a girl. The pediatrician who had shown up at some point during the event, and of whom I was unaware until he whisked away my baby, took her from me with such gentleness and efficiency that I was left staring blankly at my empty arms, before I'd even had a chance to look. So I did not know she was a girl, did not know officially, that is, but as soon as I'd glanced at her I knew she had to be a girl. I heard her cry and, unlike anytime since then, I felt no need to comfort her—the cry was a badge of her life and vitality, a song I wanted to hear. Theo began to speak but I hushed him. They brought back the baby and handed her to me. I suddenly felt so weak that I doubted my ability to hold her.

"Hold her for me," I asked Theo. "Sit close and hold her so I can see."

I lay on the bed, that narrow slab, and Theo sat in the plastic hospital seat. She was wrapped in a towel, her dark blond hair drying in the light, her chest rising rhythmically, miraculously, and settled in Theo's arms.

"She's a girl," Theo said. He'd been crying, I saw

that now. "I got a peek as they were clearing her lungs. What are you going to name her?"

I thought about that. Andy and I had run through a few names before I'd gotten pregnant but then, with all the tension that mounted as soon as the conception took place, it seemed we hadn't actually zeroed in on a particular name.

"If it was a girl, my mother wanted me to name her Elizabeth, which is what she wanted to name me but couldn't because Dad wanted Margaret. Beth thought a jazzy name like Veronica, because she's always wanted a luscious name like that, and besides Veronica was her favorite character from the Archie comics. Carla says its better to go with something androgynous so the baby isn't unduly burdened with gender."

"So it's gone to committee," Theo said.

"Hey, Theo, that was a joke. I didn't know you did jokes."

"*Branded New York* was full of jokes."

"Yeah, but they were my jokes."

"Perhaps." Theo smiled. "I was still mad at you for stealing *Swear*."

I knew that would come up. Sooner or later. "You should have been grateful I stole it," I said.

He looked up from Frances for a moment. "Oh yeah, *now* I wish you'd erased it, I will never live down that Crash Jenkins character, but *then*—" He caught a glimpse of Frances, Frances looking straight up at him, and was suddenly captured back into her spell. He stared down at her once more and kept his eyes on her small face. So, what's this beautiful baby's name?" he asked gently.

"Frances."

Wrong instructions had kept Andy away for the birth, then his phone was busy each of the many times I had the hospital call him, but he did eventually find his way to Frances's and my bedside. Not that day, of course, but this is Andy we are talking about. A pretty good effort for him meant appearing sometime within the same week. He found his way by means of Beth, whom I phoned and explained everything to. After she stopped squealing about how great it was that Frances was a girl (her feeling about infant boys is that they are cute the way that newborn tigers are cute, until they grow up and spend the rest of their days stalking those who are smaller than they are to either eat or fuck), I explained the misunderstanding with Andy and asked her if she would be so kind as to drive over to Andy's apartment in Brighton and drag him off the phone and into Massachusetts General so he could see his daughter.

"You mean Theo was with you for the birth!" Beth said. Even through the phone line I could almost see her big eyes popping out of her head. "Did he do all the father stuff, like count your breaths and cut the cord?"

"No counting or cutting, but otherwise yes."

"Wait until Carla hears *this!*"

"*Do not* tell Carla. I just don't think I'm up to the analysis of how I feel that Andy missed the birth, or what it means that Theo was there. I just want to establish now that I did not intend for Theo to be there, he just *was*."

"*Coincidentally,* because he shares a house with you," she said with a knowing tone.

"For the time being."

"Is he still really cute?"

"I'm afraid I haven't noticed."

"I don't believe you."

"Beth, I just had a *baby*."

"Is *she* really cute? Frances, I mean?"

"Adorable. I'm totally in love with her."

I was and remain completely in love with Frances. It was eight at night when she was born and by ten o'clock I was lying next to her on the hospital bed thinking that I could never have lived another day without this baby. She had an oval face and tiny, almost indistinguishable lips, and eyes that were like half moons as she slept, her small hand curled around my finger. She spent most of the time sleeping and when she did wake it was a great event that I waited for in the hazy half-dream which is new maternity. I let her out of my sight long enough to call Beth. When I returned to my room she was gently sleeping in Theo's arms.

"She looks like you," Theo said.

"She looks like Andy."

"She has your eyes."

"She has Andy's eyes."

"And your chin."

"I'm not sure she has *any* chin."

"Well," he said. "Anyway, she's lovely."

Theo was like a converted man. It was as though he'd seen God on the mountain and come back glowing with goodness. All he wanted to do was hold Frances and look into her face and then look at me, smiling. Beth was wrong to think there was anything between Theo and me, if there was a budding love affair it was between Theo and Frances. He'd allowed the hospital staff to believe he was the father—I didn't realize this until later—and was now rapidly bonding with her at a time when I was just too tired to stop him.

"Beth is getting Andy. I hope they'll let him in this late at night."

"Mmmm," Theo said, looking still at Frances.

I didn't know exactly how to word the next part. How could I tell Theo that he better trot off home now that the real father was—we hoped—on his way? It seemed a little ungrateful of me and, besides, I'm not sure that Andy deserved any particular consideration. He'd missed the last trimester of the pregnancy, as well as the birth, so there was only so much sympathy I was willing to allot him. I let Theo stay—the staff would kick him out shortly, I gathered, even though he'd managed to charm them all by informing them who he was, what his books were, and their relative position on the best-seller list. There is something about writers that allows them to do whatever the hell they want in this world, provided they are famous enough. The nurses, from what I could tell, were thrilled to have him remain exactly where he was, although he had to pop out periodically to visit their station and woo them further, promising goods as valueless as signed copies of *The Cannonbury Tales,* which, given its critical and commercial failure, and the relative unlikeliness that the nurses would have actually enjoyed the book even if it had been the slightest bit readable (it wasn't), was a little like giving a frozen turkey to a group of vegetarians.

I fell asleep—I don't remember when this happened—and when I woke up a girl of about eighteen in a striped apron was standing in my room. On the dolly before her, which she'd positioned at the foot of my bed, exactly where Frances had been (and no longer was) in her wheeled hospital bassinet, was a machine that distributed hot drinks.

"You want coffee or tea or hot chocolate?" she asked.

"Where's my baby?" I said. I sounded a little hysterical even to myself.

The girl looked around her as though to ask, *Baby? What baby?*

"I dunno," she said.

"She was here last night," I said. "Do you have any idea where she could be now?" I felt it wasn't an altogether unwarranted question considering I was in the maternity ward and there was no bassinet where previously there had been a bassinet. But the girl behaved as though I'd stopped her in the street to ask her, a perfect stranger, a peculiar question about my child.

"The nursery?" she said, as though taking a guess at a game show quiz.

I made a dash for the corridor, dressed in my maternity nightgown, the front flap of which was buttoned unevenly, and went down the long row of semi-private rooms on the ward. I thought I was moving very fast, and couldn't quite figure out why the hallway seemed to go on forever, but I was in the stooped position of an old lady with a hunchback, hobbling along at mid-speed, constricted in part by the pain, the different *today* pain that replaced the old *yesterday* pain, that had lodged itself inside my butt as though I'd spent all night getting an enema from a steel rod, and in part because there were various hallway intersections and I had no idea where the hell I was going.

"My baby!" I said upon reaching at long last a desk of nurses. They stood like a group of deer who, approached by an early morning hiker, stare with their great almond eyes at the invader who has interrupted their breakfast, just before disappearing into the brush as though vaporized. *"Someone has taken my baby!"*

Instantly, three nurses vanished. Just like that. I was left with the one who had been seated at the desk writing notes, and another who busied herself on the telephone.

"Name?" the desk nurse asked.

"Frances."

"*Last* name," she said, and blew a sigh from her lips.

"Oh, Howe."

"O'How?" She looked at a book, searching.

"No, Howe."

"Nohow?"

"Howe. H as in horse, O as in owl, W as in—"

"You are in the wrong ward. This is ward five, you are in four."

So back down the hall, moving even faster now that I'd limbered up with that early morning jaunt all the way to another ward. The nurses at the ward four desk saw me coming and dispersed immediately, except for one who look mildly pissed off as I scrambled to her desk.

"My baby, Frances Howe, H as in horse, O as in—"

"Mrs. Howe, she's in the nursery. Theo brought her to us after you fell asleep. I'll take you there."

The nursery was just as you'd expect, a long room full of babies in plastic hospital bassinets, wrapped in cotton blankets. I scanned the room, looking at all the red, round-faced, blurry-eyed newborns, which to the uninitiated look exactly alike, thinking, ugly, ugly, ugly, ugly, *gorgeous*. Frances was awake but silent, lying in her bassinet as though patiently awaiting my arrival.

"She had her morning feed about an hour ago."

"You *fed* her?"

"Yes, Mrs. Howe. "

"Who told you to feed her?"

"She did. She was crying with hunger."

"Oh well, I guess that was reasonable. What exactly did you feed her?"

"Milk, Mrs. Howe. Any objections to that?"

I thought for a moment, it seemed to me that I ought to voice some sort of objection, but I couldn't think of exactly what complaint was suitable, so I said, "Did she drink the milk?"

"Yes, Mrs. Howe."

"Can I take her now?"

"She's your baby."

I picked up Frances, who settled immediately into my arms, and started down the hall. I hadn't gotten ten feet when I was stopped by two nurses, the previously vanished nurses, who stood like police at a roadblock. One was older, with salt-and-pepper hair tied in a bun, the other was young with a long jaw and a gormless, bored-looking face. Perhaps I've seen too many *Smokey and the Bandit* reruns but the first thought in my mind was that if I could distract the one with the gray hair I could probably take the younger one.

"Mrs. Howe!" the older one declared, puffing her chest up and pursing her lips in a grand display of authority. "Wheelchair!"

She pivoted on one rubber heel and pointed with her whole arm at a wheelchair that was parked along a wall. "Sit!" she commanded. "And we will escort you to your room!"

I did as I was told. What choice did I have? I felt

as though Frances and I had been taken prisoner by a group of matriarchal aliens and that at any moment the floor would open and we would cascade down a long chute into the dungeon of this evil empire.

"A man came here last night insisting that he was your husband," she said, wheeling efficiently down the hall at a pace that would make speedwalkers envious. "He was frantic and odd, but I don't think dangerous. We had security take him away." A left turn was negotiated at great speed and I clutched the arm of the wheelchair as we whizzed past door after door. Any faster and I think we'd have been airborne. "Any idea who he was?"

"Was he tall, relatively thin, with swollen, very tired-looking eyes as though he hadn't slept in weeks?" I asked. She nodded, sucking in her lips as though she were suffering a gas pain, and punctuated this disapproving expression by stopping the wheelchair and locking it into place. "Then that would be my husband," I said meekly.

The nurse glared at me for a thin second. "What a troublemaker *he* is," she said.

The pediatrician came by at noon and declared Frances the healthiest baby he'd seen all morning and told us that unless I wanted to pay for the room privately I had to vacate.

"Next time go with SunDirect, their insurance

allows for two nights' hospital stay," was his professional advice.

I was discharged. I was practically thrown out. When the meter on your insurance expires you are shooed away like a malarial fly. We went home. My milk came in and my breasts took on the size and texture of a cauliflower. I set up a daybed in the living room where Frances and I could exist, could rest and eat and change diapers and watch television, all without having to negotiate stairs. About six o'clock Andy arrived. He rang the doorbell, which might have meant something meaningful about how he now viewed our marriage, or might have meant he lost his keys.

"Oh, hello," I greeted him at the door. "Do I know you?"

I'd been practicing this.

"The mother of my child," he said, as though he were speaking to the Virgin Mary. "You look great! I really like you fat."

"Frances," I called over my shoulder. "It's your father, all the way from Brighton, bringing insults, and I notice no gift."

"That comes later. First, you have to let me see her," he said, sweeping past me in a grand, devil-may-care fashion as though I'd been the one who kept him away all this time.

He was wearing a black mortician's-style jacket, the type you find in secondhand clothing stores and that people try to pass off as vintage when really it is just ugly, a pink shirt, and navy socks and a pair of black pants that also looked rather "vintage." I could only imagine that he'd been shopping at a *Saturday Night Fever* museum, and that the same person who did all the Christmas topiary at Boston Garden had a go at his hair. The sides had been hacked away and the back had a kind of ledge aspect to it, as though he were planning to do a little terraced farming up there. Across the front it was too long, falling over his glasses. When he looked at me, looked right at me beaming, I saw that his eyes were red in that blown firecracker way that he gets when he's not sleeping, and that there was a scab of some kind on his nose.

"I'm going for the successful bookseller look," he said, thumbing his lapels. "How am I doing?"

"You look like the butler for a whorehouse."

"Seriously," he said.

"Seriously, you look like shit."

"Bingo," he said, "that's the fashion in New York this winter. Shit."

He stepped through the house carefully, as though the floor might give way. He looked so ridiculous in his suit that it took me a moment to realize that what he was doing was tiptoeing in order not to wake Frances. His head darted left and right searching for her.

"She must be very small," he said.

"She's in the living room."

I took him in to where she was sleeping, adorable in her pink all-in-one suit with a bear embroidered across the chest.

"Daddy's little angel," Andy cooed.

"Yes, where has Daddy been for the last twenty-four hours while his little angel was being born, I'd like to know?"

He gave me a look as though I *ought* to know that. It was his dark, I've-been-betrayed-look, a look he must have learned from my mother, who has an identical expression she wheels out from time to time. "I didn't know where you were. Until Beth called me I figured you were out squatting in a cornfield somewhere."

"I might as well have been," I said.

He picked her up in an awkward, rather heartbreaking embrace, kissed her lightly on the cheek, and closed his sad, tired eyes. He stepped carefully to the couch and sat with her, told her he loved her, failed to tell me that he loved me, then lay down with a sleeping Frances over his chest, and promptly fell asleep himself.

"You are such a fuck," I said to him, and took my baby back.

Beth and David arrived to see Frances—arrived *together*—that was the first shock, and brought with them ten days' worth of food, cooked dinners, and a stuffed bear. Beth pointed at Andy on the couch and raised an eyebrow, David went over and punched him in the arm in a congratulatory manner. He went on sleeping. We all cooed over Frances, who woke briefly, ate, burped, and then went back to sleep. David peered into her basket, shook his head slowly back and forth, and mumbled something about the miracle of life. Then he went into the kitchen to baste spareribs. Beth gave me the lowdown.

"We're getting back together," she said. "We've just bought the most striking mahogany staircase with wrought-iron railings brought over from Rome. We're going for a whole new look—wood and fired tile and terra-cotta–colored walls. There will be no white in my house, only cream, and the wall between the kitchen and living room is coming down. It will be open-plan, what doors we have will open in on themselves so that the whole place exudes spaciousness and glamour. The theme is light. Light everywhere! And warmth, of course, David insists on warmth, that's why the terra-cotta paint."

Something about my disbelieving stare brought her down to earth and she looked at me sheepishly and clucked her tongue.

"Don't give me that look," she began, "this mahogany was cut down thirty years ago before we even knew we *had* a rain forest."

"You are getting back together?"

"Is that so surprising? We're *married*."

"What about the ranch house you were planning to have joined by a connecting hall to Mark's house?"

"Marianne is taking care of it. She thinks she can get two ten, maybe two fifteen. It's on the market for two fifty."

Impressive, considering Beth paid two hundred for it. Only Beth could make a profit out of leaving her husband. But that's the kind of woman Beth is, Beth steps in shit and slides uphill.

"That's how we're affording the staircase," she said, as though reading my mind. "Listen, I don't know what you did to David at Saks, but I'm telling you it was worth the three thousand dollars he wasted on that stupid panda bear. What exactly did you say anyway?"

"I wrecked his relationship with Diana. I'm good at wrecking relationships."

"You *are*, really, I mean it. I think there's a career in what you do."

Carla and James arrived later, bringing with them a stuffed dog for Frances and another ten weeks' groceries.

"I'll go buy an ice chest," David said, when he saw all the food.

Carla held Frances with a timeless perfection that is granted to all mothers. James's and her own children—Jo and Terry, one boy, one girl, named these androgynous names to keep them from overidentifying with their gender—were sixteen and fourteen now, but it didn't stop Carla from performing with ease and perfection all the various small tasks involved with a newborn as though she had two at home in diapers.

"She has an intelligent face," Carla said.

"She's a cracker!" declared James.

"She's just thrown up!" Beth said.

"Never mind," cooed Carla, dotting Frances's face with a cloth.

Carla pointed at Andy, who despite a considerable amount of coming and going, popping of corks and clinking of glasses, not to mention the baby, who let out a wail three feet from his ear, had continued to lie comatose on the couch. Carla said, "Well, at least he's sleeping."

"I thought he was *dead*, dressed in that suit," Beth said. "I thought you'd killed him and got out a suit you wouldn't mind putting in the ground."

"I kind of like the suit," David said. "I think we buried my grandfather in a suit like that."

I said, "This might even be the very same suit, exhumed."

"So how does it make you feel that Theo was at the birth?" Carla asked. "Beth told me all about it."

"I didn't tell her," Beth said. "She *guessed*."

"She said, 'Guess who was Meg's labor partner?' It took me thirty-two guesses to get Theo. I was on the phone for an hour," Carla said.

"Well, I promised I wouldn't tell," Beth said.

"I'm not talking about it," I said.

"No way," said Beth, "you have to talk about it. Did he see the baby actually, you know, *come out*?"

I threw her a glance.

"She doesn't have to talk about it," Carla said.

"Yes, she *does*."

"No, she *doesn't*."

Instead of talking about Theo we talked about all the things we used to talk about, the trivial day-to-day drivel that I am sure indicates a measure of happiness that had been altogether missing from our group for almost a year now. Carla's neighbor, a fifty-year-old advertising executive who made a vast fortune for himself by hiring young talent, stealing their ideas, and casting rumors about their fictitious drug problems throughout town before firing them, had just taken in a twenty-year-old blond, long-legged college student "as a lodger." The girl was studying media at Boston University. She was poor, Southern, and beautiful. The argument was whether it was Carla's moral obligation to tell the neighbor what a shit he was and rescue the girl before he convinced her that she had an irreplaceable, privileged arrangement with a guru of the advertising world, promising her a job and a windowed office in his very firm if only she would be his sex slave for the remainder of her student days.

"I think it's a good deal," David said. "Do you know how hard it is to get into advertising?"

"David, don't joke," said Beth. "The guy deserves to be arrested. To think he walks around, sends cards at Christmastime, just like he was a decent person."

"Maybe she really is just a lodger," said James.

"Oh please," I said.

"She's living on Brattle Street," David said. "I think she's getting a pretty good deal."

Beth glared at him. "Weren't you going to get an ice chest?"

"It's not our business," Carla said reasonably.

"Make it your business," Beth said. "Kill the guy and burn his house down."

"Not if it's the nineteenth-century colonial with the Greek revival pillars and the Victorian conservatory," I said, remembering exactly the houses to either side of Carla and James's house. "Do what you like to him, but don't hurt the house. That would be wrong."

We talked about Christmas, about what we don't like about Christmas.

"Professionally, it is a very busy time for me," Carla said. "The phone never stops ringing. *Help me, help me.* This might sound unkind but there are a lot of people out there who should just be sedated from the twenty-second of December all the way to the New Year."

"What advice do you give people on how to cope with the stress?" Beth asked.

"What do I look like, a radio call-in program?"

"Oh come on, Carla, can't you just be nice?" Beth said.

"Oh, *all right,*" Carla sighed. "I tell them the truth about Christmas, which is if you ignore it long enough it will go away. Then they tell me they can't ignore it because their mother or sister or children want this or that out of them and we talk about why they feel they have to meet all those requests."

"In other words you are no help at all," Beth said.

"No. I recommend a Prozac Christmas most of the time."

"The trouble with Christmas," David said. "Is that it doesn't happen instantly. First there's the parties to go to, then the parties to host, then all the present buying, then the decorations. The lights don't light, the tree won't stand in its tree stand, the candles don't fit in their candlesticks. You can't find the tape, you buy the wrong size, you can't find the scissors. The grocery stores close, you can't get food. A thousand details designed to drive you crazy. What we as Americans are used to is instant everything. We need an instant Christmas, a Christmas you could go order off a menu, like at a restaurant. We'd be good at that."

"Exactly," said Carla. "The problem is we're all doing it from scratch, like Julia Child. I don't even cook from scratch, so why on earth should I do Christmas from scratch?"

"Want to know how Julia Child would do Christmas?" Beth said. "First she'd have us go out in the woods and find a tree—"

"Then truss it," James said.

"Then go into the kitchen and do something with cheesecloth—" David said.

"What *is* cheesecloth anyway?" I suddenly wanted to know.

"Last year our Christmas tree died three days before Christmas," Carla said. "It was in a corner of the living room next to the piano. The needles dropped in between all the keys. We had to get a specialist out. That tree cost us two hundred dollars."

"Christmas ought to take place exclusively at shopping malls," Beth said. "The mistake was ever bringing it inside the home."

"I hate shopping," James said. "It's so aggressive. Go, get. Go, get."

"I *love* shopping," Beth said. "Except at Christmas when you are supposed to be buying for other people."

"I like shopping," I said. "If I had money I could actually take home all the things I shop for."

And we talked about Andy.

"He's got to be having an affair," Beth said. "He's been gone for nearly two months."

"So?" Carla said.

Beth replied as though this should be perfectly obvious. "So who has he been having sex with all that time?" she asked.

"Maybe nobody," Carla said. "You might not believe this, but some people go for weeks, if not months, without sex."

Beth shot a look of horror at Carla. "Oh, yeah," she said, "the terminally ill, maybe."

"Ordinary people," Carla said.

"Don't be absurd," said Beth. "Look at him, lying there exhausted. He's been having it all right."

"I think he's just afraid of the idea of being a father. You know what they say, you really know you're married when you have a child," James said.

David said, "I really knew I was married when I found this big hole in my savings account where there used to be money."

"I buy him things with *my* money," Beth said defensively. "I got him some gorgeous Rossetti patent leather pumps."

"I look like a fairy in them."

"He looks stylish."

"The things shine so much you could use them to shave by."

We ate ribs and drank champagne—well, they drank champagne, I had milk. James made a fire and we sat on the floor and debated whether or not it was ecologically sound to burn real wood. I told the story about how Andy and I used to always make love by the fire, and then how we didn't, and then how we *didn't* didn't. James told us how the houses in Kent are beamed and have their original fireplaces and stone floors and we all sighed with envy, except Beth who said that all she saw on their visit to England five years ago was mock Tudors and high-rises, and that when the Queen spoke on television on Christmas Day she was seated in front of an electric fire.

"The kind with orange tubes like a toaster," she said, "At first I thought it *was* a toaster, that the Queen was in a room with this gigantic toaster, then David pointed out it was a fireplace."

"That's because she was addressing the nation, the ordinary people," James said. "I can assure you the Queen has one or two original fireplaces."

"So it was a trick to make her look like one of the commoners?" I said. "Is that what she's doing when she dresses in bright pink with a little pillbox pink hat and a matching pink purse? Is that how she thinks the rest of England dresses?

"I'll let you in on a secret," Beth said. "You don't want to see how the rest of England dresses."

"It's got to be better than how Andy dresses," David said, giving Andy's lapel a tweak. "Imagine sleeping in these clothes, they'd give you nightmares."

Finally, about eleven, they all cleared out.

"She's so cute," Beth said. "Maybe I should get a baby."

"You mean *have* a baby. You get pregnant, and then have a baby."

"Right," Beth said, a little drunkenly.

"She's adorable," Carla said. "It makes me very nostalgic. I wish I could stay and look after her tonight while you sleep but I've got to go home and search the house for signs of what my teenagers have been up to in my absence. Good luck with . . . you know . . ."

"The corpse," I offered.

"I'm glad to see you haven't lost your sense of humor."

"I can't. I have it sewn into my abdomen."

CHAPTER TEN

I WOKE THREE TIMES WITH FRANCES, THEN ONCE with Andy, who was sleepwalking and had to be redirected back to his place on the couch. I pushed him down onto the couch with a little more force than was actually required, and warned him that if he sleepwalked again I would lock him in the cellar. The last thing I needed, I thought, was some sleepwalking wayward father tripping on my baby's basket and hurting her. Then I went upstairs with Frances and fell asleep with her beside me on the bed. I woke hours later and found the entire front of my body was glued to my nightgown by means of dried milk.

Frances went on sleeping as I rose, attempted to manually encase my breasts back in their fifty-two-dollar Robinson's bra that the measuring lady had assured me was my size, and then gave up and held them like two kittens as I went downstairs. I heard voices, Andy's and Theo's. I found them in the breakfast room, sitting across from each other, pretending to have a civilized conversation. From the crumbs on the table I assumed they'd just finished off a nice meal. When I walked in they both smiled and opened their eyes wide, whether from the pleasure of seeing me or the shock of seeing me—an outsized apparition in a milk-stained L. L. Bean flannel nightgown—I could not tell.

"I don't suppose you'd like to give me some of whatever it was you were eating," I said, launching a look of hurt and anger at Andy.

"Theo brought a marvelous array of breakfast doughnuts and some hot chocolate. It was scrumptious."

"Actually, it was for you, Meg."

"I think there is still a doughnut left here somewhere," Andy said.

He was still wearing his *Saturday Night Fever* museum suit, now ridiculously wrinkled, and with crumbs down the front. Theo was in a handknit sweater and a pair of corduroys, looking confused about exactly how to behave given the circumstances. The hospital episode had created for us a new intimacy that was at once both tender and awkward. I would have liked a few hours alone with him just to go through the whole thing—the labor, Frances's birth, the first enchanting, terrifying moments with my new baby breathing—breathing real air—beside me. He'd been there to witness what was for me the greatest event ever to transpire in my life. To talk to him about it, to clarify it all in my mind, was at that moment my only desire.

Instead, I went into the living room to see if Andy had bothered to clear up from last night's party. I decided that if it was clean, I would be nice to him. If it was a wreck, I would be mean to him. Mundane thoughts compared to the great mystery of child-birth, but I was in need of practical solutions and searching for some kind of sign from the heavens as to what I ought to do. For what it was worth, the living room gave a thumbs-down on Andy. It was un-touched. There were plates and stray forks and dinner napkins and empty glasses strewn about. Apparently, Andy had woken, surveyed the wreckage of last night's party, and promptly gone into the kitchen to devour my doughnuts. Well.

I was angry and tired and ravenously hungry, but instead of doing something useful like yell at Andy, go back to sleep, or make myself some breakfast, I started clearing up. I stacked plates and wadded nap-kins, listening to Andy in the next room as he ex-plained to Theo about the renovation of older houses, in particular those which had been mostly left to their own devices for twenty or more years like Mrs. Russell's house. He spoke eloquently of dry rot and furniture beetle and outdated wiring and fire hazards, not to mention rusted iron guttering, ruined casement windows, settlement cracks, all of which he knew Mrs. Russell's house to have. He was good at listing troubles, my Andy, and pretty effective at scaring the shit out of Theo.

"You're probably wanting to change paint or wallpaper or kitchen furniture, but don't even think about anything decorative until you've gone to work on the really important problems, the structural problems which I know this house to have. The outside has to be watertight and right now you are leaking like a rusted pipe," Andy said. "You've got guttering, roofing, pointing, and, of course, a chimney crisis. I can tell you for nothing that for the past five years Mrs. Russell has been growing flowers in front of the ventilation grilles, limiting their effectiveness. I told her not to, but she said the place needed brightening up." He spoke as though about a cancer patient who, despite all advice to the contrary, just kept on smoking. "Well, she's off the hook now, isn't she? Just grew her flowers and died. The rest is *your* headache."

When Theo spoke he sounded a little worried. "What happens when you block the ventilation grilles?"

"Wet-rot in the substructural timbers," Andy shot back.

"What about the guttering?"

"Mrs. Russell used to stand at the bedroom window and throw seed out for the birds. Anything that landed in the gutter sprouted and grew leaves."

"Which means?"

I could just imagine Andy now, leaning forward in his chair and folding his hands in front of him. "Dysfunctional guttering, leading to water ingress," he said.

"I don't dare ask about the chimneys," Theo said.

Andy let out a single "Ha" then said, "No, I don't either. I can see from the ground that there is some settlement cracking and the mortar joints are eroded. You can fix the settlement with wire ties, but as they've been uncapped for so long I fear, again, water ingress. What people don't realize is just how water kills."

"Oh my God," said Theo.

They both looked up when I came in, trailing with me a half dozen empty glasses and bottles from the night before.

"Andy, go in there and pick up all the plates and glasses."

"Where?"

"The living room, where do you think? Good morning, Theo, it is morning, isn't it?"

"Why would there be plates and glasses in the living room?" asked Andy.

"Because of all the people who were here last night. Don't act like you didn't know. I saw you there, pretending to sleep through the whole thing."

"But I *was* asleep!"

"You were faking. Don't lie. When Beth started talking about sex you got an erection."

"I was having an erotic dream. In my dream I was chanting with a crowd of bald Buddhist women in orange caftans and then they all took the caftans off."

"Wow, how do you get dreams like that?" Theo asked.

"By being formerly married to a nymphomaniac with the IQ of a vole," I said, and then to clarify I added, "I just want to point out that I am referring to his ex-wife Eloise and not, it goes without saying, to myself."

Andy said, "Eloise never shaved her head. She did have a caftan, though she wore it with high heels." He stopped and considered this. "She looked rather well in it, if you like that transvestite monk look."

"Which apparently you do. You *dream* about it."

Andy said, "On Eloise perfume would keep its scent for days. She always said it was because she had a very heavy aura."

"Her aura was very heavy, Theo," I said. "It was so heavy that she collected smells off the street. Bus-fume smells, hot-dog-grease smells, train-station smells, all clinging to her big, fat aura!"

Andy addressed Theo, "Meggy gets very strange on the subject of Eloise. I tell her there is no need. I didn't even love Eloise. I just had sex with her."

I said, "For two years every night under the banner of matrimony. Anyway, you brought her up."

"You brought her up!"

"No, you brought her . . . oh, forget it. Now listen, Andy, go to the living room and clean. First clear, then clean."

"It's fine as it is!"

"Use a rag, a laundered rag. Use disinfectant. I don't want the baby picking up any germs."

"Those *were* people who were here last night?" Andy said. "They weren't, you know, laboratory animals carrying genetically engineered viruses or anything, were they?"

I pointed at Andy. "Clean," I instructed. "It will be your first contribution toward parenthood."

He got up and left the room reluctantly. I sat down with Theo and put my head in my hands.

"How are you?" Theo asked.

"Hormonal. Water retaining. *Milk* retaining! My joints ache, some of them don't work. Look at my thumb, I can't move it, it doesn't go forward without stopping first. You know what the doctor said to me just before I had Frances? She said it is a strain on the skeleton to carry so much weight. That's not just one bone, that's an entire strained skeleton."

"You do look tired," Theo said, patting my head.

"That means I am ugly. Tired/ugly. Synonyms. No! Same word!"

"Not ugly. Not synonyms, not even homonyms, completely unrelated words."

"I'm not good at this maternity thing. I feel like I've been run over by a truck, that it backed up and ran over me again and again."

"I could run you a bath," he said.

A marvelous idea.

I could feel myself relax even at the thought of a bath. "Theo, that would be great."

Andy called from the living room, "I heard that!" Then he stormed back into the breakfast room, his hands clutching wads of paper napkins and a plate full of rib bones. "I heard that!" he repeated.

"Heard what?"

"You are being nice to him in *that* way. You know what I mean. First you get mad at me for a dream I had and then you start being sweet to Theo."

"I was just being nice, like a normal person."

"You were flirting."

"I was not," I said. "And even if I were I have the right to!"

"I have to go," Theo said.

"Don't go," I said to Theo.

"He has to!" said Andy. "He has to dig up the flowers from outside his ventilation grilles."

"Oh, stop it!" I yelled at Andy. "Theo, sit down."

"No, really I ought to go," Theo said. Then he whispered, "I'll check on you later."

Theo left. I glared at Andy.

"I could act like him, you know," Andy said. "I could say, 'Why don't I run you a bath?' in that syrupy way!"

"Then do it. Go run the bath!" I yelled.

"But I'm not trying to score points. I'm not going around fetching you doughnuts and running you baths to prove myself all over again. We are a couple."

"Maybe you *should* be proving yourself! I think that's exactly what you ought to be doing."

A parting shot. I stomped out of the room. I climbed the staircase back up to the bedroom and found Frances sleeping peacefully in the middle of our bed, her tiny face tucked down toward her chest, her little wrinkly hands curled together as though she were in prayer.

The sight of her stopped me, I felt my anger drain away. She was so perfect, so entirely beautiful, and perhaps the first thing in my life that was truly my own to love. For a long time I stood by the bed looking at her. I did not even realize Andy was standing behind me.

"She's lovely," he said.

"You missed seeing her born. That was foolish of you."

He paused, considering this last remark. "I'm here now. I can't entirely make up for what I've put you through, but I am here now."

"For the minute."

"And I don't blame you for hating me."

"That's nice," I said sarcastically. "That you don't blame me."

"Meg, give me a chance!"

"Shh! You'll wake her!" But it was too late. Frances was awake, her fists shaking, her tiny round face working its way into a mighty yell. "Now you've woken the baby," I said angrily. I picked up Frances and she stopped crying instantly and nestled against me. "You've been gone seven weeks, Andy. How many chances do you want?"

He closed his eyes, his color changed. For a moment I thought he might faint. "Just one," he said, his voice a whisper.

I didn't answer. I wasn't sure what to say.

"Are you going to fire me as a husband?" he asked.

"You walked off the job."

I sat on the edge of the bed and positioned Frances for feeding. I patted her silky head and guided her so that she could nurse.

"A couple days of motherhood and you're an expert. Look at you," Andy said.

It took me a moment to realize he was not being sarcastic. It appeared he was admiring how I could nurse Frances, and I admit I was slightly touched. I missed Andy. I missed having him near me, beside me. I said, "The outdoor lamp needs a new bulb. I want the living room tidied. And the carpet on two of the stairs has come loose."

He knew immediately what this meant; it was a language we shared, a language of domestic life, of everyday things. His face beamed. "I'll go buy some carpet tacks," he said. "The living room will be cleaner than you've ever seen it."

He started out of the room. "I doubt that," I said, as he disappeared around the corner.

C H A P T E R

E L E V E N

HE FIXED THE CARPET, FOUND A FRESH BULB for the lamp in our front porch, cleaned the living room. He cleaned it very well. He got rid of the spoils of last night's party, wiped the surfaces, dusted the skirting boards, vacuumed the rug, hand-vacuumed the sofa and chairs, swept out the fireplace, and then went into the laundry room and folded my clothes. He wanted forgiveness. He wanted me to take him back within the loving aegis of my innermost being, I knew this by the fact he changed the filter of the dryer. I wasn't sure yet if I was willing to grant him forgiveness; it was too soon to decide such things. Divorce him, take him back, I didn't know. I might never truly forgive him, but then I hadn't managed to stop loving him, either, so he had that in his favor. Also, he cleaned. And certainly I was going to do my best to suck out every last chore I could from him as he scurried for my favor. If I were ever to give any woman advice on what kind of man to marry, I would suggest one who cleaned. Millions of women out there will tell you outright that they are more dependent on their housekeepers than their husbands, that they often feel more warmth for their housekeepers than their husbands, even that they love their housekeepers more than their husbands. That is because it is hard not to love someone who cleans your house. I had a friend who, after she got a really good housekeeper, decided she didn't even need a husband—he was interfering with the housekeeper's work—and so divorced him. She was happier with just the housekeeper. If I were ever going marry again (I will *never* marry again) I would seriously consider putting an ad into the personal columns that read like this:

Wanted: Terrific, fun man with sound, uncomplicated character who enjoys cleaning my house and looking after my child so I can take kick-boxing lessons and do yoga at my local luxury health club.

I would put an ad in like this because, let's face it, this is what I really want from a husband, and though it might seem hopeless to make these, my true demands of a potential spouse, known at the outset, the theory of advertising is based on the fact that if you spread your net wide enough you will get a response from someone, somewhere.

Usually in personal ads people say they want all sorts of things that they don't really want, "romantic walks on the beach," for example. It's classic. But the enjoyment you get from a walk on the beach is based in large part on climate conditions and whether you happen to live near a beach. Driving six hours to walk a beach in winter storm conditions is not romantic. Walking on a beach with tides of polluted water and litter lapping at your feet is not romantic. I'm not pretending that a walk on the beach is a bad thing, and if I got back from the kick-boxing class and still felt like a little exercise, I might ask my husband if he wanted to go for a walk on the beach. I could do this because now I had a clean house—he cleaned it—so there is nothing stopping me from doing the beach walk thing.

Another subject that always pops up in personals: "romantic candlelit dinners." That's another one you always read about. But who pays for these romantic candlelit dinners? Or who cooks them? When a man puts an ad in the personals and says he wants candlelit dinners, he means he wants you to cook them *for him*. He wants you to clean all the pots and pans. He wants you to scrape salmon grease off the broiler once you've cooked him the dinner and he wants you to get out a wire brush once a week and clean your oven, which has a lot of built-up residue from all those gourmet dinners. Is there anything romantic about that? Am I looking for love so I can spend

twenty percent of my time with my hands up a
turkey's backside? Or a duck or a game hen? Or
buried in a sinkful of dishwashing soap? No. But
coming home to a clean house after having had a
meal out—even a not-so-good meal, even a McDonald's Happy Meal—is a great thing. You walk in, the
place is in order, you can take a bath and go to bed
and there are no dishes to clean. No surfaces to wipe,
no beds to be made, sheets to be changed, laundry to
be put away. To me, and I think to a lot of women out
there, that is nirvana. A clean house is always a good
thing, good in the purest way. You don't have to be
rich to have a clean house, you don't have to have any
particular intelligence to have a clean house, you don't
have to have a great house to appreciate when it is
clean. Clean is good, absolutely, the way that money
is good, absolutely. People who say they don't mind if
they are poor and their house is a mess are lying. Or
they are part of a strange religious cult. Or they are
students. But they are never, in any case, married
women. And here is an interesting fact: no woman in
the history of the world has ever, *ever* thrown her husband out while he was actually cleaning her house.
My advice to any man who thinks his marriage is on
the rocks is simply to get a broom and use it.

I telephoned Carla.

"He cleaned the downstairs and folded the laundry. He called upstairs to me, asking if I wanted him
to clean the bathtub, and I told him to go to the new
house and fight with the people who are installing the

central heating. I have no evidence that they've screwed it up but I'm sure they have, and I need to know in advance if we want to sue."

"What do you think about all this?" she asked.

"I wish I'd done more washing because then he'd have dried and folded that, too. As it was all I got was about two days' worth of clean clothes out of him before he went to scream at the builders."

"Well, he's doing the things I always tell husbands to do if they have wives who hate them," Carla said.

"Really?" I was interested. I never realized there was a whole school of psychology based on my theory that if husbands cleaned divorce would be anathema.

"Yes, I always advise it. You'd be surprised how many husbands don't even know how to clean a house. We run seminars for them so they can learn. The ones who pass the course usually hang on to their marriages."

"I want to divorce him, but I also want to keep him so he can clean. He's really blown it this time, the place is likely to be spotless for a year."

"Of course, I recommend counseling. I've been recommending counseling to you for five years. In fact, if you remember, I recommended counseling to you even before you were married."

"This is counseling. Here I am, on the telephone with a trained psychiatrist. That's counseling."

"No, it's not," Carla said. "When you and Andy are sitting in an office somewhere yelling and weep-

ing and begging the doctor to help you, that is counseling. I'm just a friend."

"Okay, I'll weep. I've been close to weeping anyway."

"Won't work."

"You mean I have to pay somebody?"

"Yes."

"But if I'm going to pay somebody I may as well
hire a maid and then I don't even need Andy, so I
might as well divorce him—"

Carla interrupted. "Meg, you are not sounding
like yourself at all—"

"—which defeats the whole counseling thing."

I sent Andy to the schoolhouse. I mean, to live at
the schoolhouse. I packed a bag for him, included
some bleach and Comet and disinfectant spray and
floor polish, and sent him on his way.

"I want the place ready for habitation," I said.
"You can visit Frances and me in the afternoons and
give progress reports."

"You want me to sleep there, too!" he said, as
though our new home were a chemical site. "You
want me to live out of this little bag?" he said, holding the bag by one finger, as though it contained toxic
waste.

"You can live where you want." I shrugged. "But
not here."

"Not with you!"

"Oh big shock and horror."

"You're kicking me *out*?"

"Call it what you want," I said coolly. "Maybe we can live together again, but not until you've performed certain architectural miracles on the new house. I want the upstairs finished, I want the window casings repaired. I want radiators that work and I want a skylight or two. Then I'll decide who lives where. Think of this as your penance."

"Like Prometheus," he said.

"Exactly."

Every afternoon, about four o'clock, Andy returned from the new house with tales on its development.

"The barn owls won't move," he said. "And we're not supposed to disturb them with noise, can you believe it? We've spent hundreds of thousands on the place they've taken up residence in and we're *not to disturb them!* I've had the bird society man there three times this week complaining that the erection of the upstairs beams is upsetting the birds."

I looked up from Frances, who was lying like a little cherub on the changing table, her diaper half on and half off. "Can you bribe him?" I asked.

Andy shook his head. "The central heating works, that's the good news, I don't want to tell you what they've done to the floorboards, however. They need re-laying."

"Then get the builders to re-lay them properly," I said. "For free. You have to be tough in these matters."

"I know. I'm thinking of running over the owls with the car."

Every morning I took Frances and went over to Theo's part of the house. Did you hear what I said? Theo's *part of the house*, not Theo's house. That remark alone tells you just how very chummy we had gotten—we'd reached a stage in which he left his door open for me to come through at any time. This makes sense if you consider that we used to actually live together, that for four years the only door was our mutual front door. But he did things for me that he never used to do way back in the stone age when we shared that Kenmore Square apartment and tried to be writers and lovers at the same time. For example, he cooked for me. When I entered his part of the house I could smell toasted almonds and fried chicken and bread and butter pudding, all made from recipes from his grandmother. I felt his grandmother's presence at these times, not just because of the cooking but because we spent hours in his living room sitting on his grandmother's fabulous furniture. She was named Doris, a relic of a name that nobody would ever dream of calling a child now, and it was a name she chose herself. In fact, she'd been christened Margaret but changed the name when she passed her driver's license. It occurred to her at the time they asked her name for the license, and she chose Doris on a whim while sitting at the desk in front of the clerk typing out the license. Some people might call it lying, but she saw this new name as a choice like any other. Later, she wished that she'd made up a new last name, too, as Clarkson was so ordinary. "I should have been Doris Montelaro," she told Theo some sixty years later. "I could have gone anywhere with a name like that."

"Now, *her* you ought to write about," I told Theo.

He nodded matter-of-factly. "I'm waiting until she's dead."

We talked for hours about what he was writing, what I was not writing (the book having been usurped entirely by Frances), what we would like to write, about nothing and everything. We sat together and read. He wore jeans and university sweatshirts; I wore maternity leggings and old sweaters, we were comfortable with each other. We were at ease. Sometimes we held hands, casually like old friends. Sometimes he gave me a look—what can I call it?—a smoldering look as I walked into the room. Such a promising array of emotions, it seemed almost a shame they were wasted on us. I realized, tucked up on a Queen Anne style chair with Frances sleeping on me, that I suddenly had that feeling, the feeling you get when you first walk into a really great house that is yours now, to which you hold title, to which you are fully committed, and it is your home. That same feeling you get when you meet the right person and realize that something significant has changed in your life, that a new space has opened, a space you never knew existed, that *in love* feeling. It hit me and I remembered it all over again. I'd forgotten, but not really forgotten, and I missed it so much.

One morning I told Theo, "I better stop seeing you."

I felt giddy and festive and strange and nervous. Theo took my hand and my palm was hot.

"Don't," he said. "I like it when you're here."

"I'm married."

"You are relatively married. You are married technically."

"No, I'm really married. He's erecting our upstairs right now. On his own with only builders to help him. He knows that if he gets one thing wrong, one electrical socket in the wrong place, a door hinged so it opens the wrong way, a plumbing failure, that he is in deep trouble. He's working his ass off. He's under a lot of pressure."

"He left you when you were pregnant. How can you forgive that?"

A very good question. How could I forgive that? I suppose by first understanding that this was not a surprise event. Or not entirely a surprise. After all, it took three separate attempts just to get him to show up at his own wedding. Two full-cast dress rehearsals, each of which cost us thousands of dollars. He has trouble with transitions, Andy. One of the reasons he opened a bookstore instead of climbing the publishing corporate ladder was because in order to climb the ladder you have to suffer through promotions. I say suffer, because that is what Andy did. Each time he was promoted waves of panic shot through him. He'd wake up in cold sweats, consider turning down the promotion or quitting altogether. He took sick days, declared a death in the family, went on vacation, then simply failed to show up at work before finally, painfully, settling into his new position. A few months later he would be sailing happily along, having adjusted beautifully to the demands of a new job, meeting whatever quotas he was meant to meet, charming his bosses and getting along just fine. Time would pass and he'd be put forward for another advancement and the panic would start again. The best thing he ever did was to buy the bookstore. It ensured a status quo. No promotions, no relocations. Before I got pregnant, Andy hadn't had a major upheaval in his life for five years, it was kind of due. But how could I explain this to Theo? It would just make him think Andy was even more crazy than he already thought him.

"Well, he did leave me. But he also came back," I said. "Anyway, it isn't the first time a man has left me."

I didn't realize until after I'd said it that I'd meant Theo himself—the old selfish, gruesome Theo and not this new, improved model.

"I should never have let you go," he said. "I've wasted so many years without you."

"Yeah, I know. I often think of all your wasted years becoming a literary superstar. It's a shame."

"You know what I mean," he said. He let go my hand and kneeled beside me on the rug. He removed my slipper (I hardly bothered to get dressed these mornings) and kissed my foot, then my ankle, then planted kisses all the way up the inside of my calf.

"I think I'm in love with you," he said.

"No, no, it's just a virus. Mrs. Russell had it—she died of it."

"Please keep coming by in the mornings."

It was a date we kept. Ten-thirty. Coffee would be ready, Frances would be dressed in a clean sleepsuit. There was no more talk about love. We sat together and he kissed me gingerly on the cheek when I left. Would something more have happened if I had not been a nursing mother, with sore nipples and a line of stitches that rendered me unfit for lovemaking? Perhaps. The postnatal period is not an especially libidinous one for a woman, so I was not tempted in the way I might have been had we conducted our meetings at a different time in my life. As it was, it was all so civilized. We were like two very old people whose fondness for each other cannot lead to a proper courtship, but the sentiment was still there. We sang to Frances and showed her books and she regarded us with her blurry vision. After five weeks of this, she smiled.

"I think she thinks you are her father, that is, if she has any concept of fathers," I said.

"When you two go," Theo said, "it's going to break my heart."

So, I had been warned.

I knew, even as I returned each morning to Theo's lovely house, that I was acting out of self-indulgence, and with total disregard for the effect on him. I knew that I was hurting him and that I would go on hurting him because right then, at that exact moment in time when Frances was a tiny baby and my marriage seemed so unlikely to survive, I needed him. There was so much at stake, I wanted a family for my daughter, a man in my life. I was unsure which direction to turn and so I lashed out and took what I could from all directions. I was ruthless, I would be thought ill of in the future, perhaps. But I could not help it. I realized, as I allowed Theo to further love me, as I stepped past his doorway and into the dreamy world of his grandmother's old furniture, the winter sun casting long stretches of light across the floor, and took whatever I could in those few hours each day, that I was doing what he had done to me over a dozen years previously. It was survival. It was necessity. Given the same circumstances, I'd do it all over again.

I think, perhaps, I really did love Theo. I had fallen in love with him so early in life. He was my first love. I'm not saying that he wasn't a disaster back then. He was. I remember how he used to torture me by asking if I'd read such-and-such book and then gazing at horror when the answer was no. How he used to make me feel I'd never get anywhere with my work simply because I wasn't ambitious enough. "You don't have the drive," he told me back then, on an afternoon I was supposed to be writing but was instead reading a copy of *Cosmo*. "You don't have the instinct."

A damning condemnation. I had hated him and loved him in turns. I'd wanted so much to please him. If I went to a movie—to a commercial movie, not one of the art flicks he occasioned—he saw it as an indication of a lack of talent, of intellect. Any deviation from the absolute esthetic brought me a demotion in his eyes. So I'd tried to like the right movies, to listen to the right music and, most important, to read the right books. For what? For love of Theo and for the desire to achieve that which seemed so impossible then, to be a published author. That was gone now, the desire to please him, also the thrill of seeing my name in print. Just as I could now peaceably watch Bruce Willis movies, read detective novels, and wear drip-dry maternity clothes, knowing with absolute certainty that I was not polluting my "creative talent," I knew I could go on seeing Theo and not really jeopardize my marriage. I was protected by a certain awareness of who I was; I was Meg Howe, a writer who wrote a particular kind of book and wrote it well. And I was Andy's wife.

Andy sorted out the central heating, had the boards re-laid, rid the house of plaster dust and sawdust and all the black marks from builder's boots. He got the upstairs built despite the alarm it caused the owls. Eventually the owls took the hint and relocated themselves in the wooden barn at the rear of the property, where Andy had built special owl-attracting nooks into the rafters and left a few dead mice. The conversion, though partly undecorated, was brilliant. It had been well over a year since we'd finalized the plans for it, back when we first bought the house and before I became pregnant and this whole drama began, but despite everything that had transpired since,

I still remembered each room as it had been set out on the blueprint, and sketched out in my mind. The upstairs rooms were all set along an L-shaped hallway, one side of which looked over the whole of the downstairs like a gallery. Our bedroom would face the garden, with two enormous windows overlooking the parkland adjoining the property and a hearth added into the third wall to adjoin the existing chimney. The bathroom was attached to the master bedroom and led by way of a second door into a one-time attic space which was now a nursery with its own washbasin. A third bedroom followed the nursery and my office was at one end of the hall. The day I came to see it, with Frances strapped to my stomach in one of those baby slings, her eyes dancing as we entered for the first time together our future home, Andy escorted us from room to room, excitedly pointing out all the new features he'd added to the house.

"The staircase is new, I actually watched it being put up, but it is made with antique pine and the newel post is about a hundred years old. I found that in a heap of junk most of which was beyond rescue."

The staircase was neatly tucked in a corner of the vast downstairs room. It curved gently up to the first-floor landing, lit by a host of stained-glass windows that followed the ascent. It looked so right, so perfect, that I had a hard time imagining when such a staircase hadn't existed in the house. "It's beautiful," I said. "It's inspired."

"The skylight at the top is made to look Edwardian, I had to compromise a little on how much light came through but I didn't think a plain glass pane set in timber would be right."

"No, it had to be decorative. You did the right thing."

"Wait until you see the bathroom!" he said. "It's very girly."

The bathroom was wonderful, with a handpainted pedestal sink and a tub with brass fittings and French tiles with different painted flowers and garden herbs interspersed with plain tiles on the walls. The floor was stone—we were planning to add a rug so our feet didn't freeze—and there was a heated towel rack and a gilt mirror. He'd found an old-fashioned vegetable rack from somewhere and put it up to use as shelving. It was ingenious, as was the placement of a small, oval window just behind the toilet.

"Are we really poor now that we've got all this great stuff?" I asked, smiling at my brand-new, never-been-used porcelain toilet.

He nodded. "Oh yeah."

But the best surprise was our bedroom. Or rather, it was *in* our bedroom. Without consulting me (which was very brave) Andy had bought a four-poster bed, an absolutely gorgeous four-poster bed with a carved headboard and a brand new mattress made out of lambswool and horsehair and cotton batting with a box spring with about a million springs. He'd covered it in white linen and a Shaker-style quilt. A Hudson blanket was folded into a pine blanket box at the foot of the bed.

"What do we do with our old bed?" I asked. "I mean, there's nothing wrong with it, technically, that is."

"Right now it's in the spare bedroom," Andy said. "But I think we should sell it."

"This is marvelous," I said, nodding down at our new bed. "I don't dare touch it."

"We needed a fresh start, a new bed."

"Frances is going to love living here, aren't you, Frances?"

Frances had fallen asleep. Apparently, houses just don't hold her interest the way they do mine.

We went downstairs and made ourselves some coffee and walked around in that dazed way that couples do when they buy a new house. There was still some painting to do, and I agreed that some wallpaper was probably in order. None of these things mattered, I'd papered with Andy before. I'd painted walls and put up ceiling roses and measured windows and hemmed curtains. We were a team when it came to houses. We'd laid the tile on our old kitchen floor and stripped layers of glossy paint off old pine furniture. We knew how to work together, we knew how to make a home.

So, it was decided.

Beth called.

"So is it bye-bye Theo?" she asked.

"Yes. No. Yes, I guess."

"I know this is very hard for you. I would find it

hard to walk away from a guy with those kind of looks, not to mention all that *money*," Beth said.

"It's not the money, or the looks. He loves me and Frances. But then, so does Andy."

"Andy loves Frances? Since when does Andy love Frances?"

"He does. In his Andyish way. He comes around and puts her in her baby carriage and wheels her from room to room talking to her about what it means that she is a Sagittarius. Not that he believes in any of that stuff."

"Oh, but it's true. And Sagittarius is the best sign. Everyone agrees," Beth said. "So he does love Frances."

"It would appear so." I picked up Frances now, and walked, balancing her on one shoulder and my TF700 on the other, from room to room of the apartment. Andy had brought dozens of children's books home from the store and shelved them in the bookshelf he'd had built into one of the walls of the nursery. He'd bought her a toy owl to replace the actual real owls he'd driven from the house, and a Dumbo painting that hung beside her crib. It had not been easy for him, this transition to fatherhood, but he did love his daughter. Watching her in the bath the night before, his eyes had shone with that luminous outpouring of parental love that I like to think we all feel 1at one stage or another, and he'd said, "What would we have done if she'd never been born?" This thought, like so many other similar ones, had been my very own.

Beth was saying, "Not that anyone couldn't love Frances. I love Frances. In fact, right now, I mean not this actual moment but every night—and I mean *every* night—David and I are trying to make our own little Frances. Or Frank. I guess I have to accept that it might be a boy. I read a book that said the best position for conception is the missionary position. What a bore."

"Well, keep up the good work," I said. In the kitchen I paused and peeked inside the oven. Then I went into the breakfast room and peered out onto the backyard. Theo would have a lot of work cut out for him if he planned to maintain Mrs. Russell's vegetable garden, I thought. I could still see her, bent over her patch of zucchini, kneeling on a padded mat she always used to save her knees. I would miss this breakfast room with its sunny window. I would miss remembering Mrs. Russell out pruning her roses, her hands in leather gloves, her gardening apron filled with cuttings.

"And Mark calls me, weeping. His wife wouldn't take him back, isn't that *unfair* of her? I told him what a bitch she is. Anyway, I'm glad you and Andy are getting back together. I mean, one has to have consistency in one's life, don't you think? Things were okay with Mark until he wanted to join the two ranch houses by means of a long corridor with windows on one side of it and an enormous embedded fish tank on the other. Can you believe it, a full-on eighteen-foot fish tank *embedded* into the wall! I couldn't live with that. Then we got into an argument about it. I said to him, why should I have to argue about why not to have a fish tank the length of a bus in my house! Doesn't it seem obvious that only so much aquarium is *necessary*? And then I got to thinking, what kind of woman would I be if I married a man who even *wanted* a fish tank like that? Not that he'd ever get it—there was never a chance of that!"

I said, "I think I have to agree with you there, Beth. I always had a policy not to get involved with men who like fish."

"Restaurants, fine, let *them* have aquariums. Then you eat the fish, that makes sense. But just to have them so you can clean out the scum on the inside of their little windows?"

"I know, it's very scummy," I said. I took Frances into the living room and we said good-bye to the fireplace, to the tiled hearth, to the lovely marble mantel.

Beth said, "Not even Andy is crazy enough to want an eighteen-foot aquarium!"

"Actually, Andy has a pathological fear of fish," I said.

"See, you guys would never have come to my house because of that aquarium. We'd have been ostracized, Mark and I! We'd have been the freaky fish people nobody wanted anything to do with. I am so glad David came to his senses."

"Me, too," I said. And I was. I was glad that David was back, that Andy was back. For some reason, I'd always assumed that Andy would be back. I suppose I knew, I always knew, that he would return. I remember the final wedding day we had, the day we actually got married. We'd decided that rather than risking another no-show, we'd go together to my mother's farm, spend the night in the little bedroom she insists on pretending was mine as a child, and have the wedding the next day, on the only spot of green lawn on the place not occupied by goats.

It was meant to be a quiet affair. It was meant to be just me and Andy really, but of course Beth and David and Carla and James came along, despite our insistence that it was only a to-the-point wedding that got us legally linked, not a party or anything. I had a great dress—I'd insisted on that—but I did my own hair and makeup, with Andy beside me.

"So we stand together the whole time, no walk up the aisle?" he said.

"No aisle. Not even a church. All we do is get dressed, stand together, and repeat what the preacher says."

"Who's the preacher?"

The preacher was someone named Bob I'd found through an agency that organizes weddings.

"So Preacher Bob is standing on the lawn and we come up and stand next to him?" Andy said.

"That's right. I hold flowers, you hold a ring."

"I don't get a best man?"

"No. You squandered the best man several weddings ago. You get a ring, which you have to give to me. I'm giving you a ring, too, so it's fair. Now no complaining. Help me button these buttons."

"But I wanted a best man!"

"Be quiet. If you're good we go to the Algarve for a honeymoon."

So we got dressed, polished the rings, kissed briefly, and made our debut on the lawn. Mother had arranged some flowers in milking cans, and our four guests were squeezed together on a garden bench looking somewhat ridiculous. Preacher Bob was dressed in white; standing well over six foot four he was like some kind of spirit from an Ingmar Bergman film. Behind him was a landscape of curious goats huddling at the fence and staring with their strange eyes. When Andy and I appeared they started bleating for food.

"They want to eat the flowers," Mother explained.

"Well, they can't," I said.

"Of course not, dear, now don't be so sniping. It's not good to have a bad-tempered bride."

"I'm not being bad-tempered. It's just that I never thought I'd get married in front of a crowd of goats. Isn't there any way to make them be quiet?"

"We could feed them, that would make them quiet."

So we did. We got out a wheelbarrow of hay and fed the goats. I fed the goats, Mother fed the goats. Carla and Beth fed the goats. Preacher Bob fed the goats. Andy knelt by the fence and patted them.

"Too bad there is no way to really communicate with them," he said wistfully.

"You are ruining your suit," I told him. "Go stand by the flowers."

Five minutes later we were standing in the right place. Preacher Bob said the words, Mother started to cry. Andy turned to me and said his vows. He'd memorized them. Soon enough the whole thing was over, and I don't remember a sound from the goats or anything else particularly, just that we were married and suddenly very happy. Once it was over, it felt as though we'd always been married, that it was simply the natural course of events that we should be married. It didn't feel to me to be a question of choice, or even of love. It was fate; he was my husband, we were destined to make a family, to make a life. To buy a lot of different houses that needed work and to do that work. To replumb and regrout and rewire and repaint. To churn up lawn and pull up linoleum and to spend a great deal of time sandblasting.

For people like us it is easier to talk about houses than to talk about love.

Carla said, "Why do you care so much about a house, about a mere structure?"

"It's what it *means*," I told her. And I told her this, too: Because a house means a home, or could do, because a house is there always. *Safe as houses,* isn't that the saying? Because a house is all your memories, all your touchpoints, all your life. Because you spend your life in a house, in one house or another. Remember your childhood and you will remember a house, a particular house. You will remember your grandmother's house, your best friend's house, the face of that house, the smell, the feeling you got as you walked inside.

"I'm so glad you are home," Andy said, lying in our new bed the first night we were in the schoolhouse together. He hugged me closely, "The walls echoed without you."

I said, "We need a rug downstairs. We need furniture, that's why the echo."

"No, it was a person-missing echo. The place felt wrong without you."

The place felt wrong, see how it is? The heart is a home that needs filling.